The Sword and Satchel

Robert M UnKauf

Acknowledgments

I would like to express my deepest appreciation to my wife, April UnKauf. Not only was she patient with me as I pounded away on the keyboard night after night, she waited eagerly for me to finish each new section, so she could pour over it. Your faith in me has always been unwavering, and it makes me a better man.

Thanks also to my editors, who patiently await each new book, and then expose all of my flaws so that I can keep getting better. Thank you.

Finally to the people who read my books. I am always amazed when I realize that someone out there, whether a friend or a complete stranger, is enjoying the stories I come up with. Thank you, and I hope you enjoy this one.

Prologue

Long shadows clawed their way across the field as the sun, a smoke-mantled crimson orb, settled slowly behind the towering trees that lined the once-pristine meadow. The smoke drifted lazily on the gentle breeze, disturbed only as crows fluttered among the corpses.

Banners, ragged and torn, clung limply to the broken shafts of spears and barely stirred in the faint wind, their brilliant colours muted and stained by mud and blood. The haze of the smoke and the fading light leeched what little colour remained, leaving them as lifeless as the bodies strewn across the churned and muddied field.

The torrential rain had stopped, and the ominous

purple-grey clouds had moved slowly, inexorably, east, but the clearing sky was as colourless as everything else in the ghastly field except the baleful sun. It continued to glare like a bloody eye as it sank gradually below the western horizon.

Movement on the southern edge of the clearing startled a dozen or so of the hunched crows into flight, protesting loudly as they lurched into the air, only to alight moments later on another pile of bodies a few feet away.

Two small figures, young boys no more than ten years of age, emerged into the clearing, moving with reverent silence. Their eyes were wide with a mixture of horror and excitement as they stared at the carnage spread out before them.

"I told you, Harald!" the boy in front whispered triumphantly. "I told you I heard trumpets and drums."

"Shut up, Henrik," the second boy murmured. It was obvious from their similar features that they were brothers. Both were of the same size, with dark hair, roughly cut and tangled, and dressed in ragged tunics. Painfully thin, their pale faces seemed to shine in the dying light. "I heard it too, remember? Who were they, do you think?"

"Papa says that Lord Masimor is fighting against

The Sword and Satchel

King Ryas," Henrik replied, his voice trembling with excitement. "These are probably... Hey! I bet there are swords and stuff!"

Harald moved to grab his brother, but Henrik slipped away from his grasp and dashed across to one of the corpses on the ground.

"Henrik! Don't touch them!" Harald hissed, chasing after him. "It's bad luck to touch the dead."

"That's just a silly superstition, Harry," Henrik replied with forced boldness as he stared down at the body on the ground. Still, he didn't move to touch the dead man, his eyes riveted on the torn chainmail and grisly gash that left the ribs and stomach exposed.

"It's getting dark," Harald commented, looking around uncomfortably, studiously avoiding looking at the savaged body.

"What?" Henrik forced out a laugh and quickly turned away from the sight of death. "Are you scared of ghosts?"

"Henrik..." Harald cautioned, but his brother laughed again and darted away.

Harald watched his twin dart from body to body, startled crows screeching indignantly and taking off ungainly as Henrik neared. Shaking his head, Harald trailed along behind.

"Broken... broken... bent..." Henrik muttered as he shuffled through a larger crowd of bodies. Suddenly he hooted in triumph and leaped forward towards the center of the group. "Found one!"

Harald caught up to his brother as Henrik was trying to pull a sword from the grasp of one of the fallen. Despite his protests, Harald grew excited at the sight of the weapon. Even in the dim light, the metal of the blade seemed to gleam. Harald's lips twitched as he realized that Henrik was avoiding touching the hand that still clutched the sword.

"Just..." Harald began, but suddenly Henrik shrieked and stumbled backwards. Harald stared at his brother in shock. "What?"

"He... he moved!" Henrik's face was ashen.

Harald dropped to his knees beside the fallen man, staring intently at him. "You're imagining things, Henrik," he began, but froze when the soldier's eyelid twitched.

The two boys drew back a few paces and stared at the fallen man. His face was as pale as the corpses around him, and his dark hair was stuck to his skin by a thick layer of dried blood. His right eye was swollen and grimy, and he bore a deep cut above his right temple. The tabard that covered his chainmail was shredded from the dozens of cuts he had suffered, though the armour itself seemed to still be intact. His right hand clutched the hilt of the sword as though it was the only thing holding him in this world. Again his left eyelid fluttered.

Harald glanced up at Henrik. "Go get Anika," he whispered.

Henrik swallowed hard. "She's going to be angry..." he began.

"Just do it!" Harald snapped.

Nodding jerkily, Henrik sprinted back the way they had come.

"Hold on, mister," Harald murmured. "We're getting help."

*

"Anika!"

The young woman glanced up from where she was feeding a stick of kindling into a small fire. Her long red hair was tied back in a loose knot at the base of her neck. She smiled as Henrik sprinted into the tiny clearing. "Where'd you and your brother hare off to this time?" she asked softly.

"The big meadow..." Henrik gasped. "Over the ridge..."

Anika frowned at him. "And what took you two

over there?"

"We... there's a battlefield..." Henrik managed.

Anika stood bolt upright, her eyes wide. "Where's Harry?"

"Anika..." Henrik pleaded. "We found a man alive, but he's hurt real bad. Harry's up there..."

"You *left* him there?" Anika snapped.

"Anika!"

Pursing her lips, she studied her brother. At last she nodded shortly. "Alright. Let me grab my things. We'll discuss the wisdom of charging off to explore a battlefield later."

She walked over to the bedrolls she had laid out earlier and grabbed a small pack that lay beside them. Throwing it over her shoulder, she waved Henrik on. Grinning, the boy sprinted off into the darkness. With a sigh of frustration, she hurried after him.

Her mind raced as she moved through the dark forest. A battlefield meant that the civil war her father had been talking about was drawing closer. While they were several miles away from their village, it meant that her hopes of the conflict passing them by entirely were shattered.

Henrik was waiting for her at a shallow creek, barely visible in the moonlight that filtered through the trees. He

The Sword and Satchel

was bouncing up and down on his toes. "Come on, sis!" he called. "We've got to hurry!"

"We won't be any help to this man if we get lost or fall and break an ankle, Henrik," she chided him. "Now what on earth were you doing in that clearing?"

"We heard trumpets and drums this morning, before you got up," Henrik admitted as she drew up beside him. "We... we wanted to see..."

Anika shook her head. "You two are going to be the death of me," she muttered, grabbing his hand and stepping over the tiny creek. "And this man called out to you?"

Henrik looked down as he walked, his face hidden in the darkness. "Well, no," he replied. "I wanted to see if I could find a sword or..."

"Henrik! You were going to steal a sword?"

"It's not stealing! They are all dead!"

"And taking things from the dead is so much better," she replied caustically. "You know that's a sure way to bring down a curse!"

"That's just superstition, Anika! Papa always says there's no such thing as ghosts or any of that. It's just old wives' stories."

"And Papa has never been wrong about anything, has he?"

He glanced up at her, his eyes wide. "Anika, I'm sorry."

She relented. "It's all those stories the men tell about the wars, isn't it?" she asked softly. "That's why you want a sword?"

She felt him shrug. "I guess," he murmured.

"So this man...?"

"I thought he was dead," Henrik continued. "And he was holding a really nice sword... so I grabbed it. Then he moved."

The trees gave way suddenly, opening onto the broad clearing; Anika froze, staring at the mounds lying on the ground, bathed in moonlight. She made the sign to ward off evil and straightened her shoulders. "Where are they?"

Henrik led her unerringly across the field of death to where Harald sat beside the man on the ground. The man was so still Anika thought he was dead at first, but when she touched the hollow of his throat, she could feel his faint pulse. Nodding, she opened her satchel and pulled out her waterskin. "Henrik," she murmured, placing the waterskin down and drawing her knife from her boot. She handed it to her brother. "Go cut four long sticks, about the width of your wrist and about twice as tall as you are and bring them back here. Harald, I need a few yards of cloth. See if you

The Sword and Satchel

can find something."

The two boys scampered off, and Anika studied the fallen man by the faint light of the moon.

The side of his head appeared to have been hit by a heavy object, considering the amount of bruising. The cut above his temple, while fairly deep, wasn't her greatest concern. She felt gently along his head, around the gash, but the skull itself appeared to be intact. She breathed a sigh of relief. Cuts she could deal with. Broken skulls were beyond her healing skills.

She pulled a clean cloth from her satchel and poured water onto it, attempting to clean the wound as well as possible in the darkness. The caked blood and dirt made determining the degree of injury difficult. As she dabbed lightly at the swollen flesh, the man's left eye twitched and opened slightly.

"Water..." he managed to mumble, his voice raspy and rough.

Anika moistened his lips with the cloth, gently touching the uninjured side of his face. She scanned his body for signs of a stomach wound, but the chain armour appeared intact. She placed the waterskin to his lips, and he drank greedily for a moment, coughing and sputtering as the water spilled out the corner of his mouth.

"Slowly," she soothed. His good eye fastened on her briefly at her voice, and he managed a nod. The motion obviously pained him, and his gaze drifted away. "Do you have any other injuries, other than your head?" Anika's voice remained soft and gentle.

The man blinked, trying to focus on her again. Then he shifted slightly, a groan escaping his lips around the neck of the waterskin.

"Easy," Anika murmured. "Don't move."

The man settled down, his good eye fastened on her face.

"My name is Anika," she told him, taking the waterskin away. "I'm a healer. You're very lucky my brothers found you. I'm going to help you. In a few minutes I'm going to try and shift you onto a travois, so I need to know if you have any other injuries."

He blinked again, his eye uncertain. His lips moved silently.

Gently she reached out to touch the fingers gripping the sword. "I need you to let go of your sword," she told him.

His eye grew wide, almost panicked, and he shifted again.

"It's okay," she told him, seeing the frantic look on

his face. "I'll bring it with us. But right now you need to let go."

His eye scanned her face, but at last she felt his fingers relax slightly on the hilt of the sword. She lifted the blade free and placed two of her fingers in his palm. "Squeeze my fingers," she told him. A moment later she felt his fingers tighten again. She nodded and moved to the other hand. "Again," she murmured, nodding again as she felt the slight flex of his hand. She rose and moved to his legs, placing her hand on his left foot. "I need you to push against my hand with your foot." A relieved breath escaped her as she felt his foot flex, but she repeated the process with his other foot. Nodding, she rose. At least there didn't appear to be a back or neck injury. Like skulls, there was nothing she could do about necks or backs.

She returned to kneel by his head, again wiping the blood and mud away from the gash on his temple. His eye shut in pain as she dabbed gently at the cut, but he made no sound of protest.

Once she had the worst of the grime cleaned, she pulled a small pouch from her satchel. Inside of the small leather sack were dozens of tiny bundles, each tied up securely with a brightly-coloured ribbon. The scent of herbs washed over her. Opening the pouch, she carefully selected and withdrew one of the tiny packets.

"This is pain-nettle," she told him. "I don't know what the herbalists in the cities call it, but it helps prevent the blood fever. It also dulls the pain." She balled up one of the tiny plants and placed it under his tongue. "I'm going to put some of it in the wound on your temple, too. It's going to hurt for a minute. Try not to jerk away from it, though."

The man blinked his eye slowly as though agreeing.

She poured a little water into her palm and pressed the herb into it, crushing it into a paste before taking a deep breath and smearing it into the deep gash. The soldier stiffened slightly, but didn't attempt to jerk away. A low whimper escaped his lips, and his eye watered, but he continued to gaze at her steadily.

"I'm going to wait for a moment for the nettle to take effect," she continued. "Then I'm going to stitch that gash closed. The nettle under your tongue will deaden most of the pain."

Harald stepped up beside her, several torn and bloodied banners in his hands. "This okay, sis?" he asked.

She nodded, glancing around. Across the field she could see the dim shape of Henrik marching towards them, dragging three long branches. "You've seen me make travois before, right Harry?"

"Like one of those litters?" Harald asked, wrinkling his forehead.

Anika nodded. "That's right. Do you think you and Henrik can make one? I'm going to be busy here for a moment."

Harald grinned, his teeth gleaming in the moonlight. "Sure, Anika."

Glancing back down at the soldier, Anika allowed herself a tight-lipped smile. "We're going to take you back to our camp for tonight. Tomorrow we'll take you down to our village."

The soldier moistened his lips with his tongue for a moment, then murmured, "Thank you."

Anika nodded. "What's your name?" she asked softly.

The man grimaced slightly as he whispered, "Eric."

"Well, Eric," Anika crouched down beside him. "Let's get that cut sewn up."

The pain-nettle did its job. She hadn't mentioned that in addition to alleviating pain, pain-nettle also acted as a sedative. Eric passed out before she was finished. As she placed the needle and gut-string back into her satchel, Anika glanced back at her brothers. They had managed, after much debate, to lash a rough travois together.

She motioned the boys over to her, then crouched down and grabbed Eric under the armpits. "I need to get this armour off of him," she told them. "I can drag his weight, but the armour makes him much heavier. I need you to support him once I get him into a sitting position."

The boys moved to flank the unconscious man, and Anika heaved him up, holding him steady until Harald and Henrik had securely grabbed his arms. Once he was relatively upright, she leaned him forward with the boys holding his arms outstretched and pulled the heavy chain shirt up and over his head. The boys tugged his arms free of the armour and the steel shirt slithered to the ground. His padded undershirt was damp with sweat, and there were blood stains on the dirty fabric, but Anika decided to leave it on him until they reached their camp.

Anika moved to hold Eric under the arms again. "Henrik," she instructed. "Grab the travois and place it behind me."

Her brother did as told, and she manoeuvred Eric until he was lying on the makeshift stretcher. She grabbed one of the unused banners and wrapped it around him, securing him to the branches. Then she tied another of the banners near where the two long poles met. Crouching, she slung the banner across her shoulders, grabbed the two poles, and glanced at Harald. "When I lift this, I want you to tighten the banner until I tell you to stop."

Harald nodded, and Anika heaved the travois up. Harald undid Anika's knot and tightened the support until Anika nodded. "Good enough," she told him. While the fabric support wouldn't do much, it helped reduce the strain on her arms. She glanced over at Henrik. "Head back to the camp and rekindle the fire," she told him. "Then fetch some water and get it boiling. I need to clean his wounds properly."

Henrik sprinted off, and Anika smiled at Harald. "I promised him I'd bring his sword," she said quietly. "Be careful with it. I'm guessing it's sharp."

Her brother reverently picked up the weapon, gazing at it with undisguised awe. She shook her head. "Try to make sure he doesn't roll off," she commented. Then, taking a deep breath, she started forward, dragging the unconscious soldier behind her.

Chapter 1

It was the sunlight, not the pain, which woke him, but the pain was what kept him from fading back into the comfort of sleep. Groaning, he shifted slightly.

"Anika!" a high-pitched voice called out. "He's waking up!"

He blinked, and his left eye sprang open. His right was swollen shut. The sunlight caused his head to throb. His mouth was dry and felt like something had crawled in it to die.

"Hold still, Eric," a soft, gentle voice reprimanded from beside him. "Don't try to move yet."

He tried to turn his head, but blinding pain forced him to heed the girl's instructions. He closed his left eye, and the agony subsided slightly.

"You're in pretty rough shape," the voice continued. "But I guess that's to be expected, considering."

He licked his lips and was about to ask for water, but the girl seemed to anticipate his request because before he could speak, a waterskin was pressed to his lips. He gulped thirstily.

"That foul taste is the pain-nettle," the girl, Anika he supposed, continued. "It goes away." She allowed him to drink for a second more before withdrawing the waterskin.

"Where..." he croaked. Coughing, he tried again. "Where am I?" His voice was a little less rough.

"Anidaron," Anika replied. "It's a small village near the mountains. I brought you here three days ago."

He tried to focus on what she was telling him, but his mind baulked. Anidaron. Near the mountains... what mountains? What had happened? He struggled to pierce the fog in his mind, but the throbbing pain in his skull seemed to get worse the more he tried to think.

"You need to keep still," Anika advised him. "You have a serious head injury, as well as several cracked ribs. You're lucky you aren't dead."

"What happened?" he asked.

There was a long pause. When Anika spoke again, it

was hesitant. "What do you mean?"

He cracked his left eye open and stared up at the girl who had apparently saved him. She was young, probably no more than eighteen or nineteen. Fiery red hair framed her pale, freckled face. Brilliant green eyes gazed down at him, a faint furrow of concern creasing her forehead. "How... how did I get hurt?" he asked her.

Her expression grew more concerned, and she touched his forehead lightly. "What do you remember, Eric?"

He blinked, and his head throbbed. "I..." he closed his eye, hoping it would reduce the stabbing pain. "Nothing," he said at last.

She remained silent for several moments, and he could almost feel her thinking. At length she murmured, "You were in a battle, Eric. I'm guessing you got hit in the head with an axe or a club. It's not unheard of for those kinds of injuries to cause temporary memory loss."

He relaxed a little at the word 'temporary'. "How do you know my name?" he whispered.

"You told me when I found you," she replied. "Well, when my brothers found you. Now I want you to try and rest. Do your best to keep still. If the pain is still severe, I can give you some more pain-nettle."

He gritted his teeth. "That would be nice," he agreed. "As long as it works better than it tastes."

She laughed softly, the sound soothing. "It works, and it will help you sleep. You should eat something before I give it to you, though. I'm going to prop you up a little, so you can drink some broth. It might hurt a bit."

She reached an arm under his shoulders and lifted him as gently as she could, stuffing a rough pillow under his head and neck. He grunted, and the pain nearly caused him to lose consciousness, but it was swift. He let out a gasp as she removed her arm.

"Sorry," she murmured in his ear. "I wouldn't do this unless I thought food was absolutely necessary."

He clenched his teeth and let out a pained breath, not trusting himself to speak. After a moment, he felt a bowl press against his lips. He sipped the bland broth, and his stomach growled suddenly.

"Can you hold the bowl?" she asked.

He raised his arms slowly, his muscles screaming in protest as he wrapped his hands around the rough wood of the bowl, his fingers brushing against Anika's.

"Thank you," he said after a moment.

"You're welcome," her gentle voice sounded pleased. "Drink that, and I'll be back with more pain-nettle."

He listened to her go and then focused on eating. The broth was thin and not overly warm, but he swallowed it ravenously. By the time he was finished, Anika had returned. She took the bowl from him and placed a small ball of leaves in his hand.

"Place that under your tongue," she told him. "Don't chew it. It doesn't taste very good, and it's more effective if you don't swallow it."

He did as she instructed, and then opened his eye again. "Your name is Anika?"

She nodded. "You remember that?"

"No," he admitted. "Someone called out to you when I was waking up."

She smiled, and it lit up her face. "That was my brother Henrik. He's the one who first found you."

He suddenly felt dizzy and closed his eye again. "Thank you again, Anika," he mumbled, consciousness fleeing.

*

Anika stared down at Eric, a smile playing across her lips. Despite the bruising, he was a handsome man. His features were strong, and his eyes were a dark brown that went well with his thick brown hair. The days of unconsciousness had allowed his beard to fill in, and it added to his rugged masculinity. Various old scars on his arms and chest spoke clearly of his familiarity with war, as did his toned muscles. She glanced at his only really distinguishing mark: a pair of intricate black hawks, diving with their talons extended, tattooed beneath each of his collarbones.

She rose to her feet and glanced at the cloth bundle lying beside the bed. It held his sword. The same design was carved into the pommel stone. It had to have some kind of meaning, but she didn't know what it was. She pushed the bundle under the bed with her toe.

"Anika!" her father's gruff voice called from the other room. She glanced over her shoulder.

"Coming, Papa," she replied. Looking back at Eric for a moment, she felt his forehead again briefly. The fever he had been running had diminished, she noted. She'd feared it had been the blood fever, but the wound on his temple seemed to be healing nicely. She glanced at the dark purple bruising across Eric's ribs and shoulders. She'd been quite surprised when he'd been able to reach up and hold the bowl on his own. His left arm was a mass of greenish-purple bruises that spread across his chest. His face was even worse, but the swelling had gone down. She nodded once more and darted out into the main room.

Her father sat in the rickety old rocking chair before the fireplace, gazing at the ashes in the cold hearth. It was mid-summer, and the house was sweltering, despite the doors being open. A chicken squawked and fluttered across the floor as she entered the room, bolting back out into the yard. "What do you need, Papa?" she asked as she approached.

He glanced up at her, his grey eyes cool. "How's the soldier doing?" he asked.

She shrugged. "Better. He managed to eat something. The fever has gone."

He nodded. Leif Svenson was no longer a young man, and the grey in his hair stood out in stark contrast against the brilliant red she had inherited from him. "I was beginning to worry. Is he one of the king's men?"

She shook her head. "I don't know. Maybe. He's having difficulty remembering anything."

He snorted, turning back to the empty hearth. "Head injuries," he muttered. "Well, hopefully it hasn't totally rattled his brains. How long do you reckon he'll be here?"

She glanced at her father in surprise. In all the years she'd been working as a healer, ever since her mother's death five years before, he'd never once asked after one of the patients she'd occasionally brought home. "I don't know, Papa. Why?"

He glanced back at her, and Anika saw something she'd never seen in his face before: fear. "He's a soldier, Anika. Soldiers bring more soldiers. It's the way of things. The sooner he's gone, the better. Whether he's one of the king's or one of Masimor's makes no difference. He's trouble."

"He's an injured man," Anika protested.

"He's a soldier," Leif barked. "And judging from the look of him, he's not a commoner. That makes him trouble."

She tilted her head, surprised. "What do you mean?" she asked. "Why do you say he's not a commoner?"

He grunted, not speaking. Anika walked over to lean against the wall beside the fireplace, her eyebrows raised. "Papa?"

He stared hard at the fireplace, his gaze distant. "Before I settled here, I did some soldiering myself," he admitted. "I know the look of the nobility when I see it. You've never been farther than a couple of miles from Anidaron, never been to one of the great cities, so you wouldn't understand."

"So what if he's a noble," she countered. "It doesn't

change anything."

"Damn straight it changes things!" he snapped. "If soldiers are trouble, nobles are a damn sight worse."

"Papa," she chided. "What's this about?"

He took a deep breath, and his shoulders slumped. "He's trouble, child. With this bloody civil war, having him here puts us all in danger." He looked at her, his eyes troubled. "If he's a rebel, and one of the king's patrols finds him here, we're aiding a wanted criminal. That's a death sentence for the likes of us. If he's one of the king's, and Masimor's thugs stumble into Anidaron, it won't matter that you're the healer. They'll burn this place down."

"Papa," Anika knelt down before her father. "Nothing's going to happen."

Her father frowned at her. "The sooner he's gone, the better," he repeated.

Anika shook her head and patted his knee as she rose. "Okay, Papa. As soon as he's fit to go, I'll insist he has to move on. But he's not there yet."

Nodding, Leif stared back at the fireplace, his eyes distant. "This fighting... it's not going to go away, Anika. The fact that there was a skirmish just a few miles away..."

"A skirmish?" Anika objected. "Papa, there were dozens of bodies there."

He glanced at her again, nodding. "Child, that's just a small skirmish. Chances are good that it was an advance group that got ambushed. If scouting parties are moving to the west of here..." he paused for a moment. "Anika, I need you to make sure you and the boys have emergency packs ready to go. Clothes, food, supplies. Keep the packs near the door."

"Papa, now you're just being ridiculous," she began, but his expression caused her to pause. "Do you really think...?"

"Anika," he grabbed her hand. "I've seen what war is. I never want to see it again. Places like Anidaron... they disappear when armies clash. I don't want you or the boys to be here if that happens. The village council has sent a few boys out to look around. If they come back with news of an army nearby, I want you and the boys to head for the mountains. You remember where I took you hunting? To my friend Lodi's? If I can't come with you, go there."

Anika nodded, her eyes wide. "Papa," she whispered. "I've never seen you like this."

He looked away. "Lodi and I... when we were younger, about your age, we decided that we wanted to go adventuring. We wanted to see the world. A recruiter for King Yoland – King Ryas' father – came to our village...

Lodi and I decided we'd sign up. We were young, naive... we thought armies and soldiers were glamorous.

"The War of Succession changed that. A few months after we joined up, Yoland died. Some said he was poisoned, but that was just rumour... nothing that could be proven. Still, it changed things. Yoland had two sons: Ryas and Tindal. Ryas was older, but Tindal... he was one of the most charismatic men of his time. He was a natural leader, and he was married to a very ambitious woman, the daughter of the Great Sultan Kysid from the Almeri desert.

"When Yoland died, Tindal raised his banner, and marched on the capital. It started out much like this uprising between Masimor and the King. They called it the Black Hawk Rebellion at first, when Tindal first announced his intention to take the throne. Ryas thought it would be a simple matter to crush the rebellion, but while Ryas' claim was better, many of the lords he thought were loyal preferred the idea of Tindal as king. Even more importantly, Tindal had been serving with the military for a long time while Ryas was living in the capital. Entire legions deserted and joined Tindal's rebellion.

"That's when things got ugly." Her father's gaze grew distant. "The families of rebel lords, the ones who still lived in the capital, were imprisoned. Some were executed.

Ryas even detained the families of loyal lords, holding them hostage to ensure the continued support of the nobles. Towns that didn't declare allegiance to one side or the other were razed by which ever faction happened to hold sway in a region."

He stared at Anika. "That's what I'm afraid of," he said at last. "The commoners in the villages didn't do anything, but the nobles didn't care. Even wearing the wrong colour was enough to put the towns to the torch."

"What happened?" Anika asked, her eyes wide. "With Tindal, I mean. Obviously Ryas won..."

Her father shook his head. "No one really knows. He made the mistake of seeking the support of his wife's father, Kysid. The idea of foreign troops on Prisian soil made several of his supporters abandon him. Ryas' forces moved north faster than anyone expected, striking a crushing blow against Tindal's main force... Then one day, Tindal and his wife simply disappeared.

"Ryas, of course, was suspected of sending assassins, but nothing could be proven. It wouldn't have mattered anyway. Ryas took the throne. Most of the nobles who had sided with Tindal were executed. Masimor's father was one of them, even though he'd thrown his support behind Ryas when Tindal sought aid from Kysid."

"So this rebellion is about Masimor seeking revenge?" Anika asked, startled.

Her father smiled, but it was a cold smile. "Most such wars are, child. Revenge... and power."

"Who did you fight for?" she asked in a hushed whisper.

He glanced at her sharply. "Ryas, of course," he snapped.

For the first time in her life, Anika was certain her father was lying. She nodded, though. "Why did they call it the 'Black Hawk Rebellion'?"

Leif studied her for a moment. "It was Tindal's sigil. Ryas' sigil is a white hawk on a green background. It was a statement, of sorts, the Black Hawk. Tindal believed Ryas had poisoned their father... but enough of this. It's ancient history. Those ghosts can remain buried. Go find your brothers and tell them to do their chores, then get back to tending your soldier."

Anika nodded and moved toward the door. She glanced back at her father and smiled tentatively. "Papa... I like hearing your stories. It's been a long time."

He blinked. Then he waved her out, but she saw the hint of a smile on his face.

Chapter 2

Eric stared at the roof above him. It was made of what appeared to be some kind of bark, birch most likely. He followed the overlapping layers with his eyes, testing the range he could see without turning his head too much. The swelling in his right eye had diminished, and the relief he felt at regaining his vision was indescribable. His head still hurt when he shifted, but keeping his eyes open was no longer a torment.

Anika knelt beside him, poking at his ribs. She touched a tender spot, and he shifted slightly. "They aren't quite healed," she told him. "But I think if I wrap them tightly, you should be able to get up. How does your head feel?"

"Fine," he lied.

She frowned. "Eric, I can't help if I don't have accurate information. I can tell by the lines around your eyes when you shift that you're still in pain."

He glared at her for a moment, but her expression was so earnest that he relaxed. "It's better," he told her. "The pain's down to a dull throb, and it's only there when I move too much."

She nodded and touched the skin above his temple. "The cut is healing nicely," she observed. "How's your vision?"

"Fine," he said again. At her narrowing eyes, he laughed softly. "No, really. The blurriness has gone away. I've been testing the range, and it seems good."

She nodded and leaned in, staring into his eyes. He stared calmly back, intrigued by her brilliant green irises. "You have lovely eyes," he murmured.

She jerked back, startled. Then she smiled slightly. "You've had a lot of opportunity to see them. I don't often get a chance to see them, myself."

"They're pretty," he repeated. "They suit you."

She glanced away, embarrassed. "So... any luck remembering anything?" she asked, changing the subject.

He sighed. "No," he whispered. "Nothing before

the other day."

She sat back on her heels, touching his forehead lightly. "Don't worry about it too much," she advised. "Head injuries are funny things. Chances are good that you'll see something or smell something, and everything will come back to you."

"It's just so frustrating," he confided. "I mean, it's been over a week, and still..."

She nodded. "I understand, but worrying about it won't help. Do you think you can sit up?"

He hesitated. It was the first time she'd allowed him to move since he'd awoken. That had been embarrassing, at first, but he'd gotten past the feeling of self-consciousness after the second or third time she'd helped him perform his basic necessities. The idea of sitting up... his head throbbed just thinking about it, but he gritted his teeth and braced his hands on the sides of the rickety bed frame. Slowly, he eased himself upward until he was sitting. The pain flared for a moment, and then subsided. He smiled weakly at Anika.

"Good," she grinned. "Now swing your legs over the edge of the bed and raise your arms."

He paused, suddenly uncomfortable. He was naked under the sheet, and while he'd convinced himself he was over his self-consciousness, that had been while he was completely helpless.

"Oh, get over it, Eric," Anika laughed. "It's not as if you haven't been naked this whole time."

He smiled sheepishly and took a deep breath before flinging the blanket that was covering him back. Slowly, like an old man, he swung his legs over the edge of the bed.

She smiled at him. "See? Not so hard. Now let's see if you can stand up," she said softly.

He took a deep breath and struggled to his feet. His head spun, and he staggered forward. She pressed in close, her arms wrapping around his chest, under his arms, to steady him.

They stood like that for several moments as he waited for the pain in his head to diminish. Once it did, he became intensely aware of her body against his, her breasts pressing against his chest. He cleared his throat, and she backed away to arms reach, still smiling. "Good?"

He nodded curtly, and the motion made the room spin. She moved back in to support him again, her face pressing against his neck. "I could get used to this," he mumbled into her hair as she moulded her body to his.

She laughed and leaned back to look at him, her eyes dancing. "Don't," she told him. "You don't have the stamina. It might kill you."

When she was sure he was steady, she backed away and moved to the bed to grab the blanket. "Wrap this around yourself."

"Anika..." he began, taking the proffered blanket and wrapping it around his waist. "I know I've said it before, but thank you."

"You're welcome. Now, you..." she pointed a finger at him, wrinkling her nose. "Are in dire need of a bath. Fortunately, I had Harald fill the tub before I came to check on you. Come on."

She held a hand out to him and led him slowly into the main room, where an old copper bathtub stood in the middle of the floor. He stared at it for a moment, considering the height of the sides. At last he glanced at Anika. "I'm going to need your help getting in," he admitted.

She smiled broadly. "Then let's start with the blanket."

The bath was exquisite. While the water was cool, it was refreshing. She gave him a bar of lye soap, and he washed away a week or more of sweat and grime. By the time she helped him from the tub, he felt like a new man.

She led him back into his room and had him sit on

the edge of the bed. She reached over to the dresser where she had placed a long roll of heavy cloth. "I'm going to wrap your ribs. Now raise your arms."

He lifted his arms and she leaned in and began winding the cloth around his chest. Her proximity, and the smell of her hair, suddenly gave him a new reason to become increasingly uncomfortable as his body responded to her nearness. She fought back a smile as she continued to work, and he coughed slightly. "Ummm..." he began.

"It's okay," she murmured, her breath hot against his chest as she continued her wrapping. "It's a natural reaction."

She finished winding the cloth around his torso and sat back on her heels again, smiling up at him. "How do you feel?"

"Alright," he murmured, not meeting her eyes. "Better than I have in a long time."

She studied him for a moment. "The clothing you had on was beyond saving," she explained. "Except your boots. Those are over there," she waved at a pair of worn leather boots in the corner. She tilted her head to the side. "You're bigger than my father is, but he's got a bigger waist. Wait here. I'll see if I can find some clothes for you."

She returned a few minutes later, a pair of patched

pants and a thin work shirt in her hands. "Try these on. I can take them in if they're too baggy."

The clothing was loose, and the pants and sleeves were too short, but having clothes made him feel more confident. Putting them on had been challenging, but he'd refused Anika's offer of assistance. Her nearness was too distracting. Once he was dressed, she eyed him critically.

"They'll do for now, but I'll work on them tonight," she told him. She turned and began taking the bedding off the straw mattress. "I'll bring in some new sheets. You've done enough for today, so I want you to rest until dinner. You'll eat with us tonight."

She left and returned moments later with the promised sheets. With a practised hand, she remade the rough mattress. "Rest," she said gently. "I'll come for you at dinner." Then, as she was leaving the room, she glanced back at him. "I'll bring you a razor and a mirror. You might actually be good-looking under that stubble."

He grinned back at her. "I don't know. I don't get a chance to see myself that often."

She flashed him a pretty smile and vanished into the other room.

Eric lowered himself gently to sit on the edge of the straw mattress. He placed his head gingerly in his hands.

The exertion had caused his head to throb again, but he was feeling better for having moved around. Anika returned with a basin, soap, a razor, and a tiny mirror, and placed them on the set of drawers against the wall. She hesitated for an instant before handing him the mirror, almost appearing to reconsider. He frowned slightly.

"It's just..." she paused. "There's a good chance that you won't recognize yourself. I don't want you to be too disappointed if you don't."

He chuckled softly and reached out for the mirror. She handed it to him, and he glanced at the small piece of glass.

She was right. He didn't recognize himself. A stranger stared back at him. He felt he should remember something, but her caution made sense now. He fought back a surge of disappointment and focused on studying himself.

He was, he guessed, about twenty-five, judging from the presence of very faint lines around his eyes. His skin was tanned under the fading, mottled bruising, and his eyes were a rich brown; he had fine eyebrows and a nose that looked like it might have been broken once. The stubble on his cheeks couldn't conceal his high cheekbones or the solidity of his jaw. He smiled at himself. It was odd, but he was modestly pleased to realise that his teeth were perfect.

He had a faint scar across his forehead, at the edge of his hairline, which would ultimately be complimented by the cut on his temple.

Then he noticed the tattoos.

He reached a hand up to his collarbones and brushed his fingers gently over the tiny ink hawks. Something tugged at his thoughts, a faint impression of a memory, but it was gone before he could grab on to it.

"Thanks," he murmured, returning his attention to Anika, who was waiting expectantly. "This stubble is driving me crazy."

"Nothing?" she asked softly.

He shook his head almost imperceptibly. "No, but I didn't really expect much." He raised his hand to the tattoos again. "I wonder what these mean..."

He glanced up at her, and she looked away quickly. His frown returned. "What is it, Anika?"

She bit her lower lip, then knelt down beside him and rummaged under the bed, pulling out a long, cloth bundle. "When I found you, you were holding onto your sword like it was... I don't know. You wouldn't let it go until I promised to bring it with me. Those birds... they're on the pommel of your sword, too."

She held the bundle out, and he put the mirror down

The Sword and Satchel

to take it from her.

It was heavy, but in an oddly familiar way. He peeled back the cloth slowly, tentatively. A sense of anticipation rose up within him as he let the wrapping fall away to expose the weapon contained within.

It was an exquisite sword. He didn't know how he knew, but he did. The blade was dirty, and the leather wrapping of the hilt was faded and worn, but he could see the purity of the steel under the dirt and grime. When he wrapped his fingers around the hilt, it felt... natural. Pressure marks in the leather matched the calluses on his hand perfectly, and the weight of the blade seemed to somehow complete him. He barely glanced at the pommel, where a hawk was carved into the black stone with intricate detail. He didn't need to. Even though he remembered nothing else, he knew this weapon. He touched his thumb to the blade, testing the edge. He glanced up at Anika. "I'm going to need some oil and a whetstone."

"After you shave," she chided him.

He grimaced, about to protest, but she overrode him.

"It will still be there after you've shaved. Besides, I don't know where Papa keeps the honing oil. I'll have to look for it. Shave."

He reluctantly placed the sword down and picked up

the basin and soap. She only left after he'd lathered and picked up the razor.

His gaze kept drifting to the blade resting beside him. Even though seeing it, feeling it in his hand, hadn't awakened any specific memory, it had established a sense of self he hadn't realized he'd been missing. It was distracting enough that he almost cut himself several times.

It was only when he was wiping the lather off his cheeks with the cloth the sword had been wrapped in that he realized he'd kept the hair on his upper lip and chin. He studied himself in the mirror. It felt right, somehow, keeping the beard and mustache... like that was what he always did. He stared hard at his reflection, trying desperately to remember something about himself, but at last looked away in disgust.

Nothing.

He placed the mirror down on the dresser and reached for the sword. He placed the tip on the rough wood floor and stared at the pommel.

It was a solid black stone, polished to a rich gleam, and the image of the hawk had been carved on both sides and the cuts had been filled with what appeared to be silver. He spun the blade around, staring at the stone.

He glanced up when Anika returned. She held out a

small leather flask of oil and a whetstone the size of his palm. He murmured his gratitude. Soaking a part of the cloth that had wrapped the blade in the water in the basin, he set about cleaning off the dried dirt and blood. Once that was gone, he oiled the blade, then oiled the whetstone and began sliding it along the blade in slow, almost meditative strokes.

"It's familiar," he told Anika softly. "The sword, the sharpening... while I can't actually remember anything, this feels familiar."

"I imagine you had to do it a lot," she replied, sitting on the bed beside him. "Though that sword doesn't look like it needs that much sharpening."

He nodded slightly. "It doesn't. It's made with better steel than most." He looked up at her. "But don't ask me how I know that."

She smiled encouragingly at him. "Even knowing that much is progress," she told him. "Does the image on the pommel...?"

He chuckled without mirth. "No. It means nothing to me yet. Anika, I know it's a lot to ask, but once I'm feeling better, can you take me to where you found me? If I haven't remembered anything by then, I mean."

She nodded, then reached out and touched his cheek

The Sword and Satchel

gently. "I was right," she commented softly. "You are handsome without the stubble. I'm not entirely sure about the beard, but I suppose it suits you."

Then, looking a little flustered, she rose. "My father will be back with the boys, soon. I need to get dinner ready."

"Can I help?" he inquired.

She shook her head. "You play with your toy. I'll come for you when dinner is ready. And don't mind my father. He's not exactly pleased at having a soldier here."

Eric grinned lopsidedly. "I can understand. Especially with such a pretty daughter."

She blushed and brushed an errant strand of scarlet hair back behind her ear. "I... have to go," she murmured, a little breathless.

He watched her leave. It was obvious she wasn't accustomed to that kind of attention. It made him smile. He'd always had a way with women...

He fought to hold on to the thought, to the memory, but it slipped out of reach even as he fought to isolate it.

Sighing, he turned his attention back to the blade. The sound of the stone on the steel was calming, and he let his mind go blank as he worked.

*

He heard Anika's father and brothers arrive, and quietly placed the sword down. Grabbing onto the dresser, he managed to stand up on his own. Anika appeared in the doorway and held a hand out for him. He took it and she guided him into the other room, moving slowly for him.

Her father was facing the fireplace, his broad shoulders hunched slightly. Anika cleared her throat. "Papa, this is Eric."

"So you're Anika's new project. I'm..." the aging man began, turning around. Suddenly his eyes widened, his face grew ashen, and he staggered back a step, clutching at his chest and coughing.

"Papa!" Anika shrieked, dashing across the room to support him. "Henrik! Get some water! Harald, my satchel!"

Her brother dashed out of the house and the old man stumbled over to the chair sitting by the hearth and collapsed into it, still clutching his chest. Anika pressed her hand to his throat, checking his pulse, then felt his forehead.

The entire time, the old man's eyes never left Eric.

The other brother, Harald, rushed over to one of the cupboards near the table and pulled out the satchel, bringing it to his sister.

Anika took the bag and withdrew a small pouch.

The Sword and Satchel

From it she drew out a small packet of dried herbs and held it under her father's nose. He sputtered and wheezed, twisting his face away.

Henrik reappeared with a bucket of water, which he proceeded to splash all over the floor in his haste. Anika reached above the fireplace and grabbed one of the mugs sitting there. She filled it and handed it to her father, who clutched it and gulped at it.

After a moment the old man relaxed a little and waved off the attention of his daughter. "I'm alright," he gasped. Then, with more force, "Blast it, Anika! I'm fine. Let me be."

She backed away, her face still concerned. The old man glanced up at Eric, his lips twisted into the semblance of a smile. "Forgive me," he murmured. "I fear I must have exerted myself too much this afternoon."

Eric stared at the old man, knowing the excuse to be a lie. Anika's father was hiding something. He knew better than to press the issue, however. Instead he smiled back. "I'm sure rest will help."

The old man nodded. "My name is Leif Svenson. You already know my daughter. As for the boys, one of them is Henrik and the other is Harald, but only Anika can tell them apart."

The two boys alternated between staring at Eric and glancing in rapidly diminishing concern towards their father.

"Papa," Anika began, but Leif shook his head.

"It's nothing, Anika. Let it be. I'm old. I've come to expect episodes like this. Now, why don't you and the boys play host to your soldier. I think I should go to bed. Forgive me, young man, for being such a poor host, but..."

"There's nothing to forgive, sir," Eric replied.

The old man nodded and struggled to his feet, fending his daughter off as he did so. Without another word, Leif shuffled to one of the other doorways and disappeared.

Anika stared after her father, her green eyes wide with concern. "He's never had an attack that bad before," she whispered. She rounded on the boys. "Did you make him run after you at all today? Henrik?"

The dark-haired boy on the left shook his head. "Honest, Anika! We just came back from the fields!"

"Papa was working the east quarter with Joff," Harald added. "We didn't see him until we started back. Maybe he had to do some digging... you know that's hard on him."

Anika sighed and turned back to Eric. "Well," she smiled weakly at him. "We may as well eat. I'll check on him after dinner."

The Sword and Satchel

Eric stared at the doorway for a moment, his mind spinning. What had the old man seen? The look in Leif's eyes when he'd seen him had been... terrified recognition. But how? Eric shook his head, baffled.

"Come on," Anika said, smiling at him. "The boys are eager to pepper you with questions you can't answer, and dinner is getting cold."

Eric nodded and let her lead him to the table.

The dinner was simple but filling, a thick stew consisting mostly of potatoes, peas, and carrots with a few pieces of meat. He had been restricted to broth so far, so the thicker food came as a welcome change. He wolfed the meal down eagerly, while trying to handle the rapid questions of the twins between bites. Most of the questions he couldn't answer, and he sensed their disappointment.

"I tell you what," he said at last after another question by Henrik about life as a soldier. "If it's okay with your sister, after you finish eating, I'll show you my sword."

Henrik and Harald's eyes lit up and they looked pleadingly at Anika. She frowned slightly, but finally nodded. "But not in the house. Boys will be boys, and I can see them swinging that thing around in your room. And you," she pointed at Eric, "are not to try showing them how to use it 'properly'. You're not ready for that kind of activity yet."

"Yes, Anika," Eric said solemnly, grinning at the excitement on the boys' faces.

The boys polished off their dinner in seconds, and sat, bouncing in their chairs, until Anika dismissed them with a wave. "Go!" she laughed. "Just try to be careful."

Chapter 3

It was a quaint little village. Virtually all of the buildings were made of rough-hewn timber and roofed with turf. It was amusing to see the grassy roofs, with the occasional goat perched precariously on them, munching on the greenery. He judged there to be around two dozen squat buildings, each with a stick fence enclosing the area around them. The fences were to keep in the various goats and pigs, while chickens clucked and wandered around the streets. A cat sat, cleaning its whiskers, on the step of a house across the packed-dirt street. The cat paused in its ablutions as a thin dog wandered by.

It was incredibly pastoral, he mused, with the sun beginning to sink in the west; as he looked around he felt a tension in his shoulders he hadn't noticed before ease somewhat. He took a deep breath. The air was rich with the smell of peat smoke and roasting meat, mingled with a faint hint of manure.

The boys grinned as he knelt down onto one knee, carefully placing the tip of the blade on the thick leather of his left boot. "The first thing you need to know about a sword is that it is not a toy, and it's not a tool. It's a weapon. Because of that, it needs to be treated with respect. Your life could depend on it."

The boys nodded in unison, and he marvelled at the similarity of both appearance and movement they shared. "The second thing you need to realize about a sword – and about this sword in particular – is that it is very, very sharp. Have you ever seen your father's razor?"

They stared at him with wide eyes, nodding slowly.

"This is just as sharp," he cautioned. He rubbed his cheek and grinned. "Maybe sharper." When they laughed, he rose awkwardly to stand in front of them. "Never, ever swing a sword at someone unless you intend to kill them."

That stopped their laughter.

"Swords are made for one purpose," he continued. The cautionary words came naturally, as though he had heard or said them before, but he couldn't quite put a finger on the memory. "It's not a nice purpose, but it is a necessary one. Swords are made to kill. Bows can be used to shoot game. Axes can be used to chop down trees or cut wood. Swords are used to kill people."

"Couldn't you use a sword to cut down a tree?" one of the boys – Harald, he thought – asked quietly.

Eric shook his head. "The lightness and the flexibility of the blade make it too weak to be effective... unless it's a sapling. And no swordsman would ever allow someone to ruin his blade by using it on a tree."

The boys nodded soberly.

"Now, do you still want to hold it?" he asked.

The boy on the left nodded eagerly. "Alright, Henrik," Eric said, holding the hilt out towards him.

"Hey!" the boy exclaimed in delight. "You knew my name! No one ever knows which one of us is which!"

Eric shrugged. "You look a lot alike, but your mannerisms are different. If neither of you moved or spoke, I wouldn't know the difference between you."

As Henrik took the sword from him, Harald stepped back slightly. "So how are we different?"

Eric grinned, but kept his eyes on Henrik. "You're more cautious," he replied. "You seem to think things through. Henrik is more impulsive. He acts first, thinks second."

Harald frowned.

"That's not a bad thing, for either of you," Eric told the boy. "You complement each other... though you probably end up getting in trouble because of him more often than the other way around."

Henrik grinned, gripping the sword with both hands. "Hey, this is heavier than I expected," he commented as he raised it.

"It can't be too light," Eric explained. "It has to be strong enough to deflect another sword or an axe, and it needs to have enough weight to do damage when it hits someone. There are lighter blades, but they are primarily dueling blades. They are used by people who aren't fighting someone in armour or carrying a shield. That sword is about as light as a battle sword can be. Most are much heavier."

"So it's a special sword?" Harald inquired.

Eric nodded. "It's made with very good steel, and it's an uncommon design. It's slightly longer than most swords, and it can be used with one or both hands."

Henrik swung the blade and overbalanced, stumbling slightly. Eric caught him before he fell, and the swiftness of the movement made his head spin.

"Easy," he murmured, pressing a hand to his head.

"We don't want you to fall and accidentally cut off your foot. Anika would never forgive me."

Henrik grinned and handed the sword back to him. "When you're feeling better, can you show me how to use it?"

Eric smiled slightly, his head pounding. "We'll see," he replied. "But it takes years to learn to use a sword properly. Harald, did you want to hold it?"

Harald nodded and stepped forward cautiously. He lifted the sword, feeling its weight, but didn't try and swing it around. He simply held it for a few moments and handed it back to Eric.

Eric was about to say something when he felt a prickle run down his spine. He glanced up, looking around for what had caused the faint sense of unease.

The street was empty. The chickens had returned to their roosts, and the dog that had trotted past a few minutes earlier was gone. The cat on the doorstep across the street had stopped cleaning itself, its paw still partially raised. It turned and jumped up onto the windowsill beside it and disappeared inside the house.

Then he heard it. It was faint, but the sound was unmistakable.

Hoof beats. Slow and steady. Lots of them.

"Boys," Eric said softly, keeping his tone even. "Go inside and send Anika out."

Henrik and Harald stared at him uncertainly, obviously not hearing the distant sound.

"Just send Anika out, please," he repeated.

They shrugged and went in, calling for Anika.

She appeared a few moments later, drying her hands on a threadbare apron. "What's the matter, Eric? Is it your head?"

"Listen," he whispered.

She stared at him, confused.

"Listen," he said again, motioning towards the road to the north.

She turned in the direction he'd indicated and opened her mouth slightly, tilting her head to the side.

"Do you hear it?" he asked softly.

She nodded slowly. "What...?"

"Horses," he told her. "Lots of them. I'd say twenty... maybe more."

She blinked and stared at him, her eyes wide.

"You'd better get your father," he commented. "And maybe send the boys to some of the other houses. I'd say they'll be here in a few minutes."

"What should...?"

"If you have anything of value, hide it. Chances are good they're just passing through, but it's better to be safe," he continued, his eyes distant. "Tell your father to dig out his sword and keep it beside the door."

"My father doesn't have a sword," Anika protested.

"Yes," he whispered. "He does."

She stared at him for a moment longer, then turned and hurried inside. Almost immediately the twins sprinted out of the house and raced up the street, each heading to a different house.

Anika returned a few moments later, shaking her head. Her father followed, carrying a sword that had seen some hard use. "How did you know..." Anika demanded.

"It was his posture, I think... or his eyes. Once a soldier, always a soldier." He glanced at Anika. "You need to stay inside. Keep out of sight."

She opened her mouth to object, but Leif was nodding. "He's right," he grumbled. "Do it."

Anika paused, then nodded brusquely. She looked at her father. "Don't do anything reckless," she ordered him.

Leif chuckled. "I'm too old and he's too hurt. We're just here to watch them go by." He placed his sword inside the door and motioned for Eric to do the same. Eric nodded, placed the sword out of sight but within easy reach,

The Sword and Satchel

and leaned against the doorframe.

Anika moved back inside.

"You think they're here for me, don't you?" Eric asked the old man softly.

Leif snorted. "No, boy. If they knew you were here, they'd have come a week gone. Let's just hope none of them recognize you."

"You know something you aren't telling me," Eric commented.

"I know lots I'm not telling you, boy," Leif growled. "And I'm not going to start telling you here and now. Henrik! Harald! Good enough! Get back and get inside."

"You know me, don't you?" Eric whispered.

"Never seen you before," Leif replied. "But you're the spitting image of a man I knew once. Maybe I'll tell you about it later. For right now, you focus on looking like a farmer." He glanced over at Eric and grimaced. "You had to go and shave, didn't you? Probably used my razor, too."

Despite the foreboding sense of tension, Eric had to laugh softly.

The twins scampered back and Leif jerked a thumb towards the house. "You have the packs I told you to get ready?" he asked before the boys darted inside.

"Yessir!" one of the boys told him.

"Good," he grumbled. "Have it handy. Anika knows where to go, if things turn ugly."

"You were expecting this," Eric observed.

"This, or something like it," Leif agreed. "The gods know I saw enough burned-out towns during the War of Succession to know that a place like Anidaron is nothing more than a flyspeck to an army. If they want something, they'll take it, and they'll burn the place down if they get the itch."

"Well," Eric murmured. "Let's hope they don't get the itch." He paused for a beat, and then cracked a lopsided smile. "How far is the nearest brothel?"

Leif glanced over at him, startled, and barked a loud laugh. "Different kind of itch," he chuckled. "Most of those soldiers probably already have that one."

Along the road, doors were opening as the men of the village stepped out to stand in their doorways. Each of them probably had some kind of weapon, whether a scythe or a club or an old sword, hidden out of sight behind their doors.

They waited in tense silence as the sun sank slowly towards the western horizon.

They didn't have to wait long.

The first horses came into view around the bend, a

quarter of a mile up the dirt road. They were carrying a banner, but the fading light made it difficult to see. Even so, Leif grunted. "King's men," he murmured.

"How can you tell?" Eric asked, shading his eyes and peering down the road.

"You see enough banners, you just know," the old man muttered.

"That's a good thing, though," Eric offered. "King's men won't burn a village for no good reason, will they?"

Leif spat on the ground. "Didn't stop them during the War," he snorted. "Don't see that much has changed: same king, just a different rebellion."

Eric nodded, his eyes intent on the train of horses rounding the bend. Twenty... twenty-two...

"Looks like it is just one file," he observed.

"File?" Leif queried, glancing at him.

Eric shrugged. "It's the word that came into my head. Twenty-five riders. I think it's a cavalry term."

Leif stared at him for a moment longer, his eyes contemplative. "It is, but not one that's used very often around here."

Eric turned his attention back to the group of horsemen nearing the edge of the village. They rode in pairs, relaxed and casual in their saddles. Most wore light cavalry armour, a combination of tough leather and chainmail; the chainmail jingled as they trotted. One of the men near the front, however, was dressed in a rich green overcoat with white trim, gold brocade, and shiny gold buttons. He wore a black tri-corn hat from which a long white feather bobbed and weaved as he moved. An officer, Eric decided. Judging from the look of him, it was one of his first commands. He was young, but his expression was haughty as he gazed disdainfully around at the shoddy buildings as the column trotted up the packed dirt road.

"They don't appear hostile," Eric mused softly.

"They never do," Leif's expression was guarded. "At least, not until it's too late."

The young officer raised a hand and the column slowed to a halt. Eric sensed Leif stiffen.

"I would speak to the headman of this village... or whatever he calls himself," the pale-faced youth called out in a nasal voice.

The men standing in the doorways shuffled uncomfortably, glancing across the streets at one another. At last, Leif sighed. "Beg pardon," he said loudly enough to be heard. "But we don't have a single headman. That said, I can speak for the council, I reckon."

"Fine, fine," the officer rolled his eyes, and his

spirited palomino pranced slightly in place, sensing its rider's agitation. "Come here, then."

"Are you sure you know what you're doing, Leif?" Eric asked softly.

"Either I go or he burns this place down anyway. Just be ready." He looked at Eric, his eyes fierce. "Keep them safe."

Leif strode purposefully into the street to stand beside the officer's horse. "How can we help you, sir?"

Eric found his hand moving very, very slowly around the doorframe, and his fingers closed on the hilt of Leif's sword. If things went badly, Leif would need the weapon in a hurry.

"We require all of your livestock, and any grains, tubers... well, whatever provisions you have," the officer told Leif, a coldly calculating smile twisting across his lips.

Leif hesitated, a stunned expression on his face. "My Lord," he murmured at last. "Of course..."

"Oi!" a bearded man in the house across the street yelled. "You ain't givin' away my livestock without my say so!"

"Shut up, Gannick!" Leif hissed.

"I'll be damned if I will, Leif Svenson! They've got no right to..."

The Sword and Satchel

"Corporal!" the officer called out, his smile malicious. "I would say this village is in rebellion. Kill them."

"My Lord!" Leif began to protest, but the officer drew his sword and slashed downward in a single swift motion, and Leif dropped like a stone. The soldiers in the column began to spread out, leaping from their horses and drawing their weapons as though this type of command was commonplace.

"Shit!" Eric hissed, jerking Leif's sword from where it had been leaning. Without hesitation, he hurled the weapon at the green-coated officer.

The blade hummed through the air and slammed into the officer's chest, knocking the man from his saddle in a spurt of blood. None of the soldiers even blinked at the loss of their officer.

It was going to be a massacre. Eric could see that already. While all of the men in the village had some kind of weapon, they were makeshift weapons at best. The soldiers moved towards each home, hacking through the poorly armed farmers with ruthless efficiency. Two soldiers converged on Eric, their swords drawn. The soldier on his left smiled toothlessly at him. "Nice throw, farm boy," the man chuckled. "Never liked that prick. Now whatcha gonna do, though? Not smart throwing your sword like that..."

"That wasn't my sword," Eric replied as he pulled his own weapon from behind the doorframe.

It was as if time stood still for him. All the noise, the screams from the homes around him, the howls of the men still engaged with the soldiers, seemed to disappear. The pain in his head, which had been throbbing dully before, vanished completely as he stepped between the two men advancing on him.

His blade was a blur, but each movement was precise. The toothless soldier fell before he could even lift his sword to block the strike. The second died before the first hit the ground.

He glanced down the street. Twenty-two men remained, all of them engaged in the destruction of the village. A part of him wanted desperately to charge into the fray, to cut down these monsters, but the rational part of his mind knew that he couldn't handle all of them. Now, while they were distracted, was his only chance to get Anika and the boys to safety.

He snarled in frustration and spun back towards the house. "Anika!" he snapped. "Get the boys! We need to go!"

Anika appeared in the doorway, her eyes wide and

the twins clinging to her waist. She stared at him, then looked around for her father. When she saw the crumpled form in the street, a low moan escaped her lips.

He turned and dashed into the street and grabbed the reins of the officer's horse. "Anika! Can you ride?" When she didn't answer, he stalked back and grabbed her shoulder. "Damn it, Anika! It's too late for Leif, but unless you want to watch the boys get killed, you'll take Harald, get on that horse, and ride like hell! Now move!"

He pulled her forward and then shoved her towards the palomino. Then he grabbed Henrik's hand and hurried over to one of the other horses. "Do you know how to ride, Henrik?"

The boy shook his head, and Eric swore softly. Placing his sword down, he lifted Henrik into the saddle, glancing over to see Anika doing the same with Harald. "Okay," he whispered. "Do you see that horn at the front of the saddle? Hang on to that and don't let go. Understand?"

The boy nodded and Eric retrieved his sword, grabbed the reins of another horse, a frisky bay, and climbed awkwardly into the saddle. Fortunately, there was a scabbard on the saddle, and while it was a poor fit for his sword, it freed his hands up. He moved up beside Henrik and grabbed the reins of the boy's horse. "Hold on tight," he cautioned. "Keep low, and don't let go."

He glanced up to see Anika and Harald riding double, galloping down the road, away from the village. He kicked his horse firmly, and the horse leaped forward, pulling the second horse into motion. Henrik cried out in surprise, but held on.

At the edge of the village, Eric glanced back to see if they were being followed, but no one seemed to have even noticed their hasty departure. The horses remained calmly in the street, ignoring the bodies of Leif and the officer. The rest of the soldiers were raiding homes, paying no attention to anything else. He muttered a soft prayer that it stayed that way until they were well out of sight, and urged his horse faster.

Chapter 4

Anika stared at the flames of the tiny fire Eric had permitted them to build, her expression blank. Henrik and Harald were finally asleep, though it had taken Anika over an hour to calm them after they had finally stopped for the night.

They had ridden madly until it had grown too dark for the horses to continue safely. Eric had then guided them carefully into the forest, looking for a secluded spot to get some rest. He'd known that Anika would be in no condition to do anything except care for the sobbing children.

He glanced over at her. The fire cast half her face in shadow, but the side he could see looked weary beyond her years. She looked exhausted, but her red-rimmed eyes told him more than words could that there would likely be no sleep for her that night. He considered speaking to her, saying something comforting, but decided against it. Sometimes it was better to stay quiet. Instead he rose and placed another handful of tiny branches on the flames. The fire wasn't absolutely necessary, as the summer night was still warm, but he knew that the flames provided a different kind of comfort in times of loss.

The throbbing in his head had returned once they had left the road, but it was bearable. He closed his eyes briefly. When he opened them, Anika was watching him.

"What happened?" she demanded softly, not wanting to wake the boys. "Why...?"

He shook his head slowly. "The soldiers were there to gather provisions. Your father thought he could diffuse the situation," Eric murmured. "The soldiers were going to take everything, anyway. He knew it. He agreed to let them have everything. Then one of the other villagers, Gannick, objected; the officer told the soldiers to kill everyone, then he killed Leif."

"Is that what all soldiers are like? Is that what *you're* like?" Her voice was bitter, angry.

Eric shrugged, staring into the flames. "Not all soldiers, no. Some are, I suppose. Most soldiers are simply

The Sword and Satchel

in it for the pay. Some, like that officer, are in the army because they're sick, malicious bastards. As for me... I don't know. I wish I did. I hope I'm cut from a different cloth."

He glanced up at her, and she glared at him angrily. He shook his head and returned his gaze to the flames. "Look, I know you need someone to hate right now; I get it. I don't blame you for wanting to take it out on me, but I didn't kill your father. I wish I could have saved him, but wishes can't change the past."

He rose to his feet and looked down at her. "Now, I know better than to tell you to get some sleep, but when the sun comes up tomorrow, we need to put as many miles between us and that group of soldiers as we can before we let those horses go."

She stared back at him, her eyes still smoldering. "Why would we let them go?" she demanded.

"Because they bear the army's brand," he replied. "If anyone sees us with them, we'll be hanged as horse thieves, and that would be a rather ignominious end, as far as I'm concerned."

She glared at him for a moment longer before looking away. "Do you think they'll come looking for us?"

Eric sighed. "Probably," he admitted. "Even if we hadn't stolen three of their horses, I killed three of the king's men, one of them an officer. The army rarely lets things like that go unpunished.

"You killed three of them?" she asked, incredulously.

He nodded, not looking at her. "A part of me says I should have tried to kill them all," he admitted softly. "Instead I ran away."

"No," she corrected gently. "Instead you saved our lives." She picked up a stick and poked the tiny fire with it. "I'm sorry," she whispered. "I should be grateful... I am grateful... it's just..."

Her shoulders began to shake as she fought to keep back the tears. Eric moved across to her and knelt down, wrapping his arms around her gently. With a sob she buried her face in his shoulder and wept.

Anika cried herself to sleep in his arms. He held her tenderly as her breathing slowed. Once she was asleep, he rose and threw several handfuls of dirt on the fire. The first hints of dawn were already approaching, and he felt the leaden weight of exhaustion in his arms, but he moved to the edge of the small camp, keeping watch, and waited for the sun to rise.

Once there was enough light to see, he quietly checked on the boys before disappearing back the way they had come. He spent nearly an hour carefully concealing their tracks before returning to the tiny grove they had camped in. Anika and the twins were still asleep, and he regretted having to wake them, but he crouched down and touched Anika gently on the shoulder. She blinked up at him blearily.

"We need to keep moving," he whispered. "I've covered our tracks, but if they have a scout, it won't fool him for long."

She nodded and sat up, brushing the twigs and dirt from her long red hair. "I'll wake the boys," she said softly.

He nodded, extending a hand to help her up. She smiled slightly as she took it, her eyes sad, and he went to saddle the horses.

The boys were silent and dazed as he helped them onto the horses. Anika watched from the side as he strapped his sword around his waist with an extra set of reins he'd found in the saddlebags. When he was done he tied the three horses in a line and helped her to mount before stepping in front of the lead horse and taking the reins.

"You aren't riding?" she asked. He shook his head. "There's no point just now," he replied. "We aren't going to be moving faster than a walk in this," he gestured to the heavy woods. Then he glanced back at her. "Your father mentioned that you knew where to go if things went badly..." he commented to her softly, so the boys wouldn't hear.

She stared at him blankly for a moment before her eyes flickered and she nodded. She looked around, trying to get her bearing, but the heavy brush prevented her from seeing anything specific. "He has... had a friend in the mountains, a man named Lodi," she said at last. "He said to go to him if... if we had to leave Anidaron."

Eric nodded. "West, then. Good. That will throw them off, heading back towards them. We're north of the road right now," he added. "Do we have to cross it again, or..."

She shook her head. "No," she closed her eyes, thinking. "It's north of the road."

"How far is it?"

"I haven't been up there since I was a child," she murmured, shaking her head.

"Did you get there in a day, or did you have to camp out?"

"We camped out," she said after a moment. "Two nights, at least."

"Three day trip..." he muttered. He glanced at the packs they were carrying. "I hope you packed some food."

She smiled and nodded. "Not much, but it will get us there, I think."

"Let's hope so. I'm betting that there's not much between here and the mountains, and I don't have a bow." He adjusted the sword slightly, squared his shoulders, and started off, the horses trailing dutifully behind him.

The first couple of hours went by uneventfully, but by mid-morning, the boys were complaining from sitting in the saddle for so long. He ignored it for almost another hour before he finally stopped. "Alright," he growled. "You're young, and you probably know these woods better than I do, boys. Keep in sight, and don't fall behind. If you get tired, get back on the horses. We're not stopping until nightfall."

The boys slid gratefully from the saddles and stretched their legs before scampering ahead of them. Eric glanced up at Anika. "How are you faring?"

She shrugged and dismounted gracefully. "I'm okay," she said. "But I'm not used to riding, either. Why don't we let the horses go now?"

He shook his head. "The boys are all piss and vinegar now, but in about three hours, they're going to want to stop and rest. We can't afford to. We'll keep the horses until tomorrow, then let them go. Hopefully, if anyone is following us, they'll follow the horses and completely miss our trail, but I want anyone following to be sure the horses are with us."

She stared at him for a moment. "I think you may have done something like this before," she observed quietly.

He shrugged. "It's possible," he agreed. "If I have, I hope it worked the last time."

She laughed. "You're here, so it must have."

He grinned at her. "I like your logic. Come on. We can't let the boys get too far ahead."

By mid-afternoon they had moved into territory familiar to Anika. Rather than breaking a trail through the thick woods, she was able to guide them along easier routes, which sped up their progress and reduced the visibility of their passage.

They set up camp in a narrow ravine in the shadow of the mountains. They ate sparingly, much to the chagrin of both Henrik and Harald, who were ravenous. The boys seemed in remarkably good spirits, considering the events of the previous day, but Eric was smart enough not to comment on it. Children dealt with loss in different ways than adults did, he supposed.

Anika was a different story.

The day had been hard on her, both physically and emotionally. He could see the pain in her face every time

The Sword and Satchel

she caught a glimpse of certain places, places he assumed she had visited with her father at some point. By the time the boys fell asleep, she was fighting to keep from crying, trying to keep up a strong appearance for her brothers.

"Tell me about him," Eric said at last, moving to sit beside her after the boys had finally drifted off.

She looked over at him, her eyes moist.

"It helps, sometimes," he added, "to talk about them... about the people we've lost. Don't ask me how I know. I just do."

She closed her eyes, and a tear trickled down her cheek. "He... when Mama died, Papa was the only thing that kept me going. We were both so devastated, but Henrik and Harry were only five, and they didn't really understand. I was fourteen, and it almost broke me. But Papa was so strong..."

This time she didn't try to fight the sobs that she'd been holding back. There, in his arms, she wept as she mourned the bravest, strongest man she had ever known. Eric held her until her tears were spent, gently running his hand along her long, scarlet hair. They fell asleep like that, her head on his shoulder and his arms wrapped protectively around her.

He awoke sometime before dawn, silently cursing

himself for falling asleep. He eased Anika's head from his shoulder and rose, stretching his stiff muscles lightly. He checked the wrapping around his ribs, then pressed lightly in the area where the ribs were cracked. There was still some degree of pain, but it wasn't excruciating. He was pleased to note that the headache which had plagued him for the last week was finally gone. Other than his eyes feeling grainy from lack of sleep over the last two days, he was feeling better than he could have hoped.

He glanced around the tiny camp, making sure Henrik and Harald were still snoring softly. He checked the horses, which he'd tethered to some trees at the edge of the ravine, and then he grabbed his sword and the ill-fitting scabbard. Moving quietly, he headed back down the path they had taken, doing his best to check for signs of their passage while also listening for any indicators that there was some kind of pursuit.

He'd gone nearly a mile back down their trail, and was about to turn back, when something made him pause and crouch down. He glanced around, trying to pinpoint what was out of place.

The sound of a tiny stream gurgling to his right made him shift his attention in that direction. The forest grew slightly denser there, with serviceberry and leatherleaf

The Sword and Satchel

bushes thick between the trunks of the poplar and birch trees. Slowly, very slowly, he moved through the branches, every sense alert for what had drawn his attention.

"Finish washing those pots, Jaden. We're gaining on them, and I'd like to get this over with before nightfall."

The sound of the gruff voice caused Eric to freeze. He stared through the branches towards the sound of the voice, and a flicker of movement caught his eye.

"I don't like this, Tom," a second voice muttered.

"What? Are you squeamish about killing the woman and kids?" the first voice demanded.

"No," the second man replied without rancor. There was the sound of splashing water, and the rattle of gravel in a pot. "I figure I've done that and worse. What gets me is that they only sent you and me after them. That burly fellow killed three good men... well, Jar and Ely were good enough, though the Captain was useless..."

"What are you getting at?" the first man asked.

"It's just..." the second man whined.

"Never mind," the first man grumbled. "Danik sent you because you're the best tracker we've got. He sent me to do the killing. I'll deal with that farmer. He just got the drop on Jar and Ely, and I don't believe Travis about how he killed the Captain. I figure it was that headman who did that."

Eric shifted forward slightly until he could see into a tiny clearing. One man, a thickset brute with long, greasy black hair, was sitting on a stump, picking at his fingernails with a dagger. He was shirtless, and his boots and sword were leaning against a saddle by the remains of the fire. The second man was crouched in the steam, washing the pots. He was tall and balding, and Eric could see he was missing two fingers on his left hand. Their horses were tethered across the clearing.

Eric took a moment to study the clearing, and he smiled slightly. It was covered in numerous jagged little stones, which would make moving difficult for the two bootless men. He checked to make sure the man in the creek didn't have a weapon immediately at hand. He could see a dagger strapped to the man's belt, but his bow, a standard cavalry short bow, lay unstrung beside one of the bedrolls.

Eric quietly drew his sword from the scabbard, and then untied the makeshift belt and laid it and the scabbard on the ground. Then, moving with calculated speed, he burst into the clearing with a howl.

The man in the creek stumbled backwards and fell into the water. The man on the stump jerked to his feet, clutching his dagger and staring wide eyed at Eric.

The Sword and Satchel

Eric didn't give the dark-haired man time to react. He charged across the clearing, the tip of his sword held low. The dark-haired soldier jerked his arm back to throw the dagger, but Eric was too quick. He planted his lead foot a yard from the started man and struck, the blade catching the unprepared soldier under his left ribs and slashing up through his chest.

The second soldier had splashed to his feet, and was gripping his dagger, terror in his eyes. Eric advanced slowly, stalking his prey.

The second soldier, the scout, backed away, looking for an escape. Eric's eyes narrowed as he reached the edge of the creek.

The man bolted, but Eric moved with the speed of a striking snake. The scout dropped his dagger and staggered a step more, his hands reaching up to clutch at his throat, blood pouring down the front of his leather jerkin. Then he collapsed to his knees and fell face down in the tiny brook, blood staining the swift moving water.

Eric turned and glanced back at the camp. He bent down and picked up the dagger and the pots the scout had dropped. Then he walked over and rummaged through the packs and saddlebags. Along with their weapons and food, Eric found a couple of coin purses. One was filled mainly with copper jots, but the other had several silver crowns and a gold hawk. He studied the gold coin, frowning. It wasn't unheard of for a soldier to have a few silver coins, especially if he was fond of dice, but soldiers didn't often carry gold. He shook his head and put all the coins into one purse.

He gathered up everything he felt he could use or sell and stuffed it into one of packs, tying the dead man's sword to the side. He found the dead soldier's leather and chain armour. It was simple and unadorned, and he adjusted the leather ties until it fit him. Then he retrieved his scabbard. He replaced his makeshift sword belt with the thick leather belt that had held the other man's sword. The short bow he strung, and he slung the quiver of arrows across his back.

He threw the pack over his shoulder and walked over to the horses. He wished he could alter their brand, but he knew that horse traders were always looking for that sort of thing. Instead he pulled off their halters and slapped them smartly on the rump, sending them off in different directions. Ultimately they would return the way they had come, or they'd fall prey to one of the wolves or cougars that likely lived in this forest. Either way, they wouldn't return to anyone who recognized them.

Feeling significantly more at ease, Eric gave the

The Sword and Satchel

clearing one more quick glance. The saddles and the bodies he left where they lay. The saddles, like the horses, were distinctive. No one would buy them, and without the horses, they were useless anyway. As for the bodies, no one was likely to come looking for them for some time, and by then the scavengers would have dealt with them.

He smiled coldly at the body of the dark-haired soldier. He wasn't proud of the way he'd dealt with them, but he knew better than to think he'd had any other real choice.

Chapter 5

He let Anika and the boys sleep until mid-morning. Ultimately, however, he knew they had to keep going. While there was no longer any real concern of pursuit, they still had a long way to go.

Anika's reaction to seeing him in the chain and leather armour was pretty much what he'd anticipated.

"You what?" she demanded.

"I went back down the trail and dealt with the men following us," he repeated simply.

"And you took their armour and weapons?"

He shrugged. "They weren't going to be using them anymore," he replied laconically.

"Did you kill them in their sleep?" she spat, her

expression furious.

Eric stared at her coldly. "No, but I would have if they'd been sleeping. Look, Anika, this isn't some fairy tale where the hero hands his opponent a fallen sword so they can fight a clean duel. Those men were sent to find us and kill us. Not me. Us. You, Harald, Henrik... all of us. And believe me, it sounded like it wasn't the first time they'd done something like that, so save your pity for someone who deserves it."

She opened her mouth to speak, but then shut it and turned abruptly away. "You have such a casual attitude towards death," she murmured.

He shrugged and walked over to the horses. He removed their halters and slapped each firmly on the rump. As the horses thundered away, he glanced back over his shoulder. "It's not that I am casual about death," he told her. "It's that I'm pretty damn fervent about staying alive. Now I'll pack up. Get the boys up and ready to go. We've got a long hike ahead of us."

She walked in complete silence for over an hour, pointedly avoiding looking at him, before she finally sighed in exasperation and slowed down to walk beside him. "I'm just not used to all of this," she said at last. "I've gone my whole life without ever... the closest I came to death was

The Sword and Satchel

when Mama died of the fever. Then suddenly..."

He nodded in understanding, but said nothing.

"What I'm trying to say is I'm sorry for judging you like that," she continued. "I know you did what you thought was best."

He smiled wryly. "Apology accepted."

"Is it hard?" she asked softly. "Killing someone, I mean?"

He tilted his head slightly, considering. "Yes and no," he said at last. "Deciding to kill someone, consciously deciding they have to die, that's hard. Actually killing them... I guess it depends on how skilled they are. The soldiers in the village... I just reacted. I didn't have to think. The men this morning... if I hadn't heard them talking, it would have been a difficult choice. As it was, they made it easy."

She glanced at the sword tied to his pack. It was a serviceable blade, utterly unremarkable. "Could... could you show me how to use that?" she asked softly.

He studied her for a moment, trying to read her expression. "Why?" he asked finally.

She looked away, her hands balling into fists. When she looked back at him, her expression was hard. "I don't want to feel helpless," she said finally. "Back in the village,

The Sword and Satchel

when Papa agreed with you that I had to hide... I felt useless. It was a scarier feeling than even the terror I felt when we ran out to the horses."

He took a deep breath. "Is that the only reason?"

Her face grew flushed and she looked away again. "I..." she struggled to find the words, but at last shook her head in frustration. "No," she admitted, "but the rest is more complicated."

He nodded slowly. "It's never simple," he murmured. "I have to warn you, it isn't easy. You're going to want to quit, and I won't try to stop you."

"I thought you were going to say no," she breathed, startled. "I thought you would say a woman has no need for a sword."

He laughed roughly. "Hardly," he said, his voice slightly sad. "Sometimes I think women need to know how to use a weapon more than anyone."

She frowned. "Why?"

He simply looked at her for a moment, not speaking. When she seemed confused, he sighed. "Women have something a lot of men are willing to take by force," he explained, looking uncomfortable.

Her face grew almost as red as her hair, and she stumbled. "Oh," she murmured.

He coughed and glanced around. "So," he murmured, changing the subject, "who is this person we're trying to find?"

"Lodi? He's a friend of my father's. They hunt together, every autumn. My father said they joined the army together."

Eric nodded. "That's as good a choice as any to send your family to, I suppose. Will he know who you are?"

"I haven't seen him since before Mama died, but I think he'll remember."

"I would imagine," Eric agreed. "You're a hard person to forget."

She glanced at him from the corner of her eye and smiled timidly. "Thank you."

With a sudden spring in her step, she skipped forward calling for the boys, who came scrambling back after a few moments. Eric watched her, a tiny grin tugging at the corners of his mouth.

"We're near the battlefield," Henrik exclaimed as he drew close. "Can we go back? I still want to see if I can find a sword." He glanced at Eric's sword and frowned slightly. "Or maybe a dagger."

Anika looked back at him. "Henrik's right. We're only a few minutes away. I know, before, that you said you wanted to go there...?"

Eric nodded. "I do," he replied. "If it's not out of the way, let's go."

She crouched down beside Henrik. "It's been a while since we were there, Henrik. It's not going to be a pleasant place. I'm not sure you and Harald should come with us."

Henrik cocked his head, not understanding.

"Do you remember that dead gopher last summer? The one that Gannick's cat brought in and left in the corner?"

He nodded, wrinkling his nose. "Yeah," he admitted. "It stank."

"It's going to smell like that, only a lot worse," Anika told him.

"Eww," Harald exclaimed. "How much worse?"

"Well, think about how big the gopher was, then remember how many people were lying there..." Anika replied.

"Yuck!" Henrik pretended to gag.

"Why don't we set up a little camp here?" Eric suggested. "The boys can stay here and have some food while we're gone."

Anika nodded. "I think that's a good idea." She

glanced around at the trees. "You know what to do if you see a bear or a wolf, right?" she asked the boys.

"Climb a tree," the boys said in unison.

"And get as high as you can," she instructed.

"And make sure it's not a tree the bear can push over," Eric supplied. At Anika's frown, he held up his hands. "Sorry. Just trying to help."

She pointed at a sturdy looking black ash nearby. "Show me," she instructed the boys.

They grinned at each other and sprinted across to the tree, leaping up nimbly to grab hold of the lowest limbs, then scrambling up the tree like they were squirrels.

"Good enough," she called out. "Come back down."

When the boys got back, she laid her pack on the ground and pulled out some dried meat and a half-wheel of cheese. Eric rummaged through his pack and brought out a pair of small apples, slightly bruised. The boys stared at them suspiciously. "What are those?" Harald asked.

Eric stared at him incredulously. "What do you mean what are these? Haven't you ever had an apple?"

The boy shook his head, and Eric glanced at Anika. She shrugged. "Neither have I," she told him.

He muttered something under his breath and pulled out a third apple. "I'd recommend waiting until after we get back before eating anything," he cautioned, "but here. Now you can say you've had an apple."

Henrik took a tentative bite and his eyes lit up. "Hey!" he grinned, shoving an uncertain looking Harald. "This is good!"

Eric smiled, glancing at Anika. "Let's go."

They left their packs with the twins and Anika led Eric up a small slope.

"What do you expect to learn from this?" she asked him, breaking the silence that had begun to stretch as they walked.

He frowned, his expression uncertain. "I don't know," he admitted. "Maybe nothing, but maybe something there will trigger my memory. I've been too busy the last couple of days to really dwell on it, but it's unpleasant, not knowing who I am, where I'm from..."

She reached out and touched his arm.

"I think..." he began, but then he hesitated. She raised an eyebrow in inquiry, and he glanced at her. "I think your father knew something. Just before the soldiers arrived, he said I reminded him of someone."

She leaned back, startled. "Really? Who?"

He shook his head in frustration. "I don't know. He wouldn't say. And now..."

He didn't finish, and she remained silent, her expression guarded.

"I'm sorry," he murmured. "I shouldn't have brought it up."

She smiled weakly. "It's not like I can pretend it didn't happen," she said. "It was going to happen anyway. The attacks he was having were getting worse. I just didn't expect it to be so... sudden."

He was about to say something when he hesitated, his nose wrinkling. "Gods," he muttered. "I guess we're getting close."

She nodded, coughing at the faint reek that drifted on the breeze. "It's a few hundred yards still," she added.

He looked at her. "Why don't you stay here? There's no need for both of us to have to smell that stench. I can't imagine I'll be very long. Not in that."

Her grateful look made him smile, and he set his shoulders as though he was about to march into the underworld itself. "Alright," he muttered. "Be right back."

The stench grew steadily worse as he approached the clearing. He tried breathing through his mouth, but that helped only marginally. When he finally left the trees and stepped onto the battlefield, he had to pause, retching.

The field was a charnel house. The bodies had been

ravaged by scavengers, and the smell of death and rotting meat was overpowering. He stared around at the carnage.

All told, it wasn't much of a battlefield, he decided. There were close to thirty bodies, but no more. Several tattered banners fluttered in the breeze, bearing a white hawk on a green background. It was the same banner the soldiers had carried into Anidaron, the banner of the king. Most of the bodies on the ground had traces of green in their torn and grime-covered cloaks. The bright afternoon sunlight gleamed hotly off the steel armour the dead still wore. He stared at the scene, trying to make sense of what he was seeing.

Of the fallen, he figured twenty-four or so were king's men. That left six others. Each of the others was surrounded by at least three of the king's men. Near the center of the clearing, a cluster of six of the green-cloaked figures surrounded a discarded shirt of chainmail. A broken staff with a ragged banner leaned drunkenly near the group. Almost against his will, he found himself drawn towards it, pulled by a need to know what emblem was sewn on the ragged cloth.

Coughing, he weaved his way forward, stepping over and around the bodies, trying not to look too closely at the bloated corpses.

He paused before he looked at the banner, reaching down to lift the shirt of chain links. It was lighter than he expected, speaking to the quality of the steel used. It slithered metallically in his hands as he rolled it up, tucking it under his arm. At last, after bracing himself, he looked at the torn banner.

The cloth was a rich scarlet, and in the center of the banner, fluttering in the breeze, was a black hawk identical to the ones tattooed on his collarbones.

Chapter 6

"So," Anika rose to her feet as Eric drew into sight. She'd moved back a few dozen yards, to avoid the smell of death on the breeze. "Did you... did it help?"

He frowned at the ground, stopping a few feet from her, his fingers unconsciously flexing around the steel links of the chain shirt in his hands. "I don't know if 'help' is the right word. I didn't suddenly remember anything, if that's what you mean."

"But...?" she pressed.

He rubbed a hand across the back of his neck, his gaze troubled. "I'm still trying to sort things out. The way the battlefield is just doesn't make sense to me."

She stepped closer to him, touching his arm gently.

"Explain it to me," she suggested. "I don't think I'll be able to help, but maybe explaining it will help clarify things for you."

He paused and nodded, moving to sit down cross-legged against a large poplar. She joined him, curling her feet under her in a posture that looked incredibly uncomfortable to him. "It was an ambush," he observed quietly. "But why would someone send twenty-five men to ambush a party of seven? And why not use archers?"

"Start at the beginning," Anika told him. "I didn't see much of the battlefield when I was there."

He nodded and glanced around for a few pebbles which he lay out in a circle. "Unless I missed something, there were six men with me," he told her. "They were wearing the same kind of armour as this," he patted the chainmail beside him. "No surcoats, no cloaks. It appeared as though we were trying to remain unnoticed, except for the banner." He shook his head. "That was planted in the ground near where I fell, like it was a rallying point..."

"Was it a grey banner with a blue cross?" she asked.

He shook his head. "No. It was red, with a black bird, like the one on my sword. Why?"

"The blue cross is Masimor's sigil," Anika explained. "I thought maybe..."

Eric nodded slowly. "That would have made more sense." He paused for a moment, then continued. "The men with me were spread out like this," he pointed at the pebbles, "in a circle around the banner, like they were protecting something."

"That's where you were?"

He nodded.

She frowned. "Was there anything else?"

He shook his head.

"So," she paused, looking at the pebbles. "The king sent a legion..."

"A platoon," he corrected.

"Whatever. He sent twenty-five men to the edge of the mountains to attack seven men under an unfamiliar banner. How did he know where you would be?"

Eric shook his head. "I don't know. Good intelligence, I suppose."

She frowned. "Six men formed a circle around you... leaving you as the last line of defense?"

He shrugged. "Defense of what?"

"It sounds like you were protecting something, or someone, important... except, why would something important only be protected by seven men?"

"Draw less attention," he supplied. "Seven men can

move quickly, and are less likely to be noticed than a squad or a platoon."

"It could be that you were carrying information..." she murmured thoughtfully.

"But why have a banner that declared us as not some of the king's men?" he demanded, frustrated.

"Maybe you were supposed to meet someone?"

He stared at the circle of pebbles, the aggravation in his face obvious. "More questions, but no answers. Gods, this is..." he snarled wordlessly.

She reached a hand up and touched his cheek. "Eric," she said quietly. "Don't worry about it. You'll remember."

He looked up at her and she smiled reassuringly. He stared into her green eyes for a moment. A subtle tension seemed to pass between them, and he shifted slightly, drawing nearer to her. Suddenly uncomfortable with his steady gaze, she looked away demurely.

"Anika," he began, but she rose to her feet and brushed off her rough cotton pants.

"The boys are waiting," she murmured, looking back at him. "And we've already been gone too long."

He reached up and caught her hand in his. "Anika," he repeated softly, his eyes searching hers. She blushed and looked away again.

"I'm... you make me..." she began, looking helpless and lost.

He chuckled softly and rose to his feet. "It's okay," he said gently. "Let's head back."

She shook her head. "I'm not good at this," she muttered. "Eric, I like you... but things are a mess right now. I know... I can feel that there's something between you and I, but with everything..."

He nodded and took her hands in his. She stared down at them. "Anika, it's okay," he repeated. "I didn't mean to make you uncomfortable."

She laughed at that. "Just being near you makes me uncomfortable, Eric," she said, hastening to add, "Not in a bad way... I mean..."

"I know what you mean," he told her. "Look, I'm not going to pretend I don't find you attractive, and I'm not just talking about how you look. But you've been through an ordeal, and it's not like I'm exactly myself right now, either. I can be patient. If there's really something between us... well, I think you're worth waiting for, so I'm willing to wait."

She glanced away, then looked back at him, her gaze steady. "I'm worried that... that I'll get too attached to you, and that suddenly you'll remember you left a beautiful wife in some grand palace, and the look I see in your eyes right now will be gone."

His face clouded, and he nodded. "I hadn't even considered that," he admitted. His eyes grew distant. "I wish I could remember *some*thing."

She sighed and stepped in to press her forehead against his chest. "I hope it comes back to you," she told him. "And if it does, and there's no wife waiting patiently at home, let me know."

He brushed her long red hair with his fingertips, breathing gently on the top of her head. "I will."

They stood like that for a moment more before she pulled away. He bent down and gathered up the chainmail shirt. "I'm assuming you took this off me?" he asked.

She nodded. "You're heavy enough without adding an extra twenty pounds. As it was, I had to drag you almost a mile back to our camp."

"Thank you," he said softly.

Grinning, she turned and started walking away.

The boys were asleep under the tree when they returned. Anika and Eric let them sleep for a few more minutes while they had a quick meal.

"How far do you think it is to Lodi's place?" Eric

The Sword and Satchel

asked.

She shook her head. "I don't know. I remember how to get there, and I remember the valley his cottage is in, but I can't tell you how far it is. We might get there tomorrow, but I just don't know."

He shrugged and walked over to where the boys were sleeping. "Hey!" he called, crouching down beside them and shaking them gently. As they blinked and sat up, he glanced around. "It's good to see you scared the bears off with your snores."

Anika bit back a laugh, and Eric grinned at her. "Next time," he continued, "nap in shifts. You didn't get eaten this time, but bears love the taste of little boys."

Henrik shoved him playfully, and Eric tousled his dark hair. "Come on," he said, rising. "We've got a bit of walking before sunset."

The remainder of the day passed uneventfully, except for Harald pushing Henrik into a creek. Henrik had squawked indignantly and pulled his brother in with him, and the pair had spent the better part of a quarter of an hour screaming and splashing in the water before Eric had called back for them to hurry up. They regretted their little foray after an hour of walking in soggy clothes.

They found a rough trail that Anika explained had

been used years before when there had been a quarry in the mountains. It was overgrown, but it made the hike less arduous, as the terrain had grown significantly steeper and rockier. By the time the sun dropped behind the mountain they were moving around, the boys and Anika were obviously exhausted, and Eric was feeling the week of bed-rest in every muscle.

They paused beside a fast-moving river that Anika identified as the Clearbrook. Henrik and Harald dutifully went in search of firewood while Eric set about clearing some of the stones to make sleeping less uncomfortable. He thought back to the bedrolls of the two soldiers he'd dealt with that morning with some regret. When the boys returned with the wood, Anika set about getting the fire going.

Among the things he'd found in the soldiers' packs was a spool of tough fishing line and a few simple hooks, and Eric spent the next hour showing the boys where to fish for steelhead and cut-throat. They didn't catch anything, but the boys returned to the camp grinning anyhow.

The night was significantly cooler at the higher elevation. The fire, which before had been less for warmth and more for comfort, became far more important. After their meal of dried meat and the heel of a loaf of bread, the boys curled up as close to the flames as they could safely get before drifting off. Anika and Eric sat staring at the flames for a while longer before Anika finally glanced up.

"Why don't you get some sleep?" she asked quietly. "I can stay up for a while. You haven't had as much rest as we have."

He didn't protest. The exertion and stress of the past few days had begun to catch up with him, and he nodded.

Anika came over to kneel beside him. "Take off that armour before you lie down. I want to check your ribs."

He groaned softly, but twisted to try and work on the ties. She batted his hands away and began untying the leather laces along the sides of the tough leather armour. "If you insist on twisting like that, not to mention charging in to attack people, you're never going to heal," she commented, archly.

He chuckled softly. Once the ties were loose, he raised his arms and she helped pull the armour over his head. The old work shirt she had given him, now damp with sweat, came next, and he shivered as the cool breeze prickled his skin.

With deft, practised hands, she unwound the bandage around his chest. He continued to hold his arms up while she knelt behind him, feeling along each rib and applying gentle pressure in certain places. The pain was negligible, and he didn't flinch or gasp at her touch. "Now turn around so I can see your front," she instructed.

He turned, and she repeated the procedure, testing each rib gently. "You're healing remarkably quickly," she observed. She ran her hand along his left side lightly, where the bruising had almost disappeared. "Here," she murmured. "This was a mass of bruises when I found you. It looked like a log had fallen on you."

"Mace," he murmured, his eyes drooping. "Took a blow from a mace."

His eyes opened wide suddenly. "I was blocking a sword strike," he added, a smile breaking across his face. "It left me open on that side and..."

She smiled at him, her eyes dancing. "You see? It will come back."

He nodded, and she shifted her hand to his chest, just below one of the tattoos. "There was a long, straight bruise here. It's almost gone..." her fingertip traced the faint yellowing line.

He grinned. "My shield. I was holding it too close to my body, and someone ran into my back. I fell forward..." his eyes clouded. "It's gone."

She slid her hand up his chest to cup his cheek. "It's okay, Eric. It's coming back. It may take a while, but it's coming back."

He leaned his face against her hand, his eyes on hers. Then, regretfully, he sat back, taking her hand in his. "Anika..."

She glanced down, smiling ruefully. "Just because I don't think I should, doesn't mean I don't want to," she murmured. The she glanced over at the sleeping boys. A tiny laugh escaped her and she rose to her feet. "Besides, I have two little chaperons to make sure I don't do anything I might regret."

He smiled up at her and reached for his shirt, but paused. "Do you need to wrap me again?"

She shook her head. "You're doing fine. The ribs will heal without being wrapped. But if you can make do without the shirt, I think it needs to be washed." She wrinkled her nose. "Don't take this the wrong way, but it stinks."

He grinned. "That happens. It's the price we soldiers have to pay. Wake me when you get sleepy. I'll take the second watch."

She nodded and grabbed the shirt. "Sleep. I think we're safe for now."

He lay down close enough to the fire not to feel the chill of the mountain air. Within moments, he was asleep.

The Sword and Satchel

---

*

Dark eyes, filled with pride, stared at him over the gleaming blade of a sword. "You have earned this," a rough voice told him. "I had it made for you when you first started training."

He reached out and took the hilt, feeling the warmth of the fine leather wrapping. "That was years ago, Father," he commented.

"You needed to feel you deserved it," his father told him.

Eric looked back up, smiling. Lines creased his father's tanned skin, and a long white scar ran down the left side of his face. His dark eyes, the same shade as Eric's own, looked back at him. It was how he would look in twenty-five years, Eric knew, though his skin was a few shades darker than the old man's.

"Thank you, Father," Eric whispered.

"Just remember that not all battles are fought with swords, Eric. As good as you are with a blade, you need to remember that your mind is your greatest weapon."

"Yes, Father."

His father laughed. "Listen to me, always lecturing. I suppose I come by it honestly, though. Your grandfather was much the same." The old man stared hard at Eric. "Promise me you'll be careful, Eric. This isn't some skirmish against the nomads."

Eric nodded. "I'll be careful, Father."

His father shook his head. "I don't trust him. Go there, hear him out, and get out. Make no promises..."

"Father," Eric laughed. "We've been over this a dozen times. I know what I'm supposed to do."

His father nodded, then glanced past him at the ship sitting at anchor in the bay. "The tide's coming in," he observed. "You'd best be going."

Eric nodded and wrapped his father in a rough embrace. "I'll be fine, Father. I'll be back in no time."

His father patted him firmly on his back, his beard brushing against Eric's cheek. "Good luck, Eric. Gods protect you."

"Eric!" a voice called out from the longboat. "It's time!"

*

"Eric," Anika's voice was soft. "It's time."

Eric sat up, grasping at the fading dream. For an instant, he could still feel his father's arms, could still hold on to a hint of who he was.

Then it was gone.

He sighed, rubbing his eyes. He glanced at Anika and gave her a weak smile. "I'm good," he murmured. "Get some sleep."

Chapter 7

"This is the valley," Anika exclaimed as they stood gazing down the slope of the mountain. "Lodi's cottage is at the far end, beside the river."

Eric nodded, gazing across the pristine landscape laid out before them. Tall spruce and pines carpeted the valley below, and a ribbon of silver wound its way through the dense woods. "I can see why your father came here to hunt," he commented. "I bet there's a lot of game in that forest."

She nodded. "He brought back enough to last the winter every year. Gods, we were sick of salted venison by the spring."

The Sword and Satchel

Eric smiled at her. "I can imagine." He studied the terrain for a moment. "I'd say we should be there by mid-afternoon, maybe early evening."

Anika bounced up and down on her toes for a moment, her face bright with excitement. "It feels like we've been walking for weeks," she said softly. "It will be nice to rest."

Eric bit his lower lip, frowning. "Anika," he began hesitantly, not wanting to voice his concerns, but knowing he had to. "What exactly do you want from this friend of your father's?"

She glanced at him, her eyes troubled. "What do you mean?"

He ran a hand across the back of his neck, looking at the valley. "I know your father told you to come here... but what are your plans after that?"

She opened her mouth to say something, then snapped it shut. "I don't know," she said at last. "I've been so focused on getting here..."

He studied her, his face neutral. "What do you know about Lodi, other than he knew your father?"

She shook her head. "Nothing, really," she admitted. "Except that he's a hunter."

He took a deep breath. "Well, you might want to

think about what you need from him before we get there. He's going to want to know, sooner or later, and it's usually better to have a plan in place beforehand."

She gazed out across the valley, her expression thoughtful. "You're right," she agreed. She glanced back at where the twins were throwing rocks off the edge of a small cliff, trying to see who could throw the farthest. "You're holding something back," she murmured.

"I am," he replied, "but I don't want to bring it up since it might not be relevant."

She narrowed her eyes at him. "Spit it out, Eric. If it isn't relevant, it won't matter if you tell me or not. If it is relevant, it might help me get a better grasp on things."

He pursed his lips, glancing over at her. "It's just that there are mighty few people in this world who will do something for nothing," he said at last. "Now it's possible that Lodi held your father in high enough regard that he'll help you without hesitation. I don't know because I don't know the man. But my guess is that he's going to want something, and you don't have a whole lot to offer."

She looked out across the valley, not speaking. At last she shook her head. "I hope you're wrong about him."

He nodded. "So do I."

The walk through the valley was quiet, except for

the occasional scream of delight from one of the boys as they sprinted after one another, playing tag. Anika was unusually contemplative, and Eric gave her the space he thought she needed.

By mid-day, they began to see signs of human activity. Nothing overt, just trails that were cleared slightly more than was completely natural, clearings where the trees had been stripped of branches below head height to provide better sightlines, and one or two piles of sticks that Eric explained were blinds for hiding behind while hunting.

They found the cottage an hour after mid-day. It was a snug little place in the middle of a large clearing beside a swift-moving creek. The building was made from stripped logs that had been coated with some kind of resin. The roof was peat, and the grass on top was waving gently in the light breeze. A cow glanced up at them from a rough pen near the squat building, and chickens clucked contentedly as they wandered around, pecking the ground. Except for the resin coating on the logs of the cabin, it could have passed as a respectable house in Anidaron.

A ribbon of smoke curled from the chimney, which was the only part of the building made of stone. Eric paused on the edge of the clearing, his eyes scanning the building. He held up a hand for the others to stop.

The Sword and Satchel

"What's wrong?" Anika whispered.

Eric's eyes narrowed, and he glanced at a patch of trees on the edge of the clearing, about two dozen yards away. "You can put down the bow, Lodi. We're not bandits... but you know that already," he called out.

There was a long silence, then something moved in the trees he'd been staring at. A moment later a tall, lanky figure stepped into the clearing. His long hair was mostly silver, peppered with some black, and he wore homemade leathers. His beard was bushy and wild, and he peered with bright blue eyes in their direction. He held a heavy-looking recurve bow in his hands, an arrow still notched.

"Not bandits," he agreed loudly. "I would think you'd just lost your way if you hadn't called me by name. Who are you, and what do you want?"

"We're friends," Eric replied, stepping into the clearing and motioning for Anika and the boys to follow.

"That's a mighty bold claim," Lodi grumbled. "All of my friends are either dead or older than you..." He expression suddenly grew startled for an instant before he regained his calm. It might be that he recognized Anika, Eric supposed, but he didn't think so.

"I'm Leif Svenson's daughter," Anika told him. "I used to come up here with Papa, some years back."

The Sword and Satchel

Lodi eyed her for a moment, nodding slowly. "You grew up some since then," he observed. "I reckon those are Leif's boys, then?"

Anika nodded. "My father... he told me to bring the boys here if anything happened down in Anidaron..."

Lodi's gaze returned to Eric, his expression thoughtful. "And who does that make you?"

"Eric," he replied tersely. "I helped Anika get here after soldiers attacked her village."

"I'm guessing that Leif won't be coming," Lodi commented darkly. He studied them for a moment, then turned towards the cottage. "Well come on, then. Mind you don't get too near the cow. She looks docile enough, but she kicks like a mule."

He strode across the clearing, not looking back at them. Anika glanced over at Eric, who shrugged. She took a deep breath and hurried after the aging hunter.

The interior of the cottage was spartan. A single bed occupied one corner of the large central room. A fireplace graced the far wall, with a small fire burning under a pot; a small table and two chairs sat in front of the building's only window. A door led off the back wall, to a store room, Eric presumed. Beyond that, the only things in the room were a few long limbs of some kind of aged hardwood.

Considering the man living there, Eric expected that they were ash or yew.

Lodi unstrung his heavy bow and leaned it against the wall, carefully coiling the bowstring and placing it into a leather pouch hanging at his waist. He moved over to the tiny fire. He picked up a cup off the floor and dipped it into the pot, then moved over to one of the chairs and sat down.

"Don't have much in the way of creature comforts," he commented. "Now, Anika... what can I do for the daughter of Leif Svenson?"

She stared at him for a moment, uncertain. "My father..." she began.

Lodi nodded, waving his hand. "Leif told you to come find me. I heard you the first time. But what, exactly, do you want now that you've found me?"

She stared at him at a loss, her face blank.

"Did Leif ever talk to you about helping his children if he died?" Eric asked softly.

Lodi glanced at him, his eyes narrowing. "Might be that he did," he said softly. "But I'm not talking to you just now, boy. I'm talking to the girl. Mind yourself."

Eric smiled coldly at the older man, but held his peace.

"I... don't really know," Anika admitted. "I've been

asking myself that question ever since we reached the valley. I guess... I guess I'm hoping you can let us stay here."

Lodi tilted his head, studying her intently. At last he leaned back in his chair and placed the cup down on the table. "Leif and I talked about this, once, back before your mother passed. I told him I'd think about it. You must have been thirteen or fourteen then. You're what... eighteen now?"

"Twenty in the fall," she corrected.

He raised his eyebrows slightly. "As old as that, are you? And the boys?"

"Ten," Henrik supplied. He was standing staring at the bow Lodi had leaned against the wall. "How do you bend this? It's huge!"

"Years and years of practise, boy," Lodi replied. "A man doesn't draw a bow like that right off. You start smaller and work your way up to it." He glanced at Eric. "Of course, I reckon that big hulking brute there could draw it. Don't stand there looking menacing, Eric. You don't frighten me. I'm too old to be scared, and too damn tired to try and wage a war of wills with you, so sit down and let the girl decide for herself what she wants."

Anika looked over at Eric, who was tense as a statue. "Eric? What's the matter?"

Eric glowered at Lodi. "I know where you're going with this, old man," he growled.

Lodi chuckled. "Of course you do, boy. Your father wouldn't have raised a fool. But be that as it may, I'm talking to Anika just now. I know your father taught you manners... or else that harridan you call your mother did."

"You know *his* parents?" Anika demanded. "How..."

"In good time, girl. Let's deal with you and your brothers, first."

Eric stared at Lodi, his heart pounding. How could this old man know his parents? He fought back the questions, knowing Lodi would deal with him when he felt like it and not a moment sooner. "Get to the point, Lodi."

Lodi smirked at him. "Alright, then," he looked back at Anika. "Your father and I go a long ways back. Grew up together, went to war together, moved to this part of the world together, before he met your mother. Because of that, I'm willing to consider taking in your brothers. They're young, they can help out with the hunting. For Leif, it's the least I can do. The thing is, you're not a child anymore, girl. Now, I'm willing to have you stay here, but you'd have to earn your keep."

"I can cook and clean..." she began.

Lodi laughed roughly. "Look around you, girl. Does it look like I give a damn about cooking or cleaning? No. This is the part that your hulking protector doesn't care for. You'd have to earn your keep the old fashioned way."

She stared at him for a moment, not comprehending what he was saying.

"Don't get me wrong," he continued. "I'd expect you to do the cooking, too. That's my offer. The boys can stay here no matter what. That was what Leif would have wanted in any case. You... you can either share my bed, or you can leave the boys here with me and find your own path."

"That's... that's horrible!" Anika exclaimed, outraged.

"No need to get all hissy about it, girl. You're old enough, after all. It's a simple arrangement... not much different than most marriages, truth be told. I offer you protection and a place to stay. In return, you keep me warm at night. I'd treat you well..."

"But I don't even know you!" she objected, her eyes wild.

"You'd get to know me. You don't have to answer right away, girl. You're welcome here a few days before you have to make up your mind. But think on it. It's a fair

The Sword and Satchel

offer."

She stared at Eric, her expression panicked. He did his best to remain neutral. "This is your choice, Anika. As long as Lodi's offer of hospitality extends to me," Lodi nodded, albeit grudgingly, "I'll be leaving here in a few days. If you don't want this, you can come with me."

Lodi laughed softly. "There is that," he agreed. "You can head out with him. I'll not take any offense, and I'll raise the boys as though they were my own. You have my word on that."

Anika glanced over at the twins, who were watching her with wide eyes.

"I... I'll consider your offer," she said at last, her voice cold.

"I can't ask for more than that," Lodi grinned. Then he glanced at Eric. "As for you, boy... how's your father? I always knew he'd gotten away."

"How did you know my father?" Eric asked carefully.

Lodi laughed. "I fought beside him for three long, bloody years. Me and Leif both. Didn't Leif tell you that?"

"I... didn't get a chance to talk to him for long," Eric replied. "I was hurt, and Anika was tending to me when the soldiers raided her village."

The Sword and Satchel

Lodi stared at him, squinting. A slow smile spread across the old man's face. "Head injury, was it?" he motioned to the stitches on Eric's temple. "Bad things, those. How bad was it?"

"Bad enough," Eric admitted.

Lodi's smile grew broader, and he began to laugh softly. "Now isn't this something," he chortled. "You don't have the faintest clue who your father is, do you boy?"

Eric stared back at him, his face drawn. "I was hoping you could tell me."

Lodi glanced over at Anika. "Did your father ever talk to you about the War, girl?"

She shook her head. "Not really," she admitted. "He mentioned it when I first brought Eric back to the house; he said that men like him are trouble."

Lodi laughed even louder. "There's no disputing that," he agreed. He looked back at Eric. "You're too young to have been born during the war," he said quietly. "But you're the spitting image of your father, except for your skin. That's from your mother."

Eric fought back a cry of frustration. "Who is my father?" he whispered.

Lodi picked up his cup, milking the moment for all it was worth. His lips twitched as he took a sip of whatever was in the cup. "Your father," he said at last, "is Tindal Yolandson... the Black Hawk. And unless I miss my guess, there are some people out there that would like nothing better than to get their hands on you."

Chapter 8

"Oh, settle down, boy," Lodi growled when Eric shifted, caught between excitement at finally having a hint of who he was and nervousness at Lodi's ominous prediction. "You're safe enough here. I'm not going to go running off to Ryas. I've no love for that snake, and I'd be damned if I turned over Tindal's boy to either him or Masimor." He waved a hand towards the chair across the table, which had remained unused since they entered.

"Sit down, Eric. I reckon it's time I told this to someone, and you and the girl are about as good as it gets."

Eric motioned for Anika to take the chair, but she shook her head, glancing uncomfortably at Lodi. "You sit, Eric. I'll be fine."

Eric frowned, but sat down across from the old man. Lodi stared down at the table for a moment, apparently deciding where to begin.

"Leif and me, we grew up in the north, a long ways from here," Lodi told them finally, raising his eyes to stare over Eric's head at the wall behind him. "Growing up in a small village, we wanted out. Most of the young men in the village did.

"Our village was smack dab in the middle of Tindal's lands. He was a couple of years older than we were, but he was the kind of lord who went out to visit his holdings regularly... got to know the people. It's what made him so popular.

"He was only sixteen when his father granted him the title to Jortanlund, the territory we lived in. He came out to visit in the fall, and when he came through Alund, our village, he spotted Leif and I skinning a deer we'd caught that morning. He and his guards rode over; scared the piss right out of me, but he just got down and started asking about the wildlife in the area, said he wanted to do some hunting. Leif, being the kind of kid he was and not really knowing who Tindal was, said we'd take him out, if he wanted.

"His guard protested when he agreed, but it's not

like they could stop him. He just gave him that cold stare he did so well," he glanced at Eric. "Like the one you were trying on me earlier, boy," he added.

"Anyway, he put up at my uncle's inn for the night... first time royalty ever stayed in Alund. The next day, Leif and I did as we said we would, though our folks lectured us on how we were supposed to behave around him. We ignored them. He was a damn fine shot with a bow, but he had no skill at hunting at all. We trudged through the woods for hours, but his guards had insisted they come along, and made so much noise that there wasn't any game to be found.

"Ultimately, when we'd stopped for lunch, one of us, Leif, I think, told Tindal that if he wanted to find a deer, we had to lose the guards."

Lodi smiled at the memory. "Man, he lit right up. Grinned from ear to ear, he did. I reckon he'd never done anything like that before. We led them on a merry chase, those guards, and lost them within an hour. After that, it was simple finding a good buck. We let Tindal take the first shot; he hit it, but too high on the shoulder. I brought it down before it got too far, though.

"After that, he came out to Alund more often than he probably had to; came every spring, just to visit, then every fall to spend a few days hunting.

"By the time we were eighteen, he had us convinced the army was the way out of Alund. He'd begun serving, himself, a couple of years earlier, against his father's wishes, and he had earned himself a captaincy on his own merit. He was a solid captain, respected... Leif and me joined his company a few months before Yoland died."

He shook his head. "That shook him. Yoland was a good man, a good king... and he was in good health. When rumours of poison sprang up, he didn't want to believe it... until Ryas seized the throne."

Anika blinked. "What do you mean Ryas seized the throne? My father said he was older than Tindal..."

Lodi snorted. "That's the story now," he said roughly, staring at Anika with his piercing blue eyes. "But history is always written by the victor. If your father told you that, it was because knowing the truth would get you killed, if you talked about it. Ryas was eighteen when he took the throne... Tindal was twenty. Why do you think Yoland had him marry that Almeri princess? Do you really think Kysid, that clever bastard, would let his favorite daughter marry anyone less than Yoland's heir? The throne was supposed to be Tindal's... but our company was away in the borderlands to the east when Yoland died. Even on a fast horse, that's a month-long trip. News of Yoland's death didn't reach us until the first snows. We started back right away, of course, but it was already too late. Ryas was in the capital when Yoland died, and he didn't waste any time. We were a week into the ride back when one of Tindal's friends in the capital sent word that Ryas had declared himself king, and that he'd placed a bounty on Tindal's head."

"With winter on us, and with Ryas in power in the capital, Urthingrad, we did the only thing we could; we spent the winter in the castle of Lord Jarvain, one of Yoland's oldest friends. It was close to where we were, and Jarvain had always been friendly with Tindal.

"He's the one who first suggested that Tindal raise his banners against Ryas. He said there were lords who would support Tindal's claim, that Ryas was a usurper and a kinslayer..." Lodi paused and stared down at the table. "Then Kyliandra showed up."

The name sent an unexpected shiver down Eric's back. "My mother," he whispered.

Lodi glanced up and nodded. "You remember that much, eh? Doesn't surprise me. She's a hard one to forget. Fire and steel, she was. Hot as fire and sharp as a blade. She managed to escape the capital, even though Ryas had her under heavy guard. He'd have killed her if it hadn't meant war with the Almeri. He'd have married her, even with Tindal still alive, if he hadn't known that she would kill him in his sleep. She escaped and rode through one of the worst winters I can recall to the one place she knew she would find support... not even realizing that Tindal was already there.

"That was a reunion to see, let me tell you. I never liked your mother much, boy, but she had your father's heart. When she rode in..." he paused, remembering.

"Anyhow, her presence changed everything. She agreed with Jarvain, urged Tindal to raise the Black Hawk and march on Urthingrad. It was enough to sway him. He sent out word to other lords he thought would support him. Most of the northern lords declared for him by spring, but Ryas caught word of what Tindal was doing and seized the families of the southern and western lords, holding them hostage.

"That first spring was spent in small skirmishes along the western front," Lodi continued softly. "Having the hostages ensured the assistance of the western lords, though they only sent enough men to avoid Ryas' retribution. The northern lords spent most of the spring gathering supplies and mustering their forces. The southern lords, those who had families still in the capital, spent the spring delaying. They claimed that they were planting crops for Ryas' army, but it was obvious they didn't want to get involved. That lasted until the first series of executions. After that, most of the south fell into line behind Ryas, though a few lords – those who didn't have family being held hostage – remained neutral, waiting to see which way the wind was blowing.

"We had a few major battles over the summer, and it became pretty obvious that Ryas' hold on the western lords was tenuous. They would remain on the field long enough to claim they had fought, then they withdrew. Lord Jarvain and some of Tindal's other supporters drove hard down the mountains, getting to within a hundred miles of Urthingrad before the first snows put a halt to the fighting.

"Ryas realized that something had to be done, or he was going to lose the war the next spring. That was when he staged the second set of executions. For every battle the western lords had withdrawn from, he executed one member of one of the noble families. He advised the western lords that unless they started winning, they would start receiving pieces of their loved ones by courier.

"Tindal tried to convince the western lords to join him, instead, but Ryas' hold on them was too much. They hated Ryas – still do, truth be told – but they wouldn't risk their families... not for a youth they barely knew. That spring, the fighting was more intense, and by summer, all of the gains Jarvain and the other northern lords had made were lost. By the first snow, the situation had reversed, and it was the north that was in retreat.

"That was when Tindal made his biggest mistake. Kyliandra began pushing for him to send a ship to her father, asking for support. She knew that Kysid would happily send troops... it would give the Almeri a hold on this side of the Almerinthine Sea, and it would put Tindal deeply in Kysid's debt, both financially and politically. Tindal knew it would be political suicide, but Kyliandra wouldn't let it rest.

"Ultimately, Tindal decided to send an envoy to Kysid... not for troops, but for food and equipment. He figured that if he could get supplies from the Almeri, it would eliminate the need for the northern lords to supply food as well as soldiers, freeing up a huge number of soldiers for fighting.

"Unfortunately, Ryas intercepted the envoy. He began claiming that they had been sent to Kysid for exactly the reason that Kyliandra had wanted: to invite foreign soldiers onto Prisian soil.

"That swayed the rest of the south. The Almeri are a force to be reckoned with, as Yoland's father discovered almost a hundred years ago, and the southern lands border the Almerinthine Sea. The rumour was enough to sink

Tindal. As soon as the rest of the south sided with Ryas, the majority of the northern lords recognized the futility of the fight. Some turned and threw their support behind Ryas, hoping that he would show them some kind of clemency. Others, like Jarvain, fled to the east, past the borderlands.

"Your father and Kyliandra disappeared. Some said they were killed, that Ryas sent assassins, but I never believed that." He glanced at Eric. "I always figured they went east with Jarvain, or else south to Almeri. Me and Leif, we ran... we ran as far as we could, hid our swords, and tried our best to forget Tindal and his bloody Black Hawk."

Chapter 9

The silence that filled the room was deafening as Lodi finished and went to place a couple of small sticks of kindling on the dying fire. "But no," Lodi added, not looking back at Eric. "Before you ask, I don't know where your parents are, and frankly, I don't care. Like I said, I figured they went east or south. Either way, you're a long way from home. I have to wonder, what brought you into this neck of the woods? Or do you even remember?"

Eric shook his head slowly. "I wish I knew," he murmured, staring blankly at the table. He felt fragments of his history fitting into place, and he could see the faces of his parents, now. Even so, he couldn't remember anything more than flashes, glimmers, of who he was.

Anika was staring at Eric like he'd grown a second head, but the boys, who had sat down against a wall during Lodi's tale, converged on him. "So, you're like a prince?" Henrik demanded, tugging on his sleeve.

Eric blinked. "What?"

"Not just any prince, boy," Lodi grumbled, moving back to sit at the table. "Since Ryas never married, I'd say that Eric is next in line for the throne, no matter whether it's Ryas on it or not."

Eric stood up abruptly, shaking his head. "No, it... it doesn't make any sense!"

"What doesn't, boy?" Lodi demanded, peering up at him.

Eric planted his hands on the table and stared hard at Lodi. "If word leaked out that I was here, who would want me dead?"

"I guess that depends on who invited you here in the first place, boy... and whether your father is still alive or not. What's this all about?"

Eric explained the scene he had encountered at the battlefield, his face wrinkled in confusion. "They were king's men," he continued, "but why would Ryas want me dead?"

Lodi chuckled. "You're Tindal's son, boy. That's

reason enough."

"Who would benefit from my dying here? I mean, if word got back to my father that Ryas had killed me, what would happen?"

"So Tindal's alive, then?" Lodi asked, his tone more excited than Eric had expected. Eric hesitated. He didn't know Lodi, and the man had all but said he didn't care if Eric's father was alive or dead, so the excitement seemed out of place, somehow.

"I don't know," he said at last, knowing the words to be a lie. He glanced back at Lodi, who seemed slightly crestfallen. Anika was still staring in stunned amazement. "I hope so," he added softly.

Anika shook her head, as though finally coming out of a daze. "I..." she began, moving towards the door. "I need to get some air."

Eric watched her as she left, understanding the dilemma in front of her. He wished he could help, but his mind was racing. He turned to Harald and Henrik as they moved to follow Anika. "Let her be, boys. She has a decision to make, and she needs to make it on her own."

"She's not going to leave us, is she?" Henrik whimpered.

Eric crouched down in front of the twins. "Your

father wanted you to come here, to live with Lodi, if anything happened to him. From what I know of your father, he wouldn't place that kind of faith in anyone who didn't deserve it," his eyes shifted to Lodi, who nodded at the implied compliment. "Your sister, however, isn't a child anymore. That makes this situation complicated. She wants to do what's best for you, but she also has to decide what's best for her. You want her to do what's best for her, don't you?"

Henrik frowned, but Harald nodded slowly. "Why would leaving us be what's best for her?" Henrik demanded.

Eric smiled slightly, sitting back on his heels. Before he could answer, though, Harald punched his brother in the shoulder. "Don't be an idiot, Henrik. If she stays here, she has to marry Lodi, right?" he asked, staring at the old man.

Lodi grunted. "Something like that," he agreed.

Henrik blinked. "But that's not fair!"

"It's a fair offer, boy," Lodi grumbled. "You two, you couldn't take care of yourselves in the world. You need someone to watch over you. I'm willing to do that because your father wanted it. Once you're grown up, you can move on and do what you want. Women... well, they don't have as many choices in Prisia. They can marry, or they can sometimes find work as a scullion or a servant. Most choose marriage. Sooner or later, even down in Anidaron, she would have had to find a man and gotten married. You don't have to like it, but it's the way of the world."

Henrik glared at Lodi, and the old man chuckled. "He's a fierce one, isn't he?"

Eric rose to his feet. "He is," he agreed.

"Why can't we all go with you?" Harald asked Eric softly. Henrik nodded excitedly.

Eric smiled sadly down at the boys. "I wish you could," he murmured, surprised that he actually meant it. "But right now, I'm the last person your father would have wanted you to be with. If what Lodi says is true, and I see no reason it wouldn't be, anyone that recognizes me is going to try and either kill me or capture me. I don't know who I am, or where I'm going... I don't even know where my next meal will come from. I've already put you in danger, and it's only going to get worse. As much as that sounds exciting to you, I won't put you in that kind of situation. You will be safe here. Anika will be, too, if she chooses to stay."

"And if I choose to go?" Anika asked from the doorway. "What then?"

Eric turned to face her. "If you choose to go, you

can come with me for as long as you want," he said softly. "You know what I'm facing. I don't have anything to offer, but I won't ask anything of you, either. If you decide to go your own way when we get to a city, I'll see what I can do to help you get started."

She studied him for a moment, her brow furrowed. At last she nodded. "It's good enough for me. Lodi, I... appreciate... your offer, but I just can't do it."

"So you're leaving us?" Henrik asked in a whisper.

"Only for a little while," she said, stepping into the room and wrapping her brother in a tight hug. "Once I get settled somewhere, I'll send a letter to Lodi and, as long as he's willing, he'll bring you to me."

Henrik sniffled, and Harald stared forlornly at his feet until Anika reached out and pulled him into the hug. "It's going to be okay," she promised, her voice breaking. "But I have to go. I love you both so much, but I can't stay here."

"You're sure about this, girl?" Lodi asked gently. "It's not an easy path you're choosing."

She looked over her shoulder at him, tears on her cheeks. "I'm sure," she said firmly.

"Well," Lodi shrugged. "If you get settled somewhere, I'll bring the boys to you. Until then, I'll treat them well. If you change your mind, the offer is open."

She nodded, not trusting herself to speak. Letting go of her brothers, she stood and wiped the tears from her cheeks. "I... thank you for agreeing to take care of them, Lodi. I wish I could pay you for it."

He shook his head, his grey beard waggling. "I wouldn't take anything," he grumbled. "Then I'd feel guilty for making them work around here."

She glanced at Eric. "Can we go?" she asked, her voice tremulous.

Eric blinked in surprise. "Right now?"

Lodi sputtered. "Girl, you don't have to run off right away..."

"Right now," Anika told Eric, her eyes brimming with tears. "This is hard enough; staying will only make it harder."

Eric met her eyes for a moment, then nodded. "Alright,' he agreed. He looked over at Lodi. "Thank you, Lodi. If I see my father, I'll tell him you said hello."

Shaking his head, Lodi grumbled, "If you see your father, you tell him I'm still mad at him for vanishing like that... and that he still pulls his arrows on release."

Eric smiled and extended his hand to the old man. Still grumbling, Lodi took it. "You keep that girl safe," he

The Sword and Satchel

---

growled in Eric's ear. "Or I swear by the gods I will track you down and hang your hide from a tree."

Eric gripped the old hunter's shoulder firmly. "You take care of these boys, or I swear by the gods there won't be enough left of you to feed to dogs by the time I'm done with you."

"If you're done threatening each other?" Anika commented archly. She knelt down in front of the twins and held out her arms again. With a sob, both boys ran to her. "I'll send for you," she promised again, kissing their heads tenderly.

"I don't want you to go," Henrik wept.

"Me neither," Harald mumbled into her hair.

"I know," Anika soothed. "But you need to be strong. This is what Papa would have wanted."

Eric watched the three of them, his eyes burning. At last, he grabbed his pack. The chainmail strapped to the bottom chimed against the blade of the sword strapped to the side. He adjusted his own sword and picked up the short bow.

Lodi rose and walked to the door at the back of the cabin. Opening it, he disappeared inside for a moment, returning with a heavy bow almost identical to the one he'd been carrying earlier, and a small sack. "Give that to the girl," he muttered, pointing to the short bow. "She can draw it. You take this one. You're going to have to do some hunting, I'm betting. Whether you're going east or south – and don't bother telling me because I don't want to know – either way, it's a long walk to the nearest settlement. There are a couple of bowstrings and some dried venison in the bag," he added.

Eric accepted the gift graciously, nodding his thanks. He undid the straps on his pack and stuffed the sack inside. Then he glanced at Anika, who had risen and was holding both boys tightly against her side. She nodded, and he held the short bow out to her. She let the boys go and took the bow.

"Be good," she said to the twins. "And don't get into too much trouble." Then, with a determined look on her face, she walked out.

Eric glanced at the boys. "I'll take care of her," he told them softly.

Sniffling, they nodded in unison.

Hoisting the pack to his shoulder, he nodded once more to Lodi and followed Anika out.

Chapter 10

They made it out of the valley before dusk, and set up camp in a small clearing at the edge of the creek. Anika moved jerkily, like a puppet, her eyes red and her expression blank. She hadn't spoken since they had left Lodi's, and Eric had respected her need for silence.

It wasn't until they were sitting beside the small fire he had lit that she broke down. He held her as her body shook with the force of her sobs, gently caressing her hair as she wept. When she couldn't cry anymore, she leaned her head against his shoulder. "Did I do the right thing?" she asked, her voice quavering.

"Yes," he told her, his voice firm.

She stared into the flames, silent. Eric looked up

into the night sky, at the myriad of stars glimmering above them, searching for something to say. "Sometimes," he began slowly, "the choices we face are painful. We're left wondering what we did wrong to be put in the situation where we had to make the choices we did, if there was anything we could have done differently, and if we ultimately made the right choice." He paused and stared at the flames. "You could have chosen to stay," he continued. "But you would have regretted that decision every day. Every time you looked at Lodi, you would have hated him for what you had to do. Every time you looked at the boys, you would have resented them, blamed them, for something they had no control over. It would have destroyed you, and it would have tainted everything you did. You would have been trapped in a situation you didn't deserve, and it would have eaten away at you until there was nothing left but bitterness and regret.

"By choosing to go your own way, you've given yourself hope. The boys will be okay. They're safe. In time, you'll get settled somewhere you want to be, and when you do, Lodi will bring them to you. You'll be somewhere you want to be, and instead of resenting the boys for forcing you to choose a life you despised, you'll be giving them a chance to share in the life you've made.

The Sword and Satchel

"You made the right choice," he finished lamely.

She was staring at him, he realized, and he cleared his throat. She smiled slightly and touched his cheek gently with one hand. "Thank you," she murmured.

He glanced away, uncomfortable, and she leaned her head against his shoulder again. They sat like that for several minutes, enjoying the silence.

"So..." Anika murmured, finally, "Prince Eric?"

He coughed, looking sharply at her, and she laughed softly. He smiled lopsidedly and looked back at the fire. "I guess so," he admitted. He looked down at the rough work shirt, now stained with sweat from being worn under the leather armour, despite Anika's attempts to wash it. "Some prince," he muttered wryly.

She leaned into him. "So where are we going, Lord Eric?" she inquired, her tone teasing.

"South," he said quietly. "We're going to Almeri."

She tensed. "You remember something?" she asked at last.

"Bits and pieces," he admitted. "Nothing solid, really, mostly just vague impressions, but I remember getting on a ship, and a ship means we go south. Besides," he added. "Even if my parents aren't there, my grandfather is."

"Kysid," she murmured, "the Grand Sultan of the Almeri."

"As long as he's still alive," Eric agreed, his voice distant. "Even if my parents aren't there, if anyone knows where they are, he will."

"How are we going to get there?" she demanded. "I mean, it's across the Almerinthine Sea."

"I don't know," he replied. "But I'll think of something. We have a while before we have to worry about it. What is the nearest port city?"

"Heidal," she commented softly, a trace of awe in her voice. "I've always dreamed of seeing Heidal."

"Well, then," he said, looking down at her. "I guess we're heading to Heidal. How far is it?"

She closed her eyes. "It's over a hundred miles away."

*

It took almost two weeks for them to reach Heidal. Two weeks of gruelling days, limited food, and aching muscles. Eric hunted when he could, and even managed once to shoot a small deer. They had gorged themselves that night, and spent the next day salting and smoking what remained. The rest of the time they ate what they could find, from berries to various plants that Anika was familiar with.

The Sword and Satchel

Nights were a combination of unresolved tension and quiet comfort. While Eric's memory improved daily, certain areas of his past remained hidden. He could distinctly remember growing up in his grandfather's palace, serving in the Almeri army, and the history of the Almeri capital of Kisham, but the reason for him coming to Prisia remained a mystery. So did whether he was married. The former was a source of frustration. The latter was a source of the tension at night.

Every night, after they set up camp, Eric fulfilled his promise to teach her to use the sword. He showed her basic strikes and blocks, then made her repeat them endlessly, touching her with his blade when she overextended, complimenting her when she did something right. Occasionally he allowed her to practise with his blade, showing her the differences between one and two-handed methods. She found it enjoyable, but it left her exhausted, so afterwards, they would sit for hours, nestled in each others' arms, talking about their recollections and dreams from when they were children. Invariably, however, the nearness left them both craving the other's touch, neither willing to act on their growing attraction.

Heidal was a welcome sight.

The forest they had been fighting through began to

thin after ten days. On the eleventh, they broke out of the trees onto a wide plain of neatly cultivated farmland. To the east, they were able to see the King's Road, cobbled and broad, winding its way to the south, and they angled their way over to it. Two more days of walking past villages and through small towns found them looking down from a rise on the sprawling city of Heidal and the vast Almerinthine Sea beyond.

The sight struck Anika dumb. She sat down on the edge of the road and stared, awed, at the glitter of sunlight on the blue expanse of water. "It's so big," she murmured.

"The sea?" Eric asked. At her wordless nod, he smiled. "It takes ten days of sailing to reach Kisham," he told her.

"How are we going to get across?" she whispered.

"That depends," he replied, staring at his boots, "on whether you want to come with me or stay in Heidal. I told you that if you wanted to leave..."

"Oh, shut up," she muttered, slapping him on the leg. "You know I want to come."

He smiled at her for a moment, and then his expression grew serious. "Then we'll have to buy you a dancing girl outfit and some slave chains."

She stared up at him in shock. "What?" she

demanded.

He laughed at her expression. "I'm joking," he told her, gasping. "Almeri women have significantly more freedom than Prisian women, and slavery was abolished in Almeri over two hundred years ago."

She punched him in the thigh, but he continued to laugh. "Seriously," she insisted. "How are we going to get passage on a ship? Do any even go to Kisham?"

He stopped laughing and nodded. "Trading vessels go all the time. Prisia and Almeri aren't at war... right now. Normally passage costs a few dozen silver, but..." He paused, staring blankly down at the city. It was an expression she had become familiar with over the last two weeks.

"You remember something?" she asked when he shook his head, clearing it.

"Yes. My father has connections in the city. I remember going to one of the buildings, but I can't remember the name of my father's factor here."

"So we look around until you recognize the building," Anika suggested, but Eric shook his head.

"That could take days... weeks. Take a look at Heidal, Anika. Really look at it."

She turned her focus to the city laid out before them,

and her face grew ashen. Even from where they sat, several miles away, the sight was inspiring. Huge walls, made from massive chunks of limestone, circled the city. Inside the walls, tile rooftops appeared to spread as far as the eye could see. Towers and domes seemed to leap out at her, each dozens of feet tall. She could see hundreds of buildings larger than the entire village of Anidaron, and warehouses that seemed to crouch like sleeping giants along the waterfront. A massive marble edifice, so huge it dwarfed the other enormous structures, roofed with a gleaming metal and bearing a spire nearly a hundred feet high, sat in the middle of the city; it was surrounded by what looked like a small forest.

She stared at the city for several minutes, stunned. "Gods, it's huge!" she breathed.

Eric nodded, his expression sober. "It's the largest port city on this side of the Almerinthine Sea. Nearly two hundred thousand people live there, and that's not counting the traders and ships that come and go. Walking around, looking for a single shop, would be like looking through a forest for a single pine cone."

"So, how are we going to find this factor?"

Eric stared down at the city. "We go to one of the shipping offices and see who deals with Almeri. That will narrow things down, at the very least. It's possible that I'll recognize a name, or that someone..."

"Or that someone will recognize you," she finished, looking at him in concern. "Eric, you can't put yourself into that kind of situation. How well known is your father in Almeri?"

"Father? He's... well, he's... popular, I guess is the best word for it. If my uncle Kyvin – my mother's brother – if he wasn't older than my mother, I think my grandfather would name my parents his heirs. My father is pretty well known, especially in Kisham."

"And does he look like you?" she asked softly.

He nodded.

She paused. "Then would it be possible to find a trading ship from Kisham, ask to see the captain, and negotiate passage instead of hunting through Heidal for someone you don't even know?"

Eric hesitated, looking slightly lost. "I've never had to act stealthily before. On the way over, we didn't really pause in Heidal, so I didn't have to worry about someone recognizing me and turning me in. This is all new to me."

She smiled up at him. "That makes two of us." She studied him critically for a moment. "How attached are you to that beard?"

He frowned, running his hand over the beard that had grown in over the last two weeks. "I've always had my goatee, but I don't care about the beard."

"I think we need to find a barber," she said, nodding decisively. "Clean shaven. Completely. You'll look totally different. Cut that hair..."

He ran his hand through his shaggy dark mane, looking forlorn. "My hair, too?"

Grinning, she rose to her feet, studiously avoiding looking back at the city below. "You'll look like a completely different person."

"Alright," he agreed, sighing. "But first we need to find an inn. I could use a bath."

"Yes," she muttered over her shoulder as she began walking. "You certainly could."

The final few miles before Heidal were chaotically busy. Vendors who couldn't find places in the city to market their wares set up temporary shops along the cobbled road, calling out to passers-by. Anika gawked at what was being sold, occasionally pausing to finger a bolt of cloth or a fine dress. Whenever she asked the price, however, her face grew grey.

"Everything is so expensive!" she whispered, hurrying to catch up to Eric after one such encounter.

Eric laughed. "You're used to village life, where you traded for goods rather than bought them. Wait until you get into the city. These vendors are here because they couldn't afford the rent on a stall in one of the markets. That means these are bargain prices... on second-class materials."

She stared at him, wide eyed, unable to believe things could cost more than a few coppers for a bolt of cloth.

As they neared the wall, men wearing the grey and white of the Heidal City Guards began appearing, usually in pairs, walking along the road or talking to the vendors. Once or twice, Anika saw coins being exchanged. When she asked Eric about it, he shrugged. "It's probably a shake-down. These stalls probably aren't supposed to be here, but the guards turn a blind eye if they're given a little coin. It's not a pretty practise, but it's fairly common."

She shook her head. "It's like a different world," she mused.

Eric grinned at her. "Then it's a good thing that I remember more than when you first met me. It means we won't get fleeced." He waved a hand at a small boy who came running in their direction. "Watch out for the young ones," he added softly. "They'll steal almost anything."

Anika laughed. "Then it's a good thing we don't have anything to steal." She looked down at her ragged work clothes. "And we look it."

They were stopped by a bored looking guard at the gate, who asked if they were bringing any trading goods into the city. Eric chuckled softly, and the guard smiled sheepishly. "We have to ask," the guard told him.

Eric smiled. "It must be tedious," he commented.

The guard nodded vehemently. "It is. Go on in," he glanced at the sword hanging on Eric's hip and the bow in his hand, his eyes noting the second sword and Eric's leather armour. "Mercenary?" he asked.

"Caravans," Eric replied amiably. "Know who I should talk to about work?"

"Check the docks," the guard replied. "There's always groups heading out. Try to stay out of trouble."

Eric nodded and took Anika's arm. The guard eyed her appreciatively. "If *you're* looking for work," he added, "I know a tavern down by the palace that is looking for a new barmaid. It's called The Flagon Hound. Nice place. Good clientele."

She smiled brightly at him. "Thank you. I'll remember that."

The guard smiled back and waved them on.

The noise of the city hit Anika like a hammer. She almost staggered as they stepped out of the gateway and into

The Sword and Satchel

the bustle of a massive market. Stalls of much superior construction than the ones on the road were set up in six neat rows that stretched for several hundred feet. Vendors called out over each other, and the noise of haggling and the sounds of various animals in small wire enclosures added to the din. The mass of men and women seething around the vendors was overwhelming. People in neat clothing brushed shoulders with people dressed almost as roughly as she was, sometimes cursing and sometimes laughing.

"How... how can so many people live in one place?" she gasped.

Eric held her arm firmly. "This? This is only a small market. The market district takes up this entire quarter of the city. This one is designed to attract the folks from outside of the city, who want to get their shopping done and get out. The shops start in a few hundred yards. If Heidal is like any of the other cities I've been to, the quality of the shops gets better the closer you get to the palace."

"The palace?" she whispered.

He looked at her, his eyes twinkling. "You must have seen that huge marble building in the center of the city. As a major port, it's also the seat of one of the major lords of Prisia, and a major lord has a substantial home."

She stared at him. "I thought that was a temple or

something," she breathed. "You mean it's someone's home?"

Eric shrugged. "For part of the year, I presume. Most of the major lords only come back from the capital in the autumn, before the first snows. I don't know who the lord is here, but I assume he's one of Ryas' close advisors."

He led her through the market, deftly deflecting the vendors who approached them with trinkets and garments. He would smile and laugh politely, then shift past them effortlessly as they turned their attention to more likely targets.

"Where are we going?" she asked as they left the bustle of the market behind, passing onto a wide boulevard where carts and horses joined the throng of people moving in every direction.

"Closer to the docks," he told her. "Most of the inns in port cities get cheaper the closer you get to the shipping quarter. Sailors don't get paid a lot, but they account for a huge percentage of the business in a city like this. Inns near the docks cater to sailors... and people like us."

She stopped suddenly, staring at him. "But... Eric, how are we going to pay for an inn? I don't have any money."

He tugged at her arm. "Don't worry," he said

reassuringly. "I have a little."

She frowned at him, but followed along. At last she murmured, "You didn't have anything when I found you."

"No, but the soldiers following us did," he replied in a voice low enough that she could barely hear him. "Now come on. I'd like to get us settled before dark. You don't really want to be out in the streets after dark... at least, not in the places that I can afford."

The rest of the walk through the city was a blur of colours and motion. Passing carriages rumbled along the neatly paved streets, and the sound of voices seemed to fill the air incessantly. After the silence of the forest, it was almost deafening for her. Shops, with glass in their windows, flaunted fabrics of colours so vivid they took her breath away; men and women, dressed in light, soft-looking clothes, ambled along the roads. A few of these stared after them, their expressions bemused. Anika found herself feeling awkward and out of place. To top it all off, the smell of cooking floated through the air, making her stomach growl.

At last Eric led them into a less-cared for part of the city. The buildings, while still fancy to her eyes, looked older, more weathered. The streets were narrower, and the type of people moving along the streets changed from men and women in fancy clothes to rougher-looking men who eyed Eric cautiously as they passed.

He slowed down, pausing in front of one or two inns. She clutched his arm each time they stopped. He touched her shoulder reassuringly each time before moving on. "Why do you keep pausing?" she asked after he stopped in front of the third inn in a row, with a sign declaring it The Hearth.

"I'm listening and smelling," he answered. "The last place didn't offer food. The one before that... well, let's just say that women tend to avoid inns like that. This one, though..." He glanced up at the darkening sky before nodding. "This one should do."

He smiled at her, his face calm. "I know it's a lot to take in," he said gently. "This is probably overwhelming for you, so let me handle things. Trust me."

She blinked and smiled tentatively before nodding. He pressed her arm gently and led her through the open door.

She didn't know what she was expecting, but the smell of roasting meat, fish, and fresh bread wasn't it. The room inside was about the same size as her house in Anidaron. Several empty tables sat in a rough semi-circle in front of a long wooden bar. A large man, wearing an apron,

The Sword and Satchel

glanced up from where he was sitting at one of the tables, heaved himself up and walked over to them. "Good evening," he said politely.

Eric smiled at the man. "Good evening. My wife and I are looking for a room for a couple of days."

The big man nodded. "Lucky for you I might have a room vacant just now. Room and board for two nights is two crowns."

Eric studied the bigger man. "Two crowns? I'm betting I could go down the street to the Hind's End and get a room for one and five."

"I reckon you could," the innkeeper agreed calmly. "But you and I both know you'd spend half the night listening to some whore screaming, and the other half scratching at the bed-bugs. I keep a clean establishment, the food is good, and..." he added, a smile appearing at the corners of his mouth, "there's a bathhouse in the back."

Eric grinned. "I'd almost be willing to spend two crowns for the bath alone. Done." He swung his pack off his shoulder onto one of the tables and pulled out the coin purse. He withdrew two silver crowns and handed them over.

The innkeeper tucked the coins into his apron and walked back behind the bar, returning with a key. "You're upstairs, third door on the right. Judging from the look of you two, you're used to some quiet at night, so it's off the roadway. Quietest room I have. It might get a little lively down here tonight. Usually does. You'd be wise to get cleaned up and eat before the rush."

Eric nodded. "How long?"

The innkeeper peered out the door at the street. "About two hours, I reckon. Also, ma'am, I recommend you don't go wandering around after dark – at least, not alone."

Anika nodded. "Thank you."

"There's clean linens on the bed, and a pair of towels on the dresser," the innkeeper added. "Bathhouse is through that door. It locks."

Eric placed the coin purse back and swung his pack over his shoulder. "Thanks," he said. "What's your name?"

The innkeeper smiled. "Gunther," he replied. "Now you all come down when you're ready to eat. I've got some ham roasting, some fried fish, and I think my wife's just about done baking that bread."

Eric took Anika's arm and led her to the stairs.

The room was relatively spacious, only marginally smaller than Lodi's cottage. A soft-looking bed and a dresser were there only articles of furniture. Eric slung his pack down, propped his bow beside the door, and took off his sword belt. Then he gestured at the towels on the dresser. "Why don't you go first?"

She grinned at him, grabbed a towel, and practically skipped out of the room and down the stairs.

Chapter 11

Feeling refreshed, Eric glanced at his reflection in the tiny mirror in the bathhouse. He'd managed to convince the innkeeper to lend him a razor, and the face that stared back at him seemed younger than he remembered it. He rubbed a hand across his jaw and chin, feeling the unfamiliar smoothness. His returning memories told him that this was the first time he'd been clean-shaven since he first managed to grow facial hair. He stared hard at the image reflected in the glass, and he decided he liked what he saw, and it was more than the loss of the beard.

He dried his face and looked at the rough work clothes lying on a bench beside the cast-iron tub of lukewarm water. He frowned, not wanting to put the stained

The Sword and Satchel

and dirty clothing on again, but he had little choice. Sighing, he dressed and walked out of the bathhouse and into the common room.

Two rough-looking men, dock workers by the look of them, had wandered in while he'd been bathing. One was hunched over a table on the far side of the room, but the other was leaning on a chair beside Anika, gazing intently down at her. She was staring hard at the table, trying to ignore the looming figure. The man's stance, like a predatory animal, made Eric's skin prickle. He moved over to the table and cleared his throat.

The man glanced up, a lazy grin on his lips. "Back off, farm boy," the man murmured. "I wouldn't want to have to hurt you."

Eric's answering smile was cold as death, and his eyes promised the same. The stranger paled slightly, then straightened menacingly in an attempt to cover his unexpected insecurity. Eric kept his eyes on the man, his expression never wavering. "I expect you have somewhere else to be, stranger," Eric whispered coolly.

The man hesitated, his eyes flicking past Eric to the other individual at the table across the room.

"He's too far away to help you," Eric assured him. "You'd be dead before he got here. Now go and enjoy your evening, and suggest to any of your friends that they leave us alone."

The stranger's shoulders hunched slightly, and he nodded. "No offense meant," he muttered, spreading his hands. "She was alone, and I never touched her."

"No offense taken," Eric replied calmly. "And it's a good thing you didn't. I expect Gunther doesn't take kindly to people accosting his customers."

The man glanced over at Gunther, who was watching the exchange closely. He nodded jerkily to the innkeeper, who relaxed visibly. "No, I expect he don't," the man agreed. "You folks enjoy your stay."

Anika stared at Eric when he sat down across from her. "You didn't have to say a word..." she murmured.

"A man like that has met men like me before," Eric said softly. "Dock hands and the like are often a rough bunch, but they know the difference between bullying a farm boy and coming up against a trained warrior. In his mind, a fight ends with one person spitting out teeth. In mine, it ends with them coughing up blood. If his friend had been closer, he might have tried something, but I doubt it. Did he trouble you?"

She shook her head. "No... he just asked if I wanted some company."

The Sword and Satchel

Eric glanced up as Gunther approached. The big innkeeper placed two mugs on the table and filled them with the pitcher of water he carried before he cleared his throat. "I reckon you folks would like something to eat?"

Anika nodded excitedly. "That ham smells wonderful," she murmured.

"I'll bring it right out," he said. He turned away, but paused and glanced back at Eric. "Might be that if you need to stay longer than a couple of days, I could find a job for you. Looks like you know how to handle yourself."

Eric smiled. "Hopefully we won't need to take you up on that," he answered. "But I'll let you know."

"If you're not too tired..." Gunther continued, looking awkward. "My hired man, the one that kept the door, upped and left last week. Things have gotten rough the last few days. I could see my way clear to returning half your coin if you would take his place tonight."

Eric glanced at Anika, who shrugged. A silver crown for a night's work was more than a fair price, he knew. "I'll think about it over dinner," he said quietly.

"Much obliged," Gunther smiled. "I'll be right back with your food."

Anika watched Eric over the rim of her cup. "You shaved," she observed, eyeing him appreciatively. "It looks good."

Grinning, he lifted his mug and drank deeply. "I can't believe how different I look," he admitted.

"Younger," she agreed. "Now we need to do something about that hair."

He ran his hand through his still-wet dark hair. "I'll think about it," he grumbled good-naturedly. "So, should I take the job?"

She frowned. "I don't know. I guess it depends on how much you have in that purse, and how long it's going to take before we can either find your father's factor or book passage."

He studied the mug in front of him, considering. "There's enough to last a couple more days, if push comes to shove. And some to get us something other than these rags," he motioned to their stained and ripped clothing.

"Hey!" she protested, chuckling softly. "These are solid work clothes."

Grinning, he refilled his cup as Gunther returned with a small pile of thinly sliced ham, some roasted potatoes and turnips, and a loaf of fresh bread. They thanked him and loaded their plates. "Still," Eric mused around a mouthful of potato, "having some extra coin isn't a bad idea, especially if we don't have much more of a plan than find a ship going to

Kisham. It could take a week or more before the next ship sails... and I don't think we've got the money to manage that."

She nodded, cutting up the ham daintily. "Then do it," she encouraged him. "As Gunther said, you do look like you can handle yourself pretty well... for a farm boy."

Laughing, Eric speared a turnip with his fork. "Alright," he agreed. "That's settled. And tomorrow we go looking for the companies that trade with Almeri. It's possible I'll learn something tonight."

She glanced up at him, her eyes dancing. "And I'll have the entire evening in a nice, soft bed."

He grimaced slightly, shaking his head. "Speaking of which... how do you want to..."

"Oh, come on, Eric," she rolled her eyes. "We've spent the last two and a half weeks sleeping side by side on the ground. We can do that just as well in a bed. Besides, didn't you know? According to Prisian custom, since you told Gunther that I'm your wife, we're now officially married."

He almost choked on a piece of ham.

She laughed delightedly. "Just wait until you see my dancing girl outfit."

Still sputtering, he shook his head ruefully. When

he could speak again, he murmured, "I can't believe you managed that with a straight face. You should play cards."

Her face clouded. "Papa always said the same thing."

He reached a hand out and took hers.

"It's so hard," she whispered. "Sometimes I feel like I've come to terms with it, and then it just hits me... he's gone. The boys... gods, it must be so hard for them."

"I'm sure they're doing okay, Anika," Eric soothed. "And your father would be proud of you."

She glanced up at him, tears in her eyes. "You think so?"

"He didn't strike me as a fool, and only a fool wouldn't be proud of a daughter like you." He stared understandingly into her green eyes. "He'd be so proud of you... not just for getting the boys to Lodi, but for everything. I mean, you managed to hike over a hundred miles to Heidal... you're learning to use a sword... you fought your way through one of the hardest things you could face, picked up the pieces of your life, and kept going. You have more steel in you than anyone I've ever met."

"Even your mother?" Anika murmured. When Eric frowned, she added, "That's how Lodi described her, 'fire and steel'."

The Sword and Satchel

He nodded. "It was a side of her I never really saw," he admitted. "But I guess in some ways you remind me of her."

"Is she...?"

Eric laughed softly. "Oh, she's still alive. And my father is just as besotted with her now as when they first met. I suppose it's different, now. They never talked about Prisia much, but I think their first couple of years, before the War, were... difficult. Then came the War, and running to Almeri... and my grandfather."

"Is he as terrible as everyone says?" Anika asked, her eyes wide.

Eric tilted his head to the side, his eyes distant. "Grandfather? Gods, what do they say about him?"

Anika glanced around and then lowered her voice conspiratorially. "They say he was the fiercest warrior to ever mount a horse, that he sacked entire cities in his quest for domination... that he ate the children of his enemies..."

Eric stared at her, wide-eyed. "Grandfather?" he repeated. Then he laughed loudly enough that the men at the table across the room glanced over at him briefly. "Gods," he gasped. "The only thing my grandfather eats are lentils on lettuce leaves with lemon juice. He's the gentlest man I know... at least he is to us grandchildren."

Anika sat back. "Grandchildren? Do you have brothers or sisters?"

Eric shook his head. "No, but my aunt has twelve kids. My uncle, Kyvin... now he's a fierce one. He's Grandfather's heir, and he's the commander of the Almeri army. All my childhood, he terrified me. He looks like a bloody bird of prey. I got to know him when I joined up, though. He kind of... took me under his wing."

She smiled, appreciating the way his face lit up when talking about his family. Then she cleared her throat and glanced at the door as several more burly men entered. She glanced at the empty plates and sighed. "I guess I'll head up," she said quietly. "Come up when you're done. And don't sleep on the floor. I know you're thinking about it."

He smiled sheepishly and rose to his feet with her, walking her to the stairs. "I'll see you in a bit."

She disappeared up the stairway, and Eric turned to look for Gunther.

The gratitude in the innkeeper's eyes when Eric told him he'd help was heartening. Gunther studied him for a moment, then said, "But I reckon you won't look the part dressed like that."

"I can go get my armour," Eric offered, but Gunther

shook his head.

"Armour scares off the customers," he explained. "No weapons, either. We don't want the watch coming around because you went and cut a man to bits. The fellow I told you about left a few things behind. I reckon he was running from some gambling debts. He was about your size. I'll dig them out."

He turned and disappeared into the back, behind the bar, and returned carrying a neat pile of decent clothing. He handed them to Eric. "Go get changed and take up a seat by the door. They'll know what you're there for as soon as you sit down."

Eric nodded and headed up the stairs.

Anika was already sprawled out on the bed, her soft breathing calm and even. He smiled slightly at the sight of her, with her red hair splayed over her face, one arm dangling off the edge of the bed. Quietly, so as not to disturb her, he changed and headed back down the stairs, locking the door behind him.

The common room had grown noticeably busier in his brief absence. Most of the patrons were dressed in the same kind of clothes as the two dock workers he'd noticed earlier, but a couple of individuals wore slightly better clothing. Eric pegged them as off-duty guards, out for a night of drinking. One or two women, their laugher high-pitched, were also present. By the way they were dressed, Eric could tell their profession immediately. He smiled slightly as he glanced at Gunther and moved across the room. Gunther nodded at him, and he pulled a chair up beside the doorway.

The dock worker he'd encountered earlier noticed him, then. He stared at Eric for a moment, then rose to his feet and walked over. Eric remained relaxed, his eyes following the stranger as he approached.

"I didn't know you was working for Gunther," the man commented as he drew near. "Hope what I said earlier..." he trailed off.

Eric smiled congenially at him. "Already forgotten," he replied. "Just have a care and don't start anything."

The man nodded and returned to his seat. The exchange had drawn some eyes, and Eric gazed calmly around the room. If there was any question about his purpose there, the brief conversation had solidified his role. One or two heads nodded in appreciation that there was someone to keep things orderly, and everyone went back to doing whatever they'd been doing before he turned their head.

The Sword and Satchel

The evening passed relatively uneventfully. He had to escort one of the prostitutes off the premises when she drew a knife on another prostitute for encroaching on her mark. He did his best to ignore both her screamed insults and her sudden suggestive offers as he sent her on her way. A brief scuffle broke out between two of the dock workers, but at his approach both men backed down and headed to opposite ends of the common room to keep drinking. He had to help two others out after they passed out on their tables, but that was it.

He figured that the night would end quietly, right up until a group of soldiers wearing the green and white cloaks of King Ryas came through the doors.

Chapter 12

Eric felt the mood of the room shift as soon as the six soldiers walked in. There was a moment of sudden stillness before everyone turned back to their ales. Eric glanced at Gunther, who was wringing his hands, looking nervous. Eric jabbed a thumb towards the door, raising an eyebrow in question, but Gunther shook his head.

The soldiers were young, none of them older than twenty, and they stood in stark contrast to the burly, grizzled men that were there already. They seemed oblivious to the unease that pervaded the room at their presence. They moved as a group to one of the few unoccupied tables remaining, and one of them pounded on the table, calling for ale.

The Sword and Satchel

Gunther, still looking worried, hurried over. Eric watched the newcomers carefully, assessing them. There were six in total, all still wearing their swords and armour. By the neatness of their appearance it was obvious to him that they were new recruits, fresh from training, likely on their first day-pass. That, he knew, could spell trouble. The fact that they were all already drunk, and that they had come to this section of the city, told him that they had probably already been asked to leave one or more establishments.

He glanced around at the other patrons, who were eyeing the new-comers covertly. Several of the dock workers looked somewhat nervous, but the small group of off-duty guards looked almost menacing. Eric rose from his chair and headed over to where the guards were sitting.

"Good evening, gentlemen," he murmured. "I couldn't help but notice that you look less than pleased with our new arrivals. I would ask that you respect this establishment and not start anything."

One of the guards, a man slightly older than Eric, chuckled softly. He glanced up at Eric. "We won't start anything," he said softly. Then he glanced around at the others. "Will we, boys?"

The others grumbled, but nodded. Eric tilted his head slightly in acknowledgement to the man who had spoken, who nodded back brusquely. Before Eric left, the man motioned to him. "I notice you didn't say anything to any of the others... why us?"

Eric smiled. "Because I can tell the difference between fear and anger," he replied. "Most of these others work the docks. There's fear in their eyes. They won't start trouble because those boys are wearing steel. You... you're not afraid of a little steel. And soldiers don't impress you, especially untested pups like them. The way I see it, you come to this inn to avoid louts like that because you have to deal with them every day."

"So what if they start something?" one of the other guards demanded.

"Then I ask that you let me handle it. If I can't, I'm certain your captain will be pleased that you stepped in to maintain order in one of the city's public houses on your day off."

The first man chuckled. "You had us pegged from the moment you walked in here, didn't you?"

Eric shrugged. "I know people," he replied, and walked quietly back to his chair by the door.

He saw the situation brewing. One of the soldiers was eyeing a pretty little prostitute that was draping herself across the lap of one of the dock workers. The drunk soldier was leaning out of his chair, staring at the petite blonde with obvious hunger, and his equally drunk friends noticed and began urging him on. The soldier rose unsteadily to his feet a second after Eric rose and began walking nonchalantly in the same direction.

The soldier staggered across to where the dock worker and the prostitute were sitting. The girl's shirt was unbuttoned almost to her waist, revealing smooth skin that promised much more. She was giggling and whispering in the rough-looking dock worker's ear, and the man was grinning wickedly, his hand working its way up her thigh.

"How much for a romp?" the soldier slurred drunkenly, grabbing the girl's arm roughly and pulling her off the dock worker's lap.

The prostitute squealed and fell unceremoniously to the ground, her expression hateful. "I don't do soldiers, and I don't do children. You're both," she snarled up at him.

He grabbed at her again, catching the front of her blouse and ripping the thin fabric and exposing her pert breasts as he pulled her to her feet. "That's right, whore. Show me your wares!" His laugh was vicious, and he glanced back at his fellow soldiers. "I think a couple of coppers should get you passed around a few times..."

Eric caught the soldier's wrist, pressing his fingers

into a pressure point that forced the younger man's hand to open, and twisted the surprised man's hand behind his back. With an apologetic nod to the prostitute, who was trying vainly to cover herself, he roughly guided the soldier back to the table where his friends sat in stunned silence, their jaws hanging open.

"Kindly leave the other patrons alone," Eric said softly as he deposited the soldier roughly in his chair. "And never, ever lay your hands on a woman like that around me."

There was a second of stunned silence, and then the soldier he had grabbed swore loudly at him and started to rise, his hand moving towards the hilt of his sword.

Eric moved like lightning. Stepping agilely past the rising man, he swept the soldier's feet out from under him, slamming him to the ground and following him down to hammer an open hand strike to his solar plexus, winding him. A second soldier had started to rise, and Eric's elbow caught him in the groin. As the man doubled over, Eric grabbed a handful of hair and flipped the man over him to land in a groaning heap beside his gasping friend.

After that, things got crazy.

The four remaining soldiers had all gained their feet, but Eric was quicker than they expected. Rising up like a striking snake, he caught the nearest of the four in the jaw

The Sword and Satchel

with his fist, lifting the man from his feet. The other three were on the other side of the table, so Eric snapped a kick into the side of the table, driving it into their thighs and knocking them back. Two stumbled over their chairs, falling to the ground awkwardly, and the third staggered back a step, his scabbard tangling in his legs.

Eric slid across the table top, slamming his hand down on the standing man's hilt, forcing the half-drawn blade back into the scabbard. The man grunted and looked up just as Eric caught him with a left cross, dropping him like a sack of barley.

The two remaining soldiers had scrambled to their feet and one of them charged at Eric, wrapping both arms around his waist. Eric drove his fists down on the back of the man's neck, making sure not to use too much force. The man squawked and collapsed, and Eric turned to face the last soldier, who stood with his sword drawn.

"Don't be stupid," Eric warned. "I don't want to have to really hurt you."

The soldier snarled and stepped forward, raising his sword for an overhand strike. Anticipating the move, Eric stepped in to meet him, sliding past him as the blade flashed down to bounce harmlessly off the ground. Eric's first punch landed on the soldier's kidney. His second caught the man just behind the ear, and as he started to fall, Eric brought his knee up to connect with the man's chin.

It had taken only seconds.

The three guards had risen to their feet and were staring at Eric, eyes wide. Eric nodded to them, then grabbed the first soldier, who was still lying on the floor gasping for air. He dragged the man across the room and hurled him bodily out the door onto the rough stones outside. "And don't come back," he called after him.

He turned to find the second soldier lurching to his feet, clutching his head with one hand, hunched over and holding his groin with the other. Eric moved towards him, and the soldier flinched away, stumbling out the door. Of the four remaining, only one was conscious. He lay on the floor, moaning and grabbing the back of his neck. Eric walked over and grabbed the man's hand like he had the first soldier. He guided the yelping soldier to the door and shoved him out. When he turned around, the three guards were dragging the unconscious soldiers towards the door. They dragged them into the street, turned, and walked back to sit down at their table.

The common room was silent for a moment, then there was a roar of approval from the rough dock workers. The prostitute who had been the target of the soldier's interest, her shirt dangling loose, swayed seductively over towards Eric and ran one hand across his cheek.

"How can I say thank you?" she murmured, her voice low with promise.

"Get a new shirt," he replied and moved back to his seat.

The rest of the night passed without incident. Several of the dock workers offered to buy him drinks, and the prostitute – after Gunther had gone into the back and returned with a shirt that hung loosely on her narrow shoulders – continued to playfully offer him other things. To each offer he would smile and politely decline. The dock workers slapped him on the back, and ultimately the prostitute gave up and returned to her first mark.

As the crowd began to thin, Gunther walked over to where he was sitting. "That was mighty impressive," he commented. "Are you sure I can't interest you in long-term employment?"

Eric smiled and shook his head. "No. My wife and I are just passing through."

Gunther nodded and handed him a small pouch. "I figured I'd pay you what I paid my last doorman. Room and board plus a crown a night. You earned it."

Eric dipped his head in thanks and Gunther clapped

him on the shoulder. "If you change your mind, I'd be happy to have you. You and your wife could stay, free of charge."

When Gunther wandered back to help the last of the dock workers to stagger out, the three guards approached. "You know the soldiers are going to report that, right?" the older guard said quietly. "If you need witnesses, tell whoever comes that Len Aberson can vouch for what happened."

Eric smiled at him. "Thanks," he murmured.

Aberson shook his head. "Damn, but that was something. I've never seen anything quite like it. Ever think of joining the guards?"

Laughing, Eric rose to his feet. "Nope," he admitted. "Can't say that I have."

Eric watched as the guards walked away, laughing quietly as they re-enacted the fight for one another. Turning, he nodded to Gunther and headed up the stairs.

Chapter 13

Rumour of how the doorman at The Hearth had taken on half a dozen soldiers was already bouncing around the city when Eric and Anika left to begin their search for shipping companies with ties to Almeri. Eric had asked Gunther a few general questions when he came downstairs, but the innkeeper admitted to knowing very little about the commercial side of the city. He gave Eric vague directions on how to locate a few of the shipping offices, but beyond that was of little aid.

He heard the story of his fight the night before, appropriately embellished, in a small dress shop at the edge of the market quarter. It had been recommended by Gunther's wife as having the most reasonable prices in the city.

Anika stared around the shop, her eyes wide. "What are we doing here?" she asked softly.

"I figured that we'd be less noticeable if we both blended in. I have the clothes Gunther gave me last night, but you look a little out of place. Besides, this is kind of a thank you." He handed her the small pouch Gunther had given him the night before, containing three silver crowns and a few copper jots. She glanced inside and her eyes widened.

"That's more money than I've ever had," she whispered. "Papa always paid for things, when we needed something we couldn't trade for."

Eric smiled. "Well, now you get to buy what you want. Get one dress or several."

A young woman around Anika's age noticed them hovering near the door. Her eyes took in Anika's attire, and she smiled broadly. "Oh, my dear," she said as she approached. "My name is Larissa, and you look like you might be able to use some advice on fashion." She paused, then blushed. "That came out all wrong," she murmured, looking completely embarrassed. "I meant... you look like you could stand to find something new..."

Anika's genuine smile spread across her face,

The Sword and Satchel

---

lighting it up. "It's okay, Larissa. You were absolutely right the first time. I'm Anika, and I think I might need some help."

Eric grinned at her and walked over to lean quietly against the counter as Larissa led Anika around the shop. An older woman was sitting behind the counter, knitting something without looking at it, her sharp eyes watching Larissa carefully. "My daughter," the woman explained. "She's sweet, but she always seems to say the wrong thing."

Eric leaned forward. "She's young," he replied. "She'll learn."

The woman glanced up at him, nodding. "I take it you're new to the city?"

Eric smiled. "Obvious, is it?"

The woman laughed. "Her clothes say 'fresh from the country' as loud as anything. You... you look like that shirt and those pants were given to you and that they're all you have. I could take the shirt in a bit in the waist and let it out at the shoulders for you."

He eyed her. "For how much?"

"You aren't fresh from the country, though," she observed, grinning. Her gaze grew sharp. "You've got a funny accent. Don't recognize it."

Eric shrugged. "I travelled a lot when I was young,"

he replied evasively.

She nodded gravely. "If your woman buys something, I'll tailor your shirt for free. Otherwise, two jots."

He nodded, and she glanced back down at her knitting. "So now that we've established that you're secretive," she went on, "it's time to establish that I'm nosy."

Laughing, he shook his head. "Alright then. You be nosy, I'll be secretive, and we'll see which of us is more stubborn."

She grinned up at him. "Don't often see folks like you in town," she commented casually. "When did you get in?"

"Folks like us?" Eric's lips twitched.

She raised an eyebrow, her eyes gleaming with amusement. "Oh, you're going to be fun," she chuckled. She glanced at Anika and Larissa. "A country bumpkin being escorted around by a foreign lord, who looks like he knows his way around a sword, dressed up like a peasant."

Eric studied the woman for a moment, his gaze intent. "That's an interesting observation," he said at last.

"Like I said, you get a girl's mind going," she replied, eyeing him up and down with a trace of a grin. "So

The Sword and Satchel

when did you get into town?"

"Yesterday," he told her. "We're only here for a couple of days."

She nodded. "I assume you're not staying at one of the fancy places near the palace... not dressed like that and coming in here to get her new togs."

His grin broadened. "You're pretty good at this," he commented.

The sparkle in her eyes was genuine as she set down her knitting. "Been working this shop for nigh on thirty years, son. It can get mighty boring. Being nosy only pays off if you know how to ask the right questions in the right way."

He shook his head. "We're down a ways, towards the docks."

She studied him for a moment. "Might you be that new fellow Gunther brought in to watch his place?"

Eric's eyes widened slightly. "News moves pretty quick in this town, doesn't it?"

"It can, when it's juicy," she chuckled softly. "Rumour has it you beat down a dozen armed men to protect Little Suze."

Eric laughed. "That's a little different than I remember it."

"Why don't you set the story straight, then?" she asked, leaning forward.

"Why would I do that when it's so much more interesting this way?" he replied. At her crestfallen look, he relented. "There were only six, and only one managed to get his sword out."

She winked at him. "A dozen does sound better. We'll keep the truth to ourselves." She looked over to where Larissa and Anika were peering at a dress. "Not that colour, honey. Your skin's too pale. You'll look like a ghost. Now," she turned back to Eric, "where'd you say you and your woman were going?"

Eric shook his head, his expression amused. "I didn't."

"No," she agreed. "But I'm still nosy, and you were about to."

"I bet a woman such as yourself knows almost all the shipping houses in Heidal," he mused, his lips curled in a lopsided smile.

"That would be a fairly safe bet," she agreed. He studied her for a moment, and her eyes narrowed. "You're looking for someone specific?" she added, less a question than a statement.

Eric nodded. "A short man, fat and balding, wears

his spectacles on a chain... He runs one of the shipping companies."

She stared hard at him for a moment, her mouth drawing into a thin line. Then her eyes grew very wide and her mouth gaped open. "I... it can't be..."

Eric frowned at the reaction, his eyes seeking out Anika, suddenly nervous. She was leaning in to Larissa, laughing softly. He turned back to the woman behind the counter. "What?" he demanded softly.

She shook her head, her face pale.

"What?" he demanded again, more firmly.

"You look..." she whispered. "Gods, it's been almost forty years, but I still remember that face."

He turned to call to Anika that they had to go, but the old woman reached up and touched his arm almost reverently, her knitting falling forgotten to the floor. "You're his son, aren't you? You must be."

The awe on her face made him hesitate. He stared at her, his dark eyes piercing.

"We were all in love with him," she continued in a voice that was barely audible. "All of us girls. He was so dashing, so... unforgettable. Then his brother..." she broke off, her eyes wide. "You... he must still be alive!"

Every nerve in his body tingled. For a moment he

weighed the situation, knowing this woman could destroy him if she spoke so much as a single word to the wrong person. At last it was the expression in her face that decided him. He nodded tersely, not trusting himself to speak.

She gasped at the confirmation, loudly enough that Larissa and Anika glanced over. Larissa's expression grew troubled. "Mama? Is everything okay?"

The woman nodded jerkily, her eyes never leaving Eric's face. "Yes, dear. Everything is fine," her voice was fragile.

Eric took a breath, about to speak, but the woman shook her head. "Not a soul," she whispered, a tear tracing its way down her cheek. "I won't tell a soul. He... I always dreamed..."

"Mama?" Larissa moved away from Anika, hurrying towards the older woman. "What's the matter?"

The woman laughed softly, sudden joy lighting her face. "Nothing, child. This young man happens to be the son of a very old friend... no one you'd remember. It was just wonderful to hear about him. I'd given him up for dead. Go back to the young lady, and stop showing her the discount pieces. There's no charge, whatever she chooses."

Larissa gaped at her mother. "No... no charge?"

The old woman laughed again. "Not for them, dear.

The Sword and Satchel

Not for them."

Anika stared at Eric, her expression worried, but he waved his hand slightly. He'd used a similar sign during their walk, when a potential threat had proven unfounded. She relaxed slightly. "Have you found anything?" he asked.

"Well..." she began, but Larissa shook her head.

"I was showing her... less expensive dresses. Now I have to start again. We'll be a while."

Eric nodded, turning back to the old woman as Larissa led Anika back to the rows of dresses. "How recognizable am I?" he whispered.

She reached out and cupped his cheek, her wrinkled face aglow. "Now that I've seen it, I can't help but see the resemblance," she told him. "But unless someone my age or older was looking for it, no one should make the connection. Your father grew a beard during the War. That's how most people remember him. He came through Heidal once, before the War, when I was just a teenager. To fetch his bride, I believe. I got to see him, during the procession. At the time, it was the greatest moment of my life."

He nodded.

"You might want to cut your hair, though," she mused, reaching out as though to touch it before withdrawing her hand. "He wore it almost exactly like that."

Eric rolled his eyes. "Everybody wants me to cut my bloody hair," he muttered.

She smiled, and her eyes flicked to Anika. "And the girl?" she whispered. At his cold expression, she grinned like a child. "I warned you I was nosy."

He laughed ruefully. "She... she saved my life. Beyond that... I don't know."

She nodded. "I'm Hilde, by the way," she told him, abruptly changing the subject and extending her hand formally.

"Eric," he replied, taking her hand gently.

"Well, Eric, for a man who should be trying to keep a low profile, you've made quite the entrance to Heidal. Six men? What are you doing working for Gunther?"

He shook his head. "Trying to find passage back..." he hesitated.

"To Almeri," Hilde concluded. "Oh, don't be dense," she chided at his wary expression. "The man you asked for is one of the only men in Heidal who trades exclusively with the Almeri. It doesn't take much to make a connection like that. It makes sense that your father would go there, I suppose, though why he didn't return with an army and take that monster off the throne, I'll never understand."

"Too much blood," Eric whispered, remembering the only time his father had yelled at him.

She glanced at him sharply.

Eric shrugged. "I asked him that, once, why he didn't come back. He said that doing so would be the worst kind of irresponsibility imaginable. He said that the people of Prisia would fight and die believing it to be an Almeri invasion, and that he couldn't bring himself to do that to his people... too many of them had already died. He wouldn't do that again... not for an ugly chair, an uncomfortable hat, and a job he'd hate."

She laughed loudly at the last, her eyes moist. "Gods bless him," she whispered, dabbing at her eyes. "He'd have made a great king."

Eric smiled.

Hilde glanced over at Larissa, who was escorting Anika to a small curtained area. "Looks like they're almost done," she observed. "Now, as to the man you're looking for, his name is Lars. His office is in the South Prisian Shipping Consortium building, two blocks off the Long Dock. It won't be open until tomorrow." She moved around the counter, her frame still willowy despite her age. She walked over to a short rack of men's shirts and pulled one down, handing it to him. "Now take that other shirt off and hand it to me so I can tailor it while your woman is busy changing... and for gods' sakes find a pair of pants on the rack that actually fit you. Those make you look like you're hopping around in a potato sack."

"Hilde," Eric murmured. "Thank you."

She smiled at him. "No, child. Thank you. You've given this old woman something to dream about again."

He bowed his head, unexpectedly moved by the devotion his father had aroused in the most unlikely places.

"Now get moving," she scolded. "That shirt won't mend itself."

Chapter 14

Eric and Anika walked in silence down the street, heading back to the inn. Anika was wearing one of the two dresses she had selected, a modestly cut pale green dress that clung enticingly to her hips and almost brushed the cobbles as she walked. While not fancy compared to many of the dresses worn by other women in Heidal, it flattered her skin and brought out the vibrant green of her eyes. More importantly for them, it blended in to the attire of the people in the city.

Eric ran a hand over his head, not used to the feeling of the breeze on his scalp and across his neck. His dark hair was cut very short, less than an inch long, and despite Anika's smoldering look when she saw him after he emerged from the barber, he felt uncomfortable.

"It looks wonderful," she told him again, smiling at his unconscious gesture. "And without your hair and beard, you look completely different."

He couldn't argue that. He caught glimpses of himself in the glass of the shops they walked past, and could barely recognize himself in the reflection. His long hair had apparently softened his features, and while the shorter hair made him look younger, it also made him seem somehow stronger, more menacing.

They stepped into the coolness of the common room of The Hearth, and Gunther glanced up at them. He blinked, surprised, and squinted at Eric. "Damn, boy!" he exclaimed. "I didn't recognize you two." He shook his head. "It's amazing what a day in the city will do," he chuckled. Then he glanced across the room at an occupied table. Eric followed his gaze to where a grey-haired figure in the uniform of one of the city guards sat watching them.

"Is he waiting for me?" Eric asked softly.

Gunther nodded soberly. "I told him about the scuffle, but it seems that he wants to hear about it from you."

"What scuffle?" Anika asked, clutching Eric's arm.

He lowered his head. "I forgot to mention it to you. It was just a little thing, last night. A couple of soldiers got out of hand."

"So why is a member of the city guard here if it was just a little thing?" she growled, frowning slightly.

Gunther shrugged. "Apparently one of the soldiers was the son of some rich merchant or some such. And he's not just a guard... that's Olaf Hjordson, the captain of the guard."

Eric sighed. Turning to Anika he tilted his head in the direction of the guard at the table. "I have to deal with this. I'll be up shortly."

"And you'll tell me all about this little scuffle..." she growled, then added so quietly only Eric heard, "And about what happened in that dress shop that you've been so studiously avoiding talking about."

He nodded. "I promise."

She gazed up at him for a second, then turned and headed for the stairs.

"She's got some spirit in her," Gunther observed.

"Yes," he agreed, watching her walk away. When she disappeared from view, he took a deep breath and turned towards the waiting guard.

"Just tell it like it happened, boy," Gunther advised. "You did nothing wrong."

Eric flashed a smile at the big innkeeper, squared his

shoulders, and walked over to join the grizzled captain.

The captain watched him approach, his eyes sharp. When Eric reached the table, the man gestured to the chair opposite him. "I'm Captain Hjordson. I assume Gunther told you why I'm here?"

"Something about one of the soldiers I tossed out of here last night being related to a wealthy merchant," Eric replied, sitting down.

Hjordson nodded, leaning forward. "Wealthy and influential. That's why it's me sitting here, and not one of my subordinates. I wanted to hear it straight from the source."

Eric leaned back in his chair. "Alright. A group of soldiers came in near closing. They'd obviously been out drinking most of the night. One of them grabbed another patron. I returned him to his table, and he took exception to how I did it. He went for his sword, so I put him down. I had to deal with his friends, too."

Hjordson chuckled softly, studying him. "You seem to be missing the finer points. He claims you hit him from behind with a club... his back and neck looked mighty bruised."

"Ah," Eric replied. "Him. He had me by the waist, trying to tackle me. Two hand blow, back of the neck."

The Sword and Satchel

Hjordson tilted his head, squinting. "How many were there?"

"Six," Eric answered promptly.

The captain sat back in his chair, running a hand through his grey hair and peering at Eric. "How long have you been in the city?"

"Got here yesterday," Eric replied. "Why?"

Hjordson shook his head. "You just remind me of someone. Can't place it."

Eric shrugged, trying to keep his face neutral. "Anything else?"

The captain leaned forward again. "So you took on six men, all armed, bare-handed?"

"Only one got his sword out. They were drunk and inexperienced," Eric explained. "If they had been older, or had a little seasoning, things might have gone a lot differently... mind you, if they'd been older or had more seasoning, the situation probably wouldn't have come up."

"You realize that this is a harder story to accept than that you walked up behind a soldier and clubbed him?" he asked, his voice sounding tired. "One man takes on six soldiers..."

Eric shrugged again. "Hard or not, it's the truth. You've got three guardsmen who can vouch for it."

Hjordson perked up. "The guards were called in?"

Eric shook his head. "It didn't last that long. There were three guards, off-duty, in here during the fight. They saw it."

"How do you know they were guards?" the captain demanded.

Eric laughed. "Because they looked like guards, and when I spoke to them to request that if the soldiers started anything that they keep out of it, they confirmed it."

"You knew the soldiers were going to start something? How?"

Eric rolled his eyes. "Because they were young, inexperienced soldiers, and they were drunk. That's a bad combination. The way your boys looked at them said they'd had their fill of dealing with that sort, so I asked them not to start anything."

"Can you describe the guards?" Hjordson demanded.

"One said his name was Len Aberson, and that if I needed someone to corroborate my story, he would."

"Len?" Hjordson repeated, sitting back in his seat again, startled. "I know him. He's a good man."

Eric nodded. "Seemed that way," he agreed.

"Well, that changes things," the captain muttered. "Gunther told me much the same story, though a little more

The Sword and Satchel

elaborate." He stared at Eric with newfound respect. "Six men... that's impressive. Are you a soldier yourself?"

"Used to be," Eric replied.

The captain's eyes narrowed. "Deserter?" he growled.

"If I was a deserter, I'd have bolted as soon as I saw you sitting there, Captain," Eric stated, wearily.

The captain continued to stare at him, his brows furrowed. Finally he shook his head and sat back. "True," he agreed. His face grew puzzled. "I swear I've seen you somewhere before," he muttered. "It's the damndest thing."

Eric shrugged. "I'd remember," he said, almost laughing at the irony of the statement.

"Well," Hjordson said, rising. "I'll talk to Len. If he corroborates your story, you've got nothing to worry about. If I find out you're lying, you'll go to jail and Gunther will, too, for obstructing an officer of the guard."

"Fair enough," Eric sighed, rising as well and extending his hand. "You know where to find me."

The captain shook his hand, his expression still troubled. Then he strode out of the inn, shaking his head.

Gunther approached Eric, wiping his hands down on his apron. "You feel like working again tonight?"

Eric shrugged, staring after the captain. "I'll have to

check with Anika, but I don't see any reason not to."

Anika was waiting for him, sitting quietly on the edge of the bed, staring out the window.

"So?" she asked, tapping her foot quietly on the floor.

He smiled lopsidedly at her. "Well," he said. "According to rumour, I fought twenty giants last night and ate their children for breakfast."

She reached back and grabbed a pillow, throwing it at him. "Be serious, Eric. You had me really worried in the dress shop, and then the captain of the guard was waiting for you when we got back here... and we haven't even been here for a full day!"

Eric's face grew somber. "Hilde, the owner of the shop, recognized me... or, at least recognized who I am."

Anika's face grew ashen and she glanced around the room as though looking for an escape.

"She won't talk," he assured her gently. Then, sitting down beside her, he told her the events of the night before.

"And he wants you to do it again?" she demanded incredulously when he finished.

Eric nodded.

She stared at him, her eyes concerned. "Can I be

down there tonight?"

Frowning, he glanced at her. "It's a rough crowd," he advised her. "Chances are good the patrons would assume you're a prostitute."

"So talk to Gunther and ask if I can work the tables. I just hate feeling useless... helpless."

He leaned back and lay on the bed staring up at the ceiling. She leaned back beside him, curling into the crook of his arm. "If something happened to you down there..."

He wrapped his arm around her shoulders, pulling her closer. It was meant to be a reassuring motion, but she rolled with it and sprawled across his chest, staring down at him, her lips almost brushing his, her long red hair cascading down, framing his face. She stared intently into his dark eyes, her breath mingling with his. Then, slowly, she leaned in and kissed him tenderly.

"Please," she murmured after a moment, her lips shifting to his cheek.

He nodded. "I'll ask him," he promised quietly. "Anika..."

She pulled back, smiling coyly. "I know," she said softly. "That wasn't really fair."

"No," he agreed, smiling up at her. "It wasn't."

She leaned in and kissed him again. "I told you

before that just because I knew I shouldn't didn't mean I didn't want to," she said at last, pushing herself up onto her forearms.

"I'm not," he said suddenly. She stared at him blankly, completely confused.

"I'm not married," he whispered. "There isn't some woman back home wondering if I'm coming back. A lot came back to me after I spoke to Hilde. That was why I was so quiet coming back here. I was trying to think of a good way to tell you."

She stared at him, her jaw slack. "You... you aren't? You're sure?"

"I'm sure. There's no one waiting for me... and I don't *want* someone waiting patiently at home."

She looked heartbroken until he added, "I want someone who is willing to walk a hundred miles through the forest right beside me."

It was a long time before he found his way back downstairs to talk to Gunther.

Chapter 15

"Are you here to pick a fight with me or to drink?" Eric demanded, staring coldly at the heavyset man looming over him.

"Depends," the man grinned. He was missing all of his front teeth, Eric noted, and he appeared to favor his left leg slightly. "Do you think you can take me?"

"Let's not try to find out," Eric replied calmly. This wasn't the first street tough who had come in, just the dumbest. The others had sauntered in, looking around for the 'new man'. One by one, Eric had met their gaze steadily, and they had decided that drinking looked more appealing than fighting. This one, however, had less brains than he had teeth.

"What's the matter, little man? Spineless?"

From his chair beside the door, Eric stared up at the

hulking thug in genuine amusement. "Wow," he commented softly. "I haven't heard someone use that particular taunt since I was nine years old."

"Yeah? And what'd you do then?" the big man smirked.

Eric rose smoothly to his feet and the man stumbled backwards, caught off-guard. "Same thing I'm going to do right now," Eric said, smiling, and walked over to a table where a small argument threatened to escalate. The group at the table took one look at him and settled down.

He scanned the room, spotting Anika in her serving apron and the white shirt and black skirt they had hurried back to Hilde's to buy when Gunther had agreed to let her do the serving. She was joking with the dock-hands like she'd known them her entire life. There had been one or two pinches earlier in the evening, but the sudden silence from everyone in the room who had been there the night before – and everyone but the soldiers and guards were back again – in combination with Eric's suddenly menacing expression had put a rapid stop to that. He figured he had the dock worker from the night before to thank for telling everyone that Anika was with him.

Anika caught his eye and grinned at him, then twirled gracefully and walked to the bar to get more ale.

The Sword and Satchel

Gunther was grinning, his gamble with Anika having paid off far better than he'd anticipated. Her easy manner with the patrons, and her undisguised beauty, had won over everyone – even Little Suze, who had come back looking for Eric, and had spent the first half of the evening throwing poisonous glances at Anika, was grinning and joking whenever Anika came by.

Eric glanced back toward where he'd left the toothless thug, but the man was lumbering back towards his table, glowering at everyone. He'd require some watching, Eric decided.

He returned to his chair just as Olaf Hjordson walked through the doors. He was out of uniform, and he nodded at Eric as he entered. "Your story checked out," he commented. "But I'd like a word with you later."

Not waiting for Eric to acknowledge the comment, Hjordson wound his way through the crowd to the bar, where he pulled up a stool and sat down.

Eric was about to follow the captain when he heard Anika cry out.

The toothless tough had her backed against the wall and was leaning in aggressively towards her, leering suggestively.

Eric crossed the room in a matter of strides. The

thug sensed him coming and turned around, grinning. "Thought that might get..."

He never finished the sentence.

Eric struck in absolute silence. His heel caught the man in the left knee, the weakness he'd observed earlier. When the man's leg collapsed, he followed up with two quick chops on the man's collarbones. He didn't need the man's pained cry to know he'd broken them. His knee came up and caught the big street tough in the sternum, then caught the man's flailing arm, took hold of his wrist, twisting the arm painfully behind his back until he heard cartilage begin to snap. Still silent, he heaved the man back to his feet and, ignoring the big man's agonized whimpers, forced him in front of him to the entrance, shoving him roughly back down to his knees on the cobbles.

"If you ever touch her again," he whispered in the man's ear, "I will feed you your own testicles before I kill you."

Then he shoved the man forward, slamming his chin on the cobblestones, and walked back inside. He glanced across the room at Anika, who stared at him in a mixture of gratitude and shock. He smiled slightly, looking a little abashed, and someone at the back of the room began to laugh. The sound caught on, and suddenly people were

The Sword and Satchel

raising their mugs to him, laughing and cheering. It quieted after a few moments, and Eric took a deep breath. Anika smiled at him, straightening the apron she was wearing. She walked across the room and kissed him lightly on the cheek. "Thanks," she murmured, then headed back to get the drinks she'd left on the bar.

Eric caught the captain watching him, and he walked over to where the grizzled man was sitting. "You wanted to talk?" he asked.

"In a little while," the captain replied gruffly. "I need a drink just now. It's been a long day, dealing with some unhappy, wealthy, influential people. I know where you'll be." He glanced at the door. "You were pretty hard on that fellow," he observed. "I take it the pretty one is with you?"

Eric nodded, and the captain chuckled. "And the big bastard knew it, didn't he? Serves him right, then. Go back to looking menacing. I'll come find you."

The remainder of the evening passed without incident. Most of the dock workers had to work the next morning, and the inn cleared out fairly early. When only one or two men and Little Suze remained, Hjordson rose from the bar and walked over to where Eric was sitting. "Think Gunther can spare you for a few minutes?"

Eric glanced at the innkeeper, who was watching the two of them. At Eric's questioning look, Gunther nodded and motioned towards the tables. Eric rose and walked beside Hjordson to a table, sitting so he could continue watching the door.

"You're quick and you're tough," Hjordson commented. "You didn't waste a single blow on that big fellow. He was incapacitated after the first strike, wasn't he?"

Eric shrugged. "Look, I'm not interested in joining the guards," he said quietly.

Hjordson laughed roughly. "I'm not surprised," he said. He sat in silence for a moment, then he shook his head. "It's remarkable how much you resemble him."

Eric froze.

"I told you I thought I'd seen you before," the grizzled captain continued, not seeming to notice Eric's sudden tension. "Turns out I mistook you for someone else, someone I worked with a long, long time ago."

"Really?" Eric commented, trying to remain calm.

"Yup. Good man. Fast. One of the best warriors I ever met. Fought with him during the War," the grizzled captain's bright blue eyes pierced Eric, his face a mask. "A few of us veterans came down here after the fighting

The Sword and Satchel

stopped. Well, more than a few, if the truth be told. Lost touch with him before that, of course. He just sort of disappeared. We figured he was dead."

Eric eyed the old man cautiously. "That's interesting," he murmured. "But I fail to see what it has to do with me."

The captain laughed softly. "You'll have to forgive an old man's ramblings. I forget that you young folks don't much care about the state of the world. You probably don't even know much about the War. You can't be more than, what, twenty-two?"

"Something like that," Eric replied quietly.

Hjordson smiled grimly, peering down at his ale. "It was a different place before the War," he muttered. "Before Ryas became King. His father, gods rest his soul, was a good man and a good king." He looked Eric straight in the eye, then. "So was his brother."

Eric struggled to remain calm, staring at the greying veteran. "What are you getting at, Captain?"

"Oh, I'm not a captain just now, boy. I'm just an old war vet, having an ale or two after a long day."

Eric nodded, relaxing slightly. "Reminiscing about the old days," he supplied.

Hjordson nodded slowly. "That..." he agreed, his

eyes suddenly bright, "And wondering about the future."

Anika approached from the bar, smiling warily. "Can I get you another, Captain?"

Hjordson shook his head. "No, thank you."

"Say, Captain..." Eric began.

"Olaf, boy. Right now I'm just Olaf Hjordson."

"Olaf," Eric corrected. "I don't suppose you happened to know a man named Leif Svenson, did you?"

Hjordson grinned. "Now that's a name I haven't heard in some time," he commented, and Anika's hands flew to cover her mouth. The captain glanced up at her, his eyes narrowing slightly. Then he laughed softly. "Well gods be good. You must be little Anika. Why, I remember when you were just about the size of a kitten."

She stared at him, her hands still covering her mouth. "You... know me? You knew my father?"

His brows knit at the use of the past tense, and he shook his head sadly. "I assume he's dead, then?" At her nod, Hjordson sighed. "I knew him well, years ago. Like I told your young man here, a lot of us old veterans came down this way, after the War." He glanced at Eric again. "Most of us, in fact. Gunther, Lars... almost everywhere you go in the city you'll run across a handful of us northerners."

The old man rose from his seat and placed a hand

The Sword and Satchel

gently on Anika's shoulder. "I'm sorry for your loss, child. If you need anything, you come let me know." He turned back to stare down at Eric. "As for you, boy, thanks for listening to an old man's wanderings. If by any chance you happen to run across a man that looks a lot like you, can you give him a message for me?"

Eric raised his eyebrows, but nodded.

"You tell him that we haven't forgotten him, that we miss him, and that we wish he'd come back."

Eric's eyes widened. "We?" he whispered.

The captain met his eyes, his gaze sharp. "All of his old friends," he replied. "And a few new ones we've made over the years. Oh, and tell him one other thing. Tell him that the bitch was right after all, and we all should have listened."

Nodding to Anika, Hjordson turned and strode to the door. "Goodnight, Gunther!" he called out.

"Goodnight yourself, you old horse thief," Gunther called back good-naturedly.

Anika stared at Eric for a moment. "What was that all about?" she asked finally.

"I think," Eric whispered slowly, "that the captain of the guard just asked me to tell my father to invade Prisia."

Chapter 16

The sun was creeping towards the middle of the cloudless sky by the time Eric and Anika found what the locals referred to as the Long Dock. Once in the area, it took another half hour of asking directions from hostile-looking merchants for them to locate the South Prisia Trading Consortium building.

It was exactly as Eric remembered it. Smaller than many of the other shipping offices, it had a relatively non-descript frontage, with the gold-painted sign showing signs of weather, and wooden siding grey with age.

As he reached for the door, Anika touched his arm. "Do you think you can trust this man?" she asked softly.

Eric tilted his head to the side, considering the question. "I take it you don't think I should?" he said at last.

She blinked and glanced away. "I don't know. You said you remembered this place, which means that this Lars fellow is one of the only people in Prisia who knew you were here. Someone informed Ryas... someone had to, unless it was Ryas you were supposed to meet, which isn't likely. What makes you think it wasn't Lars? He's a merchant, and that kind of information would be worth all kinds of money."

Eric shook his head. "I hadn't even considered that," he muttered. He closed his eyes for a moment. When he opened them, his expression was resolute. "I don't really have much of a choice, though. We need to get out of Heidal, and this is the fastest way. He'll know what ships are going to Kisham, and when they're scheduled to go. He can arrange our passage... and maintain our anonymity."

"Or he can sell you out to the highest bidder," she countered. Pausing, she chewed on her lower lip for a moment. "I've thought about this. Let me ask about passage." She gestured at the dress she was wearing. It was a creamy colour, with gold trim and pearls sewn along the sweeping neckline... It was a much more expensive looking one than the one she'd worn the previous day. "Why do you think I dressed like this?" she added. "I should be able to pass as a wealthy lady, shouldn't I? Let me do the talking. You look different enough that if you stay in the background, he shouldn't recognize you."

He stared at her, the corners of his mouth twitching. "That is a remarkably good idea," he said finally.

She sniffed. "I do have them on occasion," she replied archly.

Grinning, he opened the door and stepped back bowing slightly. "After you, my lady. I am your humble servant."

She laughed softly. "Don't stand so straight," she admonished in a whisper. "And keep your head down."

With that, she strode past him into the dim, shabby interior of the building.

A short man, his bald head gleaming with perspiration in the stifling warmth of the building, looked up at her, his face slightly startled. "Good afternoon," he said, rising and surreptitiously wiping his hands on his dark blue pants. "I'm Lars Andersson. How can I help you, miss?"

Anika dipped her head slightly and glanced around the room. It appeared as run-down inside as it had outside, but she could see small concessions to comfort in the plush armchair that sat in front of Andersson's desk and in the upright clock that ticked softly in one corner. The presence of the clock startled her for a moment, but she quickly returned her attention to the rotund little man. "I was told that you deal exclusively with ships that travel to Almeri."

He smiled at her and pulled his spectacles from where they rested on a gold chain in his vest pocket. He picked up a cloth and began polishing the lenses, motioning her to the chair before him. "Indeed," he agreed. "I am considered to be the principle broker with a number of families in Kisham. Please, sit down. Can I offer you some water?"

She sat down and waved his offer away. "I'm considering visiting Kisham," she said haughtily. "And I require some information."

"Of course," he smiled. "How can I assist you?"

"First, would I book passage to Kisham through you, or would I need to negotiate directly with one of the ship captains?" She pretended to shudder at the thought of dealing with such men.

"I could easily arrange passage aboard one of the vessels I deal with," he assured her. "While most are trading ships, some have private berths for individuals such as yourself, who wish to see the glories of Almeri."

She nodded. "And the price of passage?"

He considered her for a moment. "It would depend on whether you were travelling alone, of course... something which I don't really recommend for a lady. It would be extremely regrettable if anything untoward happened during your voyage."

She waved the possibility away airily. "I would, of course, be taking passage with my husband," she replied, gesturing vaguely at Eric, then leaning in and whispering, "He's terrible at getting information, so he leaves such matters to me."

Lars glanced at Eric briefly, nodding politely but not really looking at him. "I see," he murmured. "For a private cabin, you would probably be able to purchase passage for..." he stared up at the ceiling, obviously doing the calculations. "Twelve crowns apiece, I should think."

Her eyes grew wide for a moment. "Twelve crowns?" she repeated, softly.

Lars nodded, oblivious to the surprise in her voice. "The passage takes ten days to Kisham," he continued. "If you like, I can also arrange for the captain to escort you to one of the better hotels, and arrange for letters of introduction."

She cleared her throat. "I will consider that," she replied. "And when might I expect the next ship to depart?"

The Sword and Satchel

He rose from his seat and walked over to a table that sat against one wall. He flipped through a book, running his finger down the page. "Four days," he said, returning to his seat.

"And should we wish to travel unnoticed?" she hesitated, and Lars frowned.

"I would need to know the purpose of your trip," he replied, stiffly. "I maintain a respectable business, and I won't condone illicit activities, including smuggling."

She studied him for a moment, assessing him. At last she nodded. "Tell him," she said over her shoulder.

"I want to go home," Eric replied softly.

Lars glanced up at Eric, puzzled, and then his face went slack. With a cry of surprised joy, he leapt to his feet, knocking his chair over backwards. "Eric! Gods, boy! I was told you were dead! Word went back on the last ship... your father... oh, thank the gods!"

"Who told you?" Eric demanded, his face a mask.

Lars stared at him, obviously puzzled. "Why, the Almeri fellow you came here with. He came back about a week after you left, said you'd been attacked by King Ryas' men. Gods, boy, where have you been?"

"Busy," Eric grunted. "Do you remember the man's name?"

Lars paused for a moment, staring down at the ground. "Alhem? Alhmed? It was something like that."

Eric rubbed his temples, his expression pained. Finally he shook his head, obviously frustrated. "I need to get home," he told Lars softly. "If word's gone back that I'm dead, it will devastate my parents."

Lars nodded vehemently. He hurried back over to the book on the table, flipping through the pages again. Finally, muttering in disappointment, he walked back over to them. "Four days is the earliest," he repeated. "If I talk to the captain, he might be willing to leave earlier..."

Eric frowned and shook his head. "You'd have to tell him who I am to convince him, and that could be dangerous."

Lars rubbed his chin, his face thoughtful. "Where are you staying?" he asked. "I can speak to him, without telling him who you are, and send word to you..."

"I think," Anika interrupted, glancing at Eric and shaking her head, "that it might be better if you let us come to you. Someone did try to kill him, and the fewer people who know where he is, the better."

Lars nodded thoughtfully. "Perhaps that's a good idea. Not that I'd tell anyone, mind you, but... yes." Then his eyes widened. "You suspected it was me!"

The Sword and Satchel

"It wasn't outside the realm of possibility," Eric agreed.

"Eric," Lars protested. "I'm the only one your father trusted with his location. I've kept that secret for thirty-five years. If there's one person in this city you can trust..."

"She's sitting in front of you," Eric told him.

Lars glanced back at Anika, really looking at her for the first time since realizing who Eric was. "So she's coming with you?"

Eric nodded.

A grin suddenly spread across the little man's face. "It's a good thing you'll be coming back from the dead, Eric... it's the only thing that might keep your mother from killing you. Gods, I'd love to be there to see that conversation."

Anika looked up at Eric, her expression troubled. He smiled his lopsided smile and said, "I'll deal with that when we get there. Right now, my biggest concern is the cost of passage."

Lars shook his head. "Don't worry about it," he told Eric. "I'll take the money from your father's account. I'm sure he won't mind."

Nodding, Eric leaned against the desk. "What's the situation in Prisia, Lars?" he asked softly.

Lars paused, looking at him curiously. "Do you mean with Masimor's rebellion?"

Eric considered for a moment, shaking his head. "Not only that," he replied finally. "I mean generally. My father never talked much about what Prisia was like. I'm curious, I guess."

Lars ran a hand over his bald head. "That's a big question, Eric... hard to really give you a single answer. I guess things are a little rough for the common folks, what with the rebellion and all. Ryas hasn't... well, he certainly isn't the king his father was. News is scarce from the north. After the War, he set out trying to hunt down all the lords who had rebelled against him. They all fled, which left the north pretty much ungoverned. He named some of his flunkies in their place, but they're never out of the capital. Things in the north are tougher than they are down here, though we've got our share of problems. The lords down here are still angry at Ryas, so they don't bother going to court, which means that they don't really have any influence on Ryas' decisions. That costs the merchants here, since the central lords, Ryas' primary supporters, demand a lower taxation level, and then put tariffs on imported goods. Makes it hard on trade.

"The east... well, the borderlands have always been

chaotic. The Lerchan Alliance formed a few years back, a few of the tribes banding together, and the number of border raids has risen pretty steadily ever since. With Masimor's rebellion, Ryas pulled more men off the patrols, which has given those wild bastards almost free reign, and rumor has it they've started burning out villages. The eastern lords keep asking for help, but Ryas hasn't done anything about it. As for the west... well, they've been hit harder than most of us. There were a few uprisings – protests against the taxes, I think – and Ryas put them down hard. That's what they say gave Masimor enough support to start his little rebellion... which has been hard on everyone, but hardest on the peasants in the villages near the fighting."

Eric nodded silently. At last he glanced down at Anika, who rose gracefully from her seat. "We should get going. I'll come around this time tomorrow, to see if there's any news."

Lars nodded. "Eric," he added, "I'm happy to see you. Sending that message to your father was the hardest thing I've ever done. I'm damn glad I was wrong."

"So am I," Eric chuckled.

Chapter 17

"You're actually thinking about it," Anika murmured as they walked back toward The Hearth. "About... what the captain suggested."

Glancing over at her, Eric shrugged. "I just wanted to see what things were like here," he said softly. "But everything Lars told us just confuses me more," he added.

"Why does that confuse you?"

Eric frowned. "I'm still having difficulty remembering why I came here, but I think it was to meet with Masimor," he told her softly. "But with things as rough here as Lars describes, you'd think that Ryas would think twice before trying to have me killed. He can't really afford to risk a war with Almeri... not right now."

"Why do you think your death would trigger a war?" she asked, her eyes wide.

Eric grimaced. "To Grandfather, family is more important than anything else. If Ryas had me killed, Grandfather would get my uncle Kyvin to rouse the legions to seek revenge, whether my father wanted him to or not. It's one of the reasons I really, really need to get home... especially now that news of my death is on its way to my family."

"So... maybe it wasn't Ryas. Or maybe Ryas hasn't considered that," Anika argued.

Eric shook his head. "I don't think Ryas is an idiot. He's arrogant, but he's not dumb enough to start a war right now."

"So... you think Masimor betrayed you?" Anika asked. Then she shook her head. "But what would he gain from it? I mean, I can understand how he might be able to use you... and your father... but killing you wouldn't accomplish anything. Unless he was able to pin your death on Ryas..."

"Even then," Eric muttered. "He must know that killing Kysid's grandson would only lead to a bigger war than he's currently fighting. While Ryas would most likely be killed, it would only put my father on the throne, which must be what Masimor was trying to accomplish by sending to speak to father in the first place... so killing me would be..."

"Idiotic," Anika agreed. "I can see why you're confused. So if neither Ryas nor Masimor would benefit from killing you, who would?"

Eric shook his head. "That's the thing. No one would. I mean, who would want a war between Almeri and Prisia? It just doesn't make sense."

Anika fell silent, and they walked the rest of the way to the inn without speaking, each grappling with the mystery.

Gunther nodded at them as they entered. "So," he commented. "Will you be staying or going?"

"At least one more night," Eric replied.

Gunther grinned. "And?"

Laughing, Anika moved towards the stairs. "Of course we'll work again tonight, Gunther."

Something made Eric suddenly glance around the room, his skin prickling. Moving without thinking, he lunged in Anika's direction, knocking her to the floor just as a curved dagger slammed into the wall where she had been standing. "Gunther! Get down!" Eric called out loudly.

Blocking Anika with his body, Eric peered around

the room. Gunther had dropped from sight, and Eric hoped it wasn't because he was dead. From the shadows across the room, a man dressed in a curious black cloak stepped forward, his dusky skin and black hair declaring him to be an Almeri. He held another curved dagger, identical to the one in the wall. "You try to hide in plain sight, *histali*," the man smiled. "But you draw too much attention. I had thought you dead, but news of a big man with your name, killing six soldiers... I thought those *pradtha*, those swine, would fail at killing you. Fortunately, it doesn't matter. News of your death is already on its way. No one will ever know how you died."

Eric rose and plucked the dagger from the wall, still blocking Anika. "Go to the room," he told her quietly.

She hesitated for only an instant, then sprinted up the stairway.

"You care for this one?" the man demanded. "I thought you only cared for yourself, *histali*." The man sneered at the word, which meant 'honored friend'. "You don't need to worry. I will kill her quickly. I would not sully myself, as your mother did, by lying with one of these *pradtha*."

"You'll have to kill me, first," Eric vowed.

The man laughed. "Of course," he grinned. "That

was what I was commanded to do, anyway, *histali*."

Eric's eyes narrowed at the insulting tone, and suddenly the man's name sprang into his memory. "Alhamid," he murmured. "Why are you doing this? Who commanded you to kill me?"

Alhamid laughed again. "It is for the glory of the Almeri, *histali*," he replied, moving forward lazily. Eric studied him, recognizing the feline grace as that of a trained warrior. "I was chosen to grant you death, and to ensure that the blame fell upon these *pradtha*."

Eric circled away from the stairs, his eyes intent on his opponent. "Who sent you, Alhamid?"

"The Jirad, who speaks for God," Alhamid told him, his voice reverent. "But you, mongrel that you are, you will never know the glory of God. Even so, you will be serving His purpose."

"Great," Eric muttered. "A fanatic."

Alhamid lunged suddenly, and Eric jerked out of the way, feeling the blade hiss past his face. He slashed at the assassin's extended arm, but Alhamid spun away before the blade could touch him.

"This, too, is why I was chosen," the dark-haired man grinned. "It is known that you are fast... but I am faster."

He stepped in like a dancer, and their daggers clashed against each other. Eric blocked a kick with his knee, ducked under Alhamid's elbow, and danced back out of range. Alhamid grinned at him, his dark eyes gleaming. "I have dreamed of this day, *histali*," Alhamid confessed. "Ever since I first saw you fight, I have wanted to dance the blades with you."

He struck again, and Eric had to leap back to avoid the slashing dagger. He sensed, rather than saw, the table behind him, and dodged around it, spinning a chair in front of him to slow Alhamid's advance.

Eric's mind was racing. The dagger in his hand was unfamiliar, and that put him at a distinct disadvantage. The shorter blade would force him to move in closer than he was accustomed, and it appeared the dagger was the other man's preferred weapon... He also suspected that Alhamid was the type of man to poison his weapon, and Eric didn't want to find out if his suspicion was accurate.

Alhamid advanced on him unhurriedly, his expression serene. His every motion was careful, controlled. He was, Eric realized, a master at this type of fighting.

Eric eased around another table, trying to keep some distance between them. The entrance to the inn was only a few feet away, but Eric knew he couldn't leave. Alhamid would just go upstairs and kill Anika.

The thought enraged him. He fought the fury down, controlled it, harnessed it. Then he shifted to his left and struck.

Alhamid grinned and shuffled back, keeping out of range. "Good!" he exclaimed as Eric snapped a series of cuts and kicks at him, driving the Almeri back gradually. Even in retreat, however, the assassin showed no loss of control, read every strike.

Eric disengaged, darting away from a counter just in time. Alhamid tilted his head mockingly at Eric. "It has been fun playing with you, *histali*," he whispered. "But now you die."

The Almeri moved like lightning, his blade a blur. Eric was barely able to deflect a strike, before he had to dive out of the way. The assassin followed him so swiftly that Eric had to scramble backwards under a table to avoid the man's blade. He kicked out at Alhamid's legs, but the man merely stepped back, laughing. Then the assassin kicked the table out of the way, and Eric realized there was no place left to go.

Alhamid looked down at Eric. "It is almost too bad," he said softly, his smile sad.

Eric braced himself to lash out one final time, but

before he could move, Alhamid jerked to the side, blood spraying from his throat as Anika pulled Eric's sword back and struck again, this time hitting the assassin deeply in the side.

Alhamid fell to the ground, his eyes wide. He focused on Eric and, despite the gashes in his neck and stomach, he struggled to reach him.

Anika stepped over the crawling man and slammed the sword through his spine, her face contorted with fury. Alhamid jerked, and the light faded from his eyes.

Eric stared up at Anika, her crimson hair wild, and her eyes burning. She released her hold on the sword hilt and suddenly backed away, her hands flying up to cover her mouth. "Oh, gods," she gasped in horror.

Bounding to his feet, he enveloped her in his arms. She clutched at his back, her face pressed hard into his shoulder, her body wracked with intense sobs. "I killed him," she repeated, over and over.

"Shhhh," Eric soothed. "It's okay. You're going to be okay."

"But I just killed a man!" she wailed, her voice muffled and her breath hot through his shirt.

"Who was going to kill us both," he told her gently. He glanced over at the bar. "And who may have killed

The Sword and Satchel

Gunther," he added.

She pushed against him, lifting her head to stare in the direction of the bar, her eyes red and damp. She wiped her cheeks and tried to move away, but Eric kept his arms wrapped tightly around her. "Let me go," she growled.

He released his hold, and she hurried across the room to the bar.

Gunther sat against the wall, blood staining his shirt and the wall behind him. He looked up at her, his right hand pressing against a deep gash in his left shoulder. "Is Eric alright?" he asked in a whisper.

She nodded, moving around the bar to kneel beside the injured innkeeper. "Let me see," she murmured.

"It's deep," he objected weakly. "I could use a healer..."

"I am a healer," she snapped. "Now let me see."

He moved his hand away from the wound, and Anika frowned. Black streaks spread away from the deep cut, and a pungent scent filled the air as soon as the wound was exposed. "Eric," she called out. "Get my pack."

Eric, who had crouched down over the body of Alhamid, rose and sprinted up the stairs.

"The dagger looks to have had snake-fennel on it," she told Gunther.

He frowned. "Is that bad?"

"Yes," she admitted, pressing her hand down firmly on the cut. "Without tinic root, it will kill you in a few minutes. As it is... be glad I have tinic root with me."

"You're really a healer, girl?" Gunther asked, his breath coming fast.

She frowned at him. "Yes, Gunther. I'm really a healer."

He shook his head. "Then why are you waiting tables here?" he wondered, his eyes starting to wander slightly.

Eric pounded down the stairs, Anika's pack in his hands. She glanced over at him. "Give me the satchel inside," she ordered. He dug around and handed it to her. "Now get me a cup of water."

Still putting pressure on Gunther's wound, she untied the leather string around her healing supplies and opened the bag. She pulled out a couple of smaller leather bags, each with a different colour threat tying it closed. Choosing one with a deep red string, she used her teeth to help untie it. A harsh, acrid aroma wafted from it, and she took out two dried leaves as Eric returned with the cup. Crushing the leaves into the water, she stirred it with her finger and then poured a small amount of the water directly

The Sword and Satchel

onto Gunther's injury. He cried out, and his legs thrashed as he struggled to get up.

"Hold him," she snapped at Eric.

Eric dropped down and pinned Gunther in place as the big man began to wail loudly.

"What on earth..." a voice began, and Anika glanced up to see Gunther's plump wife standing in the doorway of the kitchen, her hand frozen in the act of wiping them on her apron and her face ashen.

"I need a cup of flour and some cloth to use as a bandage," Anika snapped at her. "Now!"

With a startled jerk, the heavy woman bolted back into the kitchen.

"Okay, Gunther," Anika murmured. "The next part is going to hurt a little."

Eyes wide, the big man shuddered, biting back another scream.

"Eric, can you get something for him to bite down on?" she asked. "Then I'm going to need you to hold him again."

Nodding, Eric rose and followed Gunther's wife into the kitchen. Both returned a few moments later, she with the flour and cloth, he carrying a fancy, leather-wrapped wooden ladle.

"I hope you don't mind if this gets broken," she murmured to Gunther's wife as she took the ladle.

Her face still ghastly, the round little woman shook her head. "Will he be okay?" she whispered.

Anika glanced at the wound. The black streaks had stopped spreading down Gunther's arm, and the blood flowed a rich, healthy colour from the wound. "He should be," she replied. "But first..." she poured the cup of flour into the remaining herb-steeped water and mashed it into a paste with her fingers. Then she placed the stick between Gunther's teeth and glanced at Eric. "Lay him down, then hold him."

Eric nodded and helped Gunther down to the floor. Taking a deep breath, Eric pinned the big man down, and Anika scooped out a handful of the paste. Looking at Eric, she nodded curtly, then smeared the paste into the wound.

Gunther bucked, his back arching, and his scream seemed to fill the entire room. His feet drummed against the floor, and the handle of the ladle snapped, but Eric managed to keep him from lashing out or moving too much.

The agonized shriek seemed to drag on forever, but finally Gunther's frame relaxed as the big man lost consciousness.

Anika studied the wound, watching the pinkish-greyish paste intently. After a moment, the paste seemed to darken to a sickly purple, and Anika heaved a sigh of relief. "It's drawing out the poison," she explained, glancing up at the terrified woman hovering a few feet away. "He's going to be okay."

The paste grew steadily darker, until it was almost the colour of coal. As it changed colour, it also seemed to change consistency, hardening into a solid lump which Anika removed before using the remaining paste as a second application. Again the paste gradually changed colour, but it only darkened to a deep purple. When she was certain it wasn't changing colour any more, she removed the paste, washed the wound clean, and stitched the cut with some fine gut-thread.

When she finally glanced up again, several other people stood around the bar, watching her. All of them, she noticed, wore the colours of the city guard.

Chapter 18

"No," Anika repeated. "I've never seen him before, and I don't know why he would want to kill Gunther." She glanced over at Eric, rolling her eyes. The two guards were obviously stalling, asking the same questions over and over.

The guard nodded, turning to Gunther's wife. "And you, ma'am? Do you have any idea why an Almeri would come in here, trying to kill your husband? Does he have any outstanding debts...?"

Gunther's wife, Gwynn, blinked at the guard. "Debts? No. My Gunther doesn't... what are you implying?"

"I recognized him," Eric murmured. When the guard turned to him, Eric shrugged. "I had to toss him out of here the other night. He was acting belligerent. I didn't think anything of it until he just showed up and started attacking us."

"Had you ever seen him before you threw him out?" a second guard asked, staring at the body lying on the ground.

"Not that I remember," Eric admitted. "I..." he was interrupted as the door swung open and Olaf Hjordson stormed in.

"What the hell is going on?" he demanded.

"Seems some Almeri went berserk and tried to kill Gunther, sir," the guard to Eric's left commented, straightening under the captain's intent scrutiny. "This fellow, too," he added, nodding towards Eric.

The captain frowned at the body, then looked up at Gwynn. "Is Gunther okay?"

Gwynn nodded, clutching Anika's arm. "Anika helped him," she whispered. "Saved his life."

Blinking, Olaf stared at Anika. "Are you a healer, or a barmaid?" he asked.

"Right now I'm a barmaid," she muttered. "But I was my village healer before... before my father died."

Hjordson nodded thoughtfully. "Lucky for Gunther," he said finally. He shook his head. "Any idea why this man would want Gunther dead?"

"The doorman says he had to toss him out a couple of nights back..." one of the guards began, but Olaf waved him to silence.

"I don't want the whole 'he says' thing, Thom," the captain muttered. "You and Dan return to your assigned duties. I'll deal with this, but I'll need you to send Geoff back here with the cart for the body, when you check in at your post."

The guard saluted, looking relieved. "Yes, sir." He glanced over at his partner. "Let's go, Dan." The second guard looked up from the body, his face pale, and nodded, moving towards the door.

Olaf waited until the two guards were gone, then turned to Gunther's wife. "Did you see anything, Gwynn?"

She shook her head. "I came in when I heard Gunther scream. Anika was already working on his arm. I didn't even know anything had happened until I saw Gunther..."

Olaf touched her gently on the shoulder. "He's in the back?" When she nodded, he smiled tenderly. "Go sit with him. If I have any questions, I'll come see you."

Gwynn smiled, her eyes filling with tears. "Thank you, Olaf... and thank you, too, Anika, for saving my

Gunther."

Anika reached out and pressed Gwynn's hands between her own. "I'm just glad I was here," she murmured.

Gwynn moved, a little dazed, towards the rooms she and Gunther kept in the back of the inn. Olaf waited until she was gone before he rounded on Eric. "Damn, boy! You can't be killing men in my city!"

Eric raised his hands defensively. "He attacked me," he began, but Anika raised a hand to his chest.

"Eric didn't kill him," she whispered. "I did."

Hjordson stared at her, his eyes wide with disbelief. Then he looked down at the body. He paused, crouching beside the dead man. After a moment, he looked around, taking in the overturned tables and chairs. His eyes narrowed, focusing on Eric. "Tell me everything, and give it to me straight. I don't want to have to pry answers from you."

Eric left out the details of what Alhamid had told him, but he walked the captain through the fight step by step. When he was done, the captain whistled.

"He was good enough to beat you..." he whispered. He looked at Anika. "It's a clear cut case of self-defense," he added. "No charges... but good work, girl. Your father would have been very proud of you."

The Sword and Satchel

He turned his attention back to Eric. "He was after you," he said, his tone brooking no argument. "But it's probably best if we don't mention that. I'd like to leave you out of it, too, Anika. No point in drawing more attention than we need to. Did you actually throw this fellow out, or did you say that to establish motive?"

Eric shrugged. "I made it up. It seemed like a good idea at the time," he muttered.

"It was," Olaf agreed. "I can work with it, but you've got to stop drawing attention to yourself, boy. You've been in my city three days, and I've had to come out here twice already. You need to go up to your room and stay up there until things settle a bit."

"I'm planning on being gone in four days," Eric told him.

"Four days?" Olaf nodded. "Good. The sooner you're gone, the better. You're trouble."

Anika shivered at the words, remembering her father saying almost the exact same thing.

"So a disgruntled patron came in, attacked Gunther, and you had to kill him," Hjordson told them. "If any other guards come by, stick to that story. I'll check in on Gunther." Hjordson paused. "Does he know...?"

"No," Eric replied flatly. "I met him three days ago.

I'm just his doorman."

"You're going to have to tell him," Gunther said softly. "He deserves to know why some complete stranger came in and almost killed him."

"Olaf," Anika whispered, "why are you doing this? Helping us?"

Hjordson looked at her for a moment. "I'd say I was doing it for your father, girl, but that would be a lie... I'm doing it for his. There are mighty few men in this world that I would risk anything for, do anything for... and his father happens to be one of them."

The captain turned and began to walk away, but he stopped a few feet from Eric. Turning around, he licked his lips. "I just want to know one thing, boy," he said at last. "Is... is he still alive?"

Eric's lips twitched slightly. "Yes," he replied, his words quiet enough that only the captain could hear him. "Tindal Yolandson is still alive."

Hjordson's eyes brightened. Then he raised a cautionary hand. "Don't..." he began.

"You needed to hear me say his name," Eric interrupted. "But I'm not stupid enough to say it out loud again."

"Good," Olaf grunted, a silly little smile on his lips.

"I'll go check in with Gwynn, and see how Gunther's doing."

Eric bent and retrieved his sword from where it lay beside the body on the floor. He closed his eyes for a moment, and then he turned to look at Anika. "This is the second time you saved my life," he told her softly. He looked away, uncomfortable. "And all I seem to do is bring pain and horror into yours..."

"Eric," she stopped him, her lower lip trembling. "Don't. I..." she glanced at the body on the floor for a moment before looking away. "I don't want to be down here anymore."

He nodded and took her hand, leading her up the stairs.

She sat down on the bed, placing her face in her hands, as he closed the door. He moved to sit beside her, placing one arm protectively around her shoulders. She dropped her arms and leaned in to him. "I want to cry, to be upset," she whispered, shivering slightly. "But I just feel numb."

Eric looked at the pallor of her skin, frowning. "Shock," he explained to her, shifting to pull up the blanket and wrap it around her shoulders. "It's fairly common for new soldiers after their first battle."

She nodded, staring at the wall in front of her. "I felt like this after Anidaron," she murmured. "After Papa died, and we had to run."

Eric rubbed the back of her neck gently. "You saved my life down there," he repeated, changing the subject. "Gunther's, too."

She hung her head, her arms slack at her side. "I'm a healer," she said softly. "I'm not supposed to kill people."

"You're a healer," he agreed, shifting his hands to knead the muscles of her shoulders. "But you're much more than that, Anika. Saying you're just a healer is like saying the sun is just a light in the sky. It's true... but it's only one part of who you are. When I told you to go upstairs..." he shook his head. "I underestimated you. I thought you would hide in the room. I forgot that underneath the healer, underneath the barmaid, underneath the pretty girl, there is a warrior with a heart as fierce as any I've ever known."

She sighed, and he felt the tension in her muscles ease. "And under the warrior, you're a poet," she told him. Then she looked at him, her colour rising. "But if you even think about trying to tell me it's not safe being around you, you're going to find the warrior inside me isn't buried all that deeply right now."

He shifted uncomfortably. "Anika..." he began, but

she elbowed him.

"Forget it, Eric. I'm not walking away, so don't even bother. You didn't get me into anything I don't want to be in. Now, spill it."

He cocked his head to the side, not following.

"What you didn't tell Hjordson," she explained, rolling her eyes. "And don't pretend that you didn't hide anything. I know you better than that."

He chuckled softly, shaking his head. "Alright," he agreed. "I knew the man downstairs. He came over with us. His name was Alhamid. He's probably the one that told Lars I was dead."

Anika's face grew troubled. "That's a hard coincidence to swallow," she muttered.

Eric frowned. "I don't think it was Lars," he told her.

Anika stared at him, one eyebrow raised in disbelief. "Really? We showed up at Lars', and less than an hour later an Almeri assassin tried to kill you... and you don't think there's a connection?"

Eric shook his head. "I think he was waiting here, in case I showed up. From the way he talked about Prisian people, I don't think he trusted the men he hired to kill me to get the job done properly."

"Fine," she said, not convinced. "But how did he know you were here? Lars..."

"That's the thing," Eric interrupted, shaking his head. "Lars doesn't know where we are staying. We came straight back from that meeting, and Alhamid was *waiting* for us. He knew where I was. There's no way Lars could have discovered where we were staying, gotten word to Alhamid, and still manage to arrange for him to get here before us."

Anika chewed on her lower lip for a moment, and Eric was relieved to notice that her shivering had stopped and her colour was improving. "Alright," she agreed. "I can see your point. So if he was so intent on killing you, why didn't he stick around to make sure you were dead in the first place? And more importantly, who sent him?"

Eric sighed. "He was our liaison. He was supposed to go ahead and let the people we were supposed to meet know that we had arrived. I'm guessing he didn't bother to check because he had to get back to send word over as soon as possible, to get things moving in Almeri. As for who sent him... he was one of the Jiradin, a group of fanatics in Almeri who believe it is the destiny of the faithful to conquer the entire world.

"Remember how I couldn't think of anyone who

would benefit from a war between Prisia and Almeri?" he added wryly. "I suddenly have a pretty fair guess."

"So who is their leader?" Anika asked.

Eric shook his head. "No one knows. He's called 'The Jirad' and the Jiradin revere him as a prophet. My grandfather has tried to infiltrate the Jiradin, to root them out, but none of the spies ever come back. The worst part is that a lot of Almeri are sympathetic to them, even if they don't want to rule the world. The Jiradin feel that all other races are inferior, that only the true Almeri are worthy. Unfortunately, that's a pretty common sentiment among the Almeri. That's why I am the perfect target, as far as the Jiradin are concerned. I'm Kysid's grandson, but I'm only half Almeri... a mongrel, he called me."

Anika stared at him, stunned. "So they want to start a holy war, and killing you is the fastest way to do it?" Suddenly she giggled. "They're going to be so furious when you turn up alive."

"We have to get there, first," Eric warned. "It's a long way from Heidal to Kisham... and any Almeri we meet could be one of the Jiradin."

Grimacing, she murmured, "This just gets better and better, doesn't it? Alright... so, how are we going to get you home without anyone suspecting who you are?"

Eric stared at the wall, his eyes vague. "I have no idea."

Chapter 19

"I owe the two of you my thanks," Gunther said quietly. The big innkeeper lay on his bed, his wounded arm wrapped tightly. He was pale, but otherwise he appeared much improved. "If you hadn't called out, boy, that dagger would have hit me in the chest." He looked at Anika and smiled gratefully. "And if you hadn't been there..."

"It's my fault in the first place," Eric told him. "He was after me. You just happened to be in the wrong place at the wrong time. He didn't want to leave any witnesses."

Gunther frowned at him. "What are you saying, boy?"

"I'm saying that he was an assassin hired to kill me, Gunther."

The Sword and Satchel

There was a long pause, and then the big man laughed loudly. "Listen to you! Boy, just because you upset a few soldiers doesn't make you..."

"I'm the son of Tindal Yolandson," Eric said very softly, and Gunther's laughter died in his throat, the blood draining from his face. "And that man was sent to kill me in order to start a war between Prisia and Almeri."

Gunther's eyes widened, and he slowly raised his good hand up to touch Eric's cheek. "Gods be good..." he whispered. "It can't be. Tindal died..."

"No," Eric replied. "Tindal vanished. He left Prisia and went to stay with my grandfather, Kysid."

Gunther's jaw worked, but no sound emerged. His eyes scanned Eric's face, disbelief gradually changing to stunned amazement. "You're..." he choked out finally. "You... how did I not notice?"

Eric smiled. "You weren't looking for it. It's been thirty-five years since my father disappeared."

Gunther's eyes grew distant. "After he... left... I saw his face on every stranger who came in here. I chased after people on the streets..." he focused on Eric again. "And now his son..." Tears found their way to his eyes at last. "Gods, boy! How is he?"

"He was well when I left," Eric told him.

"And you... what are you doing in Prisia?"

Eric shook his head slightly. "That's a question for another day, Gunther. I owed you the truth, after what happened here today. You deserved to know why an assassin almost killed you. I'm the reason. I'm sorry."

Gunther gazed at him, tears running down his cheeks. "If I'd known I would never have let you expose yourself like that, acting as a doorman... it's disgraceful! You're the rightful heir to the bloody throne, and you've been thumping heads in my inn like a common thug..."

Eric frowned. "I thought I did a slightly better job of it than a common thug," he protested.

There was a momentary pause, and then Gunther broke into heartfelt laughter. "Gods be blessed, you did, boy... I mean, my lord."

"Hey," Eric cautioned, raising his hands. "None of that. If you start addressing your doorman by that, people are going to talk. We've drawn enough attention to ourselves already. As it is, I'm a wanted man... both by Ryas and by whoever sent that assassin. We're due to leave here in a couple of days, and I really don't want anything to interfere with that."

"Ryas knows you're in Prisia?" Gunther demanded, struggling to sit up.

"I don't know," Eric admitted. "But I... might have killed a few of his soldiers a couple of weeks back, up in Anidaron. That sort of thing doesn't really ever go away."

Gunther frowned. "And then you went and humiliated that group of boys the other night..." His eyes widened. "That's why Olaf insisted that Almeri had been in here the night before last. He knows, doesn't he?"

"He knows," Eric agreed quietly. "He's trying to keep things as quiet as he can, but a death in his city... especially the death of a foreigner..."

Nodding slowly, Gunther looked up. "You need to hide out for a while, Eric. Stay in your room. The inn will be closed tonight, anyhow. If anyone comes looking for you, I'll say the attack scared you off.

"Why does everyone insist I need to hide?" Eric grumbled.

"Because you're too dense to realize it yourself," Anika snapped. "Now we need to let Gunther get some rest. While the poison's out of his system, he still lost a lot of blood."

Gunther chuckled softly. "Oh, your mother's going to love her," he murmured.

Infuriated, Anika threw her hands up and whirled on Eric. "Everyone you talk to makes some kind of comment about your mother, or about how she's going to react when she learns about me. Lodi, Olaf, Gunther... even Lars. What is it about her that I don't know?"

"Lodi?" Gunther asked. "Why in the blazes would you go visit that old hermit?"

"My father told us to," Anika told him, tersely. "Just before Ryas' soldiers attacked my village."

Gunther's eyes narrowed. "The soldiers you 'might have killed'? In Anidaron?" he asked softly. Then he chuckled. "That would make you Leif's daughter, then? Gods, it's like a reunion of all of Tindal's personal guard..."

"Quit trying to change the subject!" Anika growled. "What is so terrifying about Eric's mother?"

Gunther looked at Eric for a moment, fighting a grin. "You know," he murmured, leaning back to lie against the pillows. "I think I might need to rest after all. Eric can explain it to you, I'm sure."

Frowning, Eric glanced at Anika. "Come on," he grumbled. "I'll tell you upstairs... while I'm busy hiding."

She followed him upstairs, her arms crossed under her breasts and a scowl on her face. As soon as he closed the door, she spun around to face him, her green eyes blazing. "So?"

Eric threw himself onto the bed, staring at the

ceiling. "I suppose a lot of people find Mother... intimidating."

"Intimidating? So she's the proverbial dragon woman?"

"No!" Eric protested. "I mean, she can be pretty strong willed, I guess, but..."

"So why does everyone seem so entertained by the thought of her meeting me?" she demanded.

A smile flickered across his lips. "I don't know if it's just because of her. You come across pretty strong, yourself."

A flush of indignation spread across her pale skin, and she glared at him.

"It's just... I don't think Mother has ever encountered another woman with the same kind of fire as she has. You have it. Most of the women in Grandfather's palace are so terrified of her that they huddle like mice when she enters a room. You..." he looked at her, his dark eyes gleaming. "I can't imagine you huddling in fear of anyone. Ever." He paused for a moment, and then added, "Which could cause a few sparks between the two of you."

"And I bet she's got the perfect bride already picked out for you," Anika muttered, averting her eyes.

"Actually," he countered, "she fought my father

tooth and nail every time he brought up the idea. She hated the fact that her father arranged her marriage. It turned out happily enough, but she has always insisted that I make my own choices... of course, the fact that she despised everyone my father suggested might have had something to do with that."

She frowned at him. "Your mother sounds... complicated," she muttered, moving to sit beside him on the bed.

Laughing, Eric nodded. "That about describes her. But you don't have to worry, Anika. I'm sure she'll love you."

Anika snorted, then covered her face, blushing. Eric grinned at her. She shook her head, her face suddenly crumbling. "But look at me, Eric!" she wailed. "We're from different worlds! You... you're the grandson of kings, son of the true heir to the throne of Prisia. I'm a village healer who doubles as a barmaid. I'm about as common as it gets."

Eric took her hands, shaking his head. "You may be a village healer, Anika, but you are anything but common. And it doesn't matter. What matters is that I'm in love with you, not with some foreign princess. That's what my mother will see." He glanced away for a moment. "My father will be a harder sell... and my grandfather..."

Anika leapt to her feet. "See! I don't belong in that world..." she began, but Eric rose up with the speed and grace of a hunting cat, wrapping her in his arm.

"You belong in my world," he told her firmly. "And I can't imagine my world without you. If you feel you can't live in my world, the world of kings and princes, I promise you I can live in yours."

The blood drained from her face, and she reached up to touch his cheek tenderly, tears in her eyes. "You'd give it all up?" she whispered.

He nodded, looking calmly into her eyes. "Of course," he told her. "I seem to be pretty good at this doorman thing. It's an easy life. If it's what you want, after we've seen my parents, so that they know I'm not dead, we can find someplace they've never heard of me..."

Her eyes shone for a moment, and she pressed her face into his chest. "No," she whispered. "No... I can learn. Your family... I can't imagine what that would do to them. I don't have anyone except the boys..." her eyes suddenly widened. "What will we do with the boys?"

Eric smiled his lopsided smile. "Well, we could leave them with Lodi," he suggested. "He seems pretty kid-friendly..." She punched him lightly in the arm, and he laughed. "Once we get to Kisham, we can send word to Lodi and have him bring them to Heidal. We'll arrange for passage for them, and we can set them up with us."

"With us..." she whispered.

"I know I'm putting the cart before the horse," Eric admitted. "But I was kind of hoping..." he broke off and shook his head. "That's the wrong way to do this," he said, stepping back and falling to one knee. "Anika," he began. "Will you..."

Someone pounded on the door of the room, causing Anika to jerk backwards and fall onto the bed, while Eric was on his feet with his sword in his hands at the first sound.

"Eric!" a woman's voice called from the hall. "Eric, open the door!"

Frowning at Anika, his eyes troubled, he cautiously opened the door a fraction and peered out, his sword still in his hand.

Hilde, the dress-shop owner, stood in the hallway, her hands clutched together. She was glancing around the hallway nervously.

"Hilde?" Eric asked, confused.

"Eric," she sighed, her creased face frightened. "Some of King Ryas' soldiers have been poking around town, asking about some folks from the country. A man and a woman and a pair of young boys. The description they gave..."

Eric's lips tightened, and he nodded. "Right," he murmured. "It never rains but it pours."

"It's only a matter of time before they hear about you," she added. "None of the folks from around here are going to say anything to them, but those soldiers you beat up..."

Eric closed his eyes, thinking the situation through. "Alright," he said at last. "Thanks for the warning, Hilde. We'll get moving."

She nodded, reaching out to touch his cheek gently. "Don't let them catch you, child. I don't know what you did, and they weren't telling, but whatever it was, I'm sure they earned it. Good luck."

Eric closed the door and looked back at Anika, who was already beginning to pack up their few possessions. "We need to see Lars," he told her. "He has to speed things up with that ship."

She blinked at him, nodding slowly. "I'll go. If those soldiers are around, they might recognize you."

Running a hand through his short hair, he chuckled softly. "I doubt it,"

"We can't take that chance," she snapped. "They

might have seen me and the boys as we were leaving, but you were standing out with Papa as they rode up. You stay here..."

"If someone in this quarter does talk, they'll come straight here, Anika. It's safer if we both go."

She hesitated. At last she nodded. "We should tell Gunther."

Nodding his head, Eric opened his pack and pulled out the chain shirt. The links, surprisingly light, slithered against one another. "He said he'd tell people we'd run off. This will mean he doesn't have to lie for us." He glanced around and found the old work shirt Anika had given him weeks earlier. She had washed it the previous day, and while it was still stained, it no longer stank. He changed out of the shirt he was wearing, then struggled into the leather armour, finishing by slipping the chain shirt over top. It was heavier than just wearing the leather, but it transformed him from looking like he was a simple mercenary into appearing something much more. Anika stared at him, surprised.

"They're looking for two country commoners," he explained. "You don't look the part anymore, with the dresses you chose. And as for me, well... no farmer could afford this." He strapped his sword belt over the steel links, and she shook her head.

"You look... impressive," she told him softly. "Like a... prince."

He grimaced slightly. "Not really. I have more ornate armour at home. This is my service armour. It's what Almeri soldiers tend to wear... or high-paid Almeri bodyguards. There are enough Almeri bodyguards in Heidal that it won't draw too much attention."

"Doesn't it get hot?" she wondered.

He nodded. "Especially in Almeri, when you're patrolling in the desert reaches."

He stuffed his newer clothes into his pack. The tiny pack bulged, but he managed to cram everything inside. "Good thing we don't need to pack food."

She nodded, picking up her own pack. The short bow and a deer-hide quiver Eric had made her during their hike to Heidal were strapped to the sides. He shook his head. "That will completely ruin the impression that I'm your bodyguard, Anika. We'll have to leave the pack with Gunther."

"Then you'll have to put my satchel in your pack," she replied, sighing. "I don't go anywhere without my herbs."

He began pulling things out of his pack. Everything he'd taken from the two soldiers he'd killed in the mountains got piled beside the dresser. It left enough room for his clothes, her second dress, and her healing satchel. Frowning, he glanced at the short bow. Shrugging, he strapped it to the side of the pack opposite the second sword and put the rest of the arrows into his own quiver. It left Anika's pack completely empty.

"Now we don't have to come back for anything," he said.

She glanced down at the quiver he'd made her. "Can you use that quiver instead?" He raised one eyebrow, and she shrugged. "It has sentimental value."

He changed quivers and picked up the heavy recurve bow that Lodi had given him. "I think I'll leave this with Gunther," he said softly. "It's not the sort of weapon bodyguards usually carry."

Giving the room a final look, he nodded to himself. Then, glancing at Anika, he motioned toward the door. "Ready?"

She sighed. "I was really starting to actually like it here," she complained as they headed downstairs to break the news to Gunther.

Chapter 20

The sun was beginning to sink as Eric led Anika through the streets of Heidal. They had left the shipping district behind and returned to the shopping district. His path led them deeper into the city, and Anika immediately noticed that the buildings around them began to change dramatically. Where the shops and inns that had lined the roughly cobbled streets of the shipping district had been older and slightly run down, the buildings they now passed were significantly larger and better kept. The paint on the siding of the shops was immaculate, and the signs hanging in front of the shops and inns were hand-carved with intricate designs.

Anika had expected them to draw eyes as they

walked down the street. Instead, she found that most of the passing men and women paid them little heed at all.

Noticing her confused expression, Eric whispered, "We fit in, here. That dress is all that they need to see. You look the part." He lifted his chin at a pair of men lounging outside of what appeared to be a bank of some sort. Both were dark-haired and dark-skinned, and wore armour similar to Eric's. "Like I told you, there are a number of Almeri bodyguards in Heidal."

The two Almeri guards nodded at Eric, who returned the greeting. "Look annoyed," he whispered to her.

"*Istan, tali*," one of them said.

"*Istan*," Eric replied. "*Tu sinna prei?*"

The guards shrugged. "*As tinna prei*," one of them answered. "*Tu?*"

"*Tinna*," Eric agreed. Anika glared at him for a moment, and he bowed to her slightly. "Forgive me," he murmured. "My lady dislikes when I speak Almeri, friend," he explained. "We wonder if you know of a good inn?"

The Almeri guard on the left nodded, his lips twitching. "Our master feels the same about our tongue," he agreed. "He chose The Nightingale to stay in. It is... acceptable, *por pradtha, tali*. I have been to Heidal before, and suggested The Silver Chalice, but our master... listens to

The Sword and Satchel

his friends, not his servants. Both are north, towards the palace."

Eric nodded politely. "My thanks," he said, and the guards nodded back.

"*Tu isal miel, tali. Tul misra es anlian,*" the second man added, eyeing Anika.

Eric grinned broadly, glancing briefly at Anika. "*Si,*" he agreed. "*As isa miel.*"

Gesturing for Anika to continue, he waved back at the two Almeri. Once they were out of earshot, Anika frowned at Eric. "What did they say?"

"That we want to be at The Silver Chalice. He said the Nightingale was fit for pigs." He paused. "And the other guard said I was lucky to have such a beautiful mistress."

"I didn't know you spoke Almeri," Anika commented softly.

Eric blinked. "I've lived there my entire life, Anika. We only spoke Prisian at home, when my father was around."

She stared at her feet as they walked. "Do many people in Kisham speak Prisian?"

"Yes," he assured her. "It's almost as widely spoken as Almeri. Kisham is a very cosmopolitan city, and Prisian is a common trading language. It's taught in schools, as are the Lerchan and Ithani languages. And everyone in my grandfather's household is versed in multiple languages."

She nodded. "So I won't be..." she swallowed. "Helpless."

He shook his head. "No," he agreed. "And I can teach you to speak Almeri, if you would like. We'll have ten days on the ship. That will be enough time for you to get the basics. It's similar to Prisian in a lot of ways."

She beamed at him. "You will?" Glancing away shyly, she added, "I've always wished I could speak another language."

"*As isa miel*," he murmured after a moment. When she titled her head, he added, "It means 'I am fortunate.' Most people... they're content to live their lives how they are. It doesn't matter if they're born in a palace or in a village, they never care to see what else there is. They don't dream of anything else. You aren't like that. You have dreams, you want to learn. *As isa miel*. I am fortunate to have found you."

He paused in front of a massive marble building. Huge fluted columns lined the front, supporting an intricately carved lattice of stone. A simple sign in front bore a silver cup, and the name of the inn: The Silver

Chalice.

"It's my turn to do the talking," he told her. "Stand slightly behind me, and don't react when they say how much it's going to cost."

"How much is it going to cost?" she demanded, her eyes wide.

He smirked. "From the looks of this place, twenty to thirty silver crowns a night."

She gasped, her jaw dropping. Finally she swallowed. "It's a good thing I asked out here," she breathed.

He guided her inside, and she bit back a surprised squeak. The entryway had two broad stairways leading to a second floor. Above them, an intricate chandelier hung suspended from the ceiling, the crystals reflecting the light of over a dozen candles. A small fountain, with a statue of a man holding a sword, spilled clear water into a shallow pool in the middle of the lobby. A black stone counter stood directly behind the pool, where an immaculately dressed man with a pencil-thin moustache stood watching them carefully.

Eric glanced around briefly, his eyes taking in all the details, hovering on the stairways and the two doors behind the counter. At last, he moved across the polished stone floor to stand before the black counter. "My mistress requires a suite, with a servant's room adjoining."

The man behind the counter peered at Anika, inclining his head gracefully. "Indeed," he murmured. "And how long does your mistress intend on staying?"

"No more than a week," he replied coolly.

The man studied Eric for a moment. "Will this be reserved by cash or credit?"

"I can arrange for her agent to open a line of credit with you," Eric told him. "Though I expect you will require a deposit?"

The concierge dipped his head slightly. "Indeed," he agreed. "One night deposit, and if you can arrange to have a letter of introduction from her local agent, the remainder can be applied to her credit."

Eric nodded brusquely. "Acceptable."

"That will be twenty-five crowns," the man added calmly, watching Eric carefully.

Eric removed the purse from where he had tied it to his sword belt. He casually withdrew the gold coin and placed it on the counter. "I will, of course, expect the change."

The man smiled politely and took the coin. "Of course," he said. "Please wait here for a moment."

The Sword and Satchel

He disappeared through one of the doors behind him returning with a small pouch. He counted out twenty-five silver crowns, poured the rest back into the pouch and handed it to Eric. "And what name shall I place on the register?"

"Lady Anika Liefsdottir. Her luggage was delayed," Eric added. "If it arrives tonight, please have it delivered."

The man bowed. "If you will just follow Willhem," he motioned toward a young man, dressed impeccably in neat black pants and a starched white shirt, who stepped out from the back room. "He will escort you to your room."

Eric paused. "I will need to have a separate tour of this inn, with emphasis on entrances and exits."

The concierge nodded. "That is expected. Willhem will provide you with your keys, and then show you the premises."

Eric nodded, and Willhem stepped forward, bowing deeply to Anika. "My lady, if you will follow me?"

Anika inclined her head and smoothly followed the youth up the stairs. Eric tucked the purse the concierge had given him under his belt and followed them.

The room was stunning, even to Eric. Huge windows, framed with light curtains and heavier black drapes, opened onto a grand view of the gardens leading to the palace nearly a mile away. Tastefully designed candelabras clung to the walls at regular intervals, and small statues rested on pristine white-marble pillars in each corner. A vast mural covered the ceiling, surrounded by finely carved, gilt-covered wooden beams. The main room was obviously designed for entertaining, with small couches placed around a low polished-wood table and a fireplace taking up the wall beside it. The hearth was cold, but Willhem indicated a small wood box beside it, in case the weather changed suddenly. He then led Anika into the bedroom; a massive canopy bed and several dressers did little to take away from the space of the room. Here the window looked down upon the ocean, and a small balcony allowed the guest to enjoy the gentle breeze off the water. Willhem indicated a porcelain basin on one of the counters. "If you would like to freshen up after your journey, my lady, I will show your servant to his quarters."

Anika smiled graciously, and waved them off. Willhem bowed, and Eric followed him to a small door off the main room. Inside was a tiny room with a single cot. Eric glanced at it and nodded, dropping his pack on the cot. "It will suffice," he said, then placed a silver coin in Willhem's outstretched hand. "Now, show me around."

The hotel was pretty much what Eric had expected.

The second door behind the concierge's counter led into a spacious kitchen, which opened into a large courtyard with a stable at the back. Eric took a few moments to look around, and then he nodded to Willhem. "Have dinner brought up to my lady's chambers in an hour," he told the boy.

"Very good, sir," Willhem said before heading back into the kitchen.

Eric returned to the room to find Anika sprawled across the huge feather bed. "This is completely surreal," she told him as he leaned against the door.

"It's impressive for the price," he agreed. "I'd expect a place like this to cost more."

"More?" she demanded, sitting up. "You just spent more money for one night than..." she shook her head, unable to continue.

"At least we know the soldiers won't look for us here," he said softly, walking toward the bed. "And in the morning I'll go see Lars and find out how long we'll be staying here. I'll have him draft a letter and arrange a line of credit."

"Won't that raise some questions?" Anika asked.

Eric laughed softly. "He won't use my father's name, though he might draw it on my grandfather's account. That would ensure the concierge downstairs treats you like royalty."

Anika lay back on the bed, staring up at the canopy. "As much as I can't quite grasp the idea of spending twenty-five silver crowns a night to sleep somewhere... I think I could get used to this. Have you felt this bed?"

"No," he smiled.

She glanced up at him, her green eyes smoldering. "Well," she said softly. "Let's correct that."

Chapter 21

Anika strode into the office at the South Prisian Trading Consortium like she owned it. Eric followed her in, his armour gleaming in the sunlight that streamed in through the windows.

Lars glanced up at the two of them from where he sat at his desk, studying a sheet of paper intently. He smiled brightly at the sight of them, and then he blinked at the armour Eric was wearing, his smile fading. He glanced at Anika, who appeared every inch a lady of distinction, and nodded slowly. "Come in, and tell me what's going on."

Anika stepped forward, giving Eric space to glide smoothly past her, and he loomed over the diminutive man at the counter. "How soon can that ship be ready?" Eric asked quietly.

Lars frowned. "I spoke to the captain last night," he replied. "His men are scattered through Heidal. He said it would be almost impossible to get them rounded up before tomorrow morning, but that it would be reasonable to sail before nightfall... for a price."

Eric studied Lars for a moment. "How much?" he demanded at last.

"Why the sudden rush?" Lars countered. "You didn't seem so concerned yesterday..."

"That was before an Almeri assassin tried to kill me after we visited here," Eric snapped. "And before we found out that Ryas' men are searching for us."

Lars sat back in his chair, the blood draining from his face. "An Almeri assassin... Ryas' men... gods, boy! What have you been up to?"

"Hiding," Eric snapped. "Now what kind of price are we looking at?"

Lars waved the concern away. "Nothing I can't cover," he replied. "But he's insisting on knowing why he has to sail so soon."

Eric shook his head. "He can't know. No one on the ship can have any idea that it's me."

Lars looked about to object, and Eric glared at him.

"No one can know," he repeated. "The Almeri was a member of the Jiradin. For all we know, there could be others like him on the ship. Tell the captain that an important lady is being escorted to meet with my grandfather. I will act as her bodyguard."

"He'll want to know who she is," Lars cautioned.

"So drop hints that she's promised to someone in the family. That shouldn't be too hard. Grandfather has been seeking alliances in Prisia for decades."

Lars nodded slowly. "It would ensure she's treated with respect," he added. "It will be a rough trip for you, though. If they suspect that you're... dallying with the bride of one of the royal family, they'll heave you over the side."

Eric smiled coldly. "I am her guard and her instructor in Almeri court etiquette. I'll need to be stationed close to her, preferably in an adjoining cabin." When Lars appeared skeptical, Eric added, "I think I can behave like a gentleman for ten days, Lars. Make it happen."

"Alright," Lars agreed. "I'll make the arrangements. Is there anything else you need?"

Eric nodded. "A letter of introduction for Lady Anika Leifsdottir, as her agent in Heidal, and I need you to open a line of credit on Grandfather's account."

Lars stared at him for a moment. "Expensive inn, I

take it?" he commented at last.

Eric shrugged. "The place we were staying at didn't work out. Besides, if Anika's going to pass as the betrothed of one of the royal family, she's going to need luggage suitable to her station... both at the inn and for loading on the ship. If we show up with nothing but the clothes on our backs, it will raise questions we can't afford to answer."

Lars sighed and nodded, drawing a sheet of heavy paper from his desk. "I trust you'll explain this to your grandfather?" he murmured as he plucked his feathered quill from the inkpot beside him. "I would hate for him to think I'm stealing from him. The assassins would come for me, next."

Eric laughed softly. "Of course," he replied.

Lars wrote out a letter of introduction, including permission for the bearer to draw up to 10,000 gold hawks from the account of Kysid ab Kyr'lasi. He unlocked a cabinet and withdrew a small strongbox. Unlocking it, he took out a heavy signet stone, poured red wax on the bottom of the letter, and stamped it carefully, sprinkling sand lightly on the seal to dry it. He glanced at Eric before handing the page to him. "That," he murmured, "is worth my life if you lose it, you realize."

Eric nodded. "I don't think Grandfather would be

overly pleased with me, either."

Lars snorted. "True. Is there anything else?"

Anika leaned forward. "Get word to Captain Olaf to keep an eye on Gunther's inn. There might be soldiers heading there to look for us, and I'd hate for Gunther to get hurt again."

Lars eyebrows arched upwards. "Olaf? Gunther? Gods, boy... do you know..." he paused. "Of course you do. You must." He face suddenly paled. "Is there anything else I ought to know, Eric?"

Eric shook his head. "Nothing like that," he reassured the balding man. "We met them both by chance. Coincidence."

"Do they know about you?" Lars demanded.

Eric nodded. "Olaf figured it out, and I told Gunther after the assassination attempt."

Lars ran a hand over his bald head. "They're both going to be furious at me for not telling them about your father..."

"You were following his instructions," Eric told him. "They'll understand."

Lars grimaced. "You don't know them as well as I do," he muttered. "I'll be buying them drinks until I'm old and grey."

Eric smiled. "I appreciate your help, Lars. Get word to that captain to expect Anika's luggage by mid-afternoon tomorrow." He gestured at the letter of introduction. "Which bank do I draw this on?"

"Stirling's," Lars replied. "It's near the palace. You can't miss it. Look for the second biggest building in Heidal."

Eric extended his hand to the other man, who took it in a firm grasp. "Thanks again," he said quietly.

Lars smiled at him. "Give my best to your father, when you see him. Tell him I'm sorry for sending the wrong information."

Turning, Eric glanced at Anika. "Anything else?" he asked.

She shook her head. "Let's go."

*

The remainder of the day was a blur for Anika. After Eric led her to the bank, where an unctuous man stared with bulging eyes at the letter of credit before sending for the manager of the bank, who ushered her politely into a fine room in the back of the bank, things got a little surreal. Eric acted the part of a stoic bodyguard, and Anika became the center of attention. The bank manager bowed and scraped, eager to please. He immediately sent a messenger to their inn, guaranteeing funds for as long as Anika wished to remain. Next, while offering her various drinks and refreshments, he provided her with a small letter he informed her would be sufficient for her to use at all of the establishments around the palace in lieu of coin. She would be required to sign the invoices at whichever shops she visited, he explained, which would then be forwarded to the bank to dispense the appropriate payments. He gave her a small purse, containing fifty gold hawks, for what he called "incidentals". She did her best to appear haughtily indifferent, as though this were customary for her, but by the time she and Eric shuffled back onto the street in front of the four-story bank that stretched an entire city block, she was dazed and numb.

"Are you feeling okay?" Eric asked softly.

She stared at him with glazed eyes. "Not really," she admitted. "I... I'm a little bewildered."

"I can believe it," he murmured. "But you're doing great. If I didn't know better, I'd have sworn you were born to this." He waved at a passing carriage, which slowed to a halt before them. "Let's head back to the inn..." he began, but she shook her head.

"If we go there, I'll find excuses to put off coming back out," she told him. "Let's get this over with."

He smiled and helped her into the carriage. "Alright," he agreed. He looked at the driver of the carriage. "My mistress requires some new additions to her wardrobe. Take us someplace appropriate."

The driver nodded curtly. "Very good, sir."

He climbed into the carriage and sat beside her on the plush velvet seat. "This next part might be a little overwhelming," he told her.

Her eyes bulged. "More overwhelming than that?" she demanded. "How?"

His lips twitched, as though he was fighting to keep from smiling at her discomfort. "Here they just bowed and scraped. Where we're going, they'll do that while they're poking and prodding you with pins and needles. I have to admit, I don't envy you."

Groaning, she leaned back and closed her eyes. "You're enjoying this, aren't you?"

"Maybe a little," he agreed.

She jabbed at him with her elbow, not even bothering to open her eyes.

The store the driver took them to was stunning. Dresses of fabrics that shimmered in the sunlight greeted them from behind windows larger than the front of her home in Anidaron had been. A man stepped forward and opened the carriage door for them, bowing as Anika stepped down. "Welcome to Estana's, my lady."

Eric hopped down and escorted Anika inside. "Let me do the talking, here," he whispered. "Just act... like you don't care for anything."

A middle-aged woman approached them as soon as they entered the room, her sharp eyes narrowing at the sight of them. "Good day," she murmured, eyeing the dress Anika was wearing disdainfully. "Forgive me, but perhaps you have come to the wrong establishment..." she added archly.

Eric stared at her coldly. "Perhaps," he said, his tone matching his expression. "But I think not. Send for the owner, and I suggest you don't dawdle. She won't thank you."

The woman sniffed and spun on her heel, heading towards the back of the shop. A moment later an elegantly dressed woman with long, silver hair emerged and approached them, a smile dancing on her lips. Despite her almost painfully perfect posture, there was something endearing about her. "Good afternoon," she murmured as she approached. "I am Estana."

Eric nodded. "My mistress is in need of a new wardrobe for an extended stay in Kisham," he told her.

"Indeed?" she asked, glancing at Anika. Her smile was genuinely warm. "And what takes you to Almeri, my dear?"

Anika smiled at her slightly, feeling more at ease around the elderly woman. "I'm going to meet my betrothed's family," she said softly.

"Well he's a fortunate man," Estana commented, extending her hands to Anika. "Is the family well connected?"

Anika's lips twitched. "I suppose you could say that," she agreed.

Estana's eyebrows lifted slightly. "Really?" she asked, sensing the understatement in Anika's tone. She glanced over at Eric as though for clarification.

"She will require attire appropriate for joining the household of Kysid ab Kyr'lasi, Sultan of Almeri," Eric told her.

Estana blinked once, her face going pale. She paused for a moment to regain her composure. At last she bowed slightly to Anika and murmured, "I am honored you chose my establishment. I presume you will be using credit?"

Anika produced the note the bank had given her and handed it to Estana. The older woman glanced at it and returned it to Anika. "Very good," she breathed. "Well then..."

Eric cleared his throat. "Your pardon, Estana, but my mistress' ship departs tomorrow."

Estana whirled and clapped her hands loudly. Several women emerged from the back of the building, their expressions startled. "Drop everything," Estana announced. "This client has priority."

The woman who had approached them to begin with rolled her eyes. "Surely..." she began.

"Sharlene," Estana rebuked her firmly. "When I require your input, I will seek it. Until then, hold your tongue. I require cloth, flattering to..." she paused and turned to face Anika. "I'm sorry, my dear... I didn't catch your name."

"Anika," she whispered.

"Sharlene, find a range of cloth that flatters Anika's skin tone and hair... jewel tones, I think. Light cottons, primarily, good for a hot climate. Erin..." Estana began barking orders too quickly for Anika to follow. She glanced over at Eric, feeling lost. He grinned.

"I will go arrange for a trunk for your new garments, my lady. I trust I leave you in good hands," he said quietly, bowing and backing away.

Estana peered at Eric, her eyes narrowing. "You might want to get more than one," she said simply and turned back to Anika. "Come along, my dear. Let's get you measured."

Throwing a final, panicked look over her shoulder at Eric, Anika followed Estana towards the back of the shop.

Chapter 22

"I can't believe you just left me there!" Anika grumbled as she pressed a cool cloth against her forehead as she lay back on the huge bed. She was wearing nothing but her shift, and her shapely legs were curled demurely beside her. The dress she'd been wearing was lying in a puddle on the floor, and two large trunks, stuffed with clothing and shoes, lurked along one wall.

"Well, it's not like I was going to be able to come back into the fitting rooms with you, anyhow," he argued, folding up his chain armour and placing it on one of the dressers, beside the porcelain wash basin. "Guards aren't normally recommended to be around their mistresses while they are dressing. I would have been standing around in the front of the shop, getting in the way. Besides, I hate shopping."

She took the cloth from her eyes and glared at him. "You enjoyed it," she accused.

"No," he countered. "*You* enjoyed it. You're playing up the indignant, maligned country girl, but you can't fool me."

An impish grin flashed across her face, and she threw the cloth at him. "Okay," she admitted. "I might have enjoyed it a little. But what am I going to do with twelve dresses?"

"Wear them, I would suspect," Eric replied. "You would have needed something to wear in Almeri, in any case... actually, my aunt will probably want to take you shopping in Kisham sooner or later, too."

Anika sighed. "I made do with one set of clothes for my entire life," she muttered.

"And you had pigs in your yard and chickens in your living room," Eric pointed out. "Think of going to my grandfather's palace as though you were going to war... you wouldn't want to go to war without armour, would you? The clothes you got today are a kind of armour. It's soft and pretty armour, but it's what will deflect the sharp tongues and cutting glances of the other women in the palace."

Anika stared at him. "Can't I just use the sword?"

He laughed. "Some women do," he admitted. "Though duels between women are less frequent than duels between men, they do happen."

"Duels?" she asked softly.

He nodded. "There are two parts to the judicial system in Almeri," he told her. "There is the civil level, and the criminal level. Most civil matters are settled through duels or through financial recompense. Criminal behavior is usually dealt with by the courts; however, if the crime impacts an individual or a family, it can be settled out of the court system through a duel."

"Are duels... to the death?" her eyes were bright with curiosity.

Eric shrugged. "It depends on the terms of the duel," he answered. "A duel is a legally binding form of arbitration, and can only be entered into between agreeing parties. The general agreement is that the act which triggered the duel will be forgiven, win or lose. If the wronged party can't agree to that, it generally goes to litigation. It's up to the challenger to set the terms of the duel. Most are to first blood, but some are to the death. Those particular duels must be supervised by an impartial judge, which the courts provide. It's a cheap solution.

Lawyers aren't overly liked in Almeri, so people will usually duel rather than pay the legal fees associated with litigation."

She shook her head. "I have a lot to learn," she whispered.

Eric shrugged. "It's not entirely different from Prisian law," he argued. "In civil matters, consenting parties here can also use dueling as a method of resolution, but people seem to have forgotten that. Most people take their grievances to court here. It's why there are so many bloody lawyers in Prisia."

She stared at him. "Do you know a lot about the laws of Prisia?"

Eric looked a little shy. "My parents insisted I learn everything I could about governing, both in Almeri and in Prisia. They drummed the laws of both countries into my head since I could talk. When I was very young, I treated it like a game. It made things easier."

Anika yawned suddenly. "Gods," she murmured. "Is it only mid-evening? I'm exhausted."

"Why don't you try and get some sleep, then?" he suggested. "Tomorrow could be a long day, and I don't know how you'll do on the ship. You might find sleeping... challenging."

She frowned, sitting up. "What do you mean?"

"A lot of people get ill on the ocean," he explained. "It makes for a pretty miserable voyage."

She groaned and fell back onto the pillows. "Great..." she began, but a knock at the door to the suite interrupted her.

Eric was on his feet in a flash; he grabbed his sword from where he had placed it beside the bedroom doorway and walked cautiously to the main door. "Who is it?" he demanded.

"Willhem, sir," the voice on the other side responded. "I have an invitation card for Lady Anika."

Eric relaxed slightly and opened the door. He was still dressed in the leather armour he wore under the chain shirt, and the sword in his hand added to the menacing appearance of an alert bodyguard. "An invitation from who?" he demanded of the young servant standing at the door.

Willhem shook his head. "I don't read the invitations, sir," he explained. "I just deliver them as they arrive."

Eric reached out and took the proffered card. Willhem looked at him expectantly, and he grudgingly handed the young man a silver coin. "Thank you," he added.

Willhem bowed and backed away, and Eric shut the

door, turning the envelope over in his hands. The card was addressed to Lady Anika Liefsdottir. Frowning, he walked back to stand at the foot of the bed. "Apparently your presence in Heidal hasn't passed unnoticed, my lady."

She sat up, reaching out for the card. "Who...?"

He handed her the card, and she tore the envelope open. "Lady Anika," she read. "You are cordially invited to evening tea with Lord Ahrlon Dersain, Duke of Floreni, and his lady wife, Rehann. Please present yourself no later than nine o'clock."

Eric groaned. "Damn," he muttered.

Anika's face paled. "I... we don't have to go, do we?"

Eric closed his eyes. "Unless you want to insult the most powerful lord in the entire south... yes, we do." Something about the invitation tickled a part of his memory, but he couldn't place what it was. Frowning, he growled, "How in the blazes did he learn about you?"

Anika laughed nervously. "Oh, it could have been the banker... or Estana... or one of her seamstresses... or the concierge... or..."

Eric glared at her for a moment, and then glanced out the window. "Alright," he muttered. "We have about two hours. Get dressed... wear one of your new outfits. I'll

The Sword and Satchel

walk you through the basics of Prisian etiquette for evening tea." He paused, then asked, "Did you buy any make-up?"

She shook her head. "I've never worn make-up," she whispered.

He nodded, then stalked back to where a small rope hung beside the door. He tugged lightly on it, and a moment later there was a soft knock. "Service?"

He opened the door and stared coolly at Willhem. "I need you to deliver a note to Estana. You know of her, I trust?"

Willhem nodded politely. "Of course, sir."

Eric walked over to the low table and opened the drawer, withdrawing a small stack of cards and envelopes and a quill with a tiny, sealed inkpot. He broke the seal, dabbed the quill into the dark blue ink, and scribbled a few lines. He placed the card in one of the envelopes and handed it to Willhem. "Deliver this and return with Estana's reply within ten minutes, and there's a hawk in it for you."

The servant paled. "Yes, sir. At once." Without looking back, he sprinted out the door.

Anika, still in her thin white shift, was peering at him from behind the doorframe of the bedroom. "What... how did you know there would be paper there? Why are you sending for Estana?"

Eric glanced at her. "All quality inns provide their guests with the means of communication," he replied. "As for Estana... I would have sent for Larissa or Hilde if it wouldn't have aroused curiosity. Sending for the dressmaker, after a purchase like you made today, isn't unheard of. I asked her to bring some basic cosmetics. Hopefully she'll read between the lines. I think she's fairly astute. Now, get dressed."

As Anika began donning one of the stunning dresses from that afternoon, Eric began walking her through the proper forms of address for Prisian nobility. "You'll be announced," he told her. "They'll ask for your title, but decline telling them. Say something like, 'Lady Anika will do nicely'. When you are introduced to the duke and duchess, curtsy deeply, but keep your face raised, head tilted slightly to the left..."

When Willhem returned, just over ten minutes later, Anika was nearly dressed and Eric had moved on to discussing the proper way to hold her tea cup.

"Sir," Willhem panted when Eric opened the door. "Madam Estana says she will be here momentarily."

Eric nodded and handed the man a gold hawk. "Very good, Willhem. If my mistress has further need of you..."

"I am at my lady's service," he assured Eric hastily. "I will escort Madam Estana up upon her arrival."

"Excellent," Eric nodded politely as he led the youth to the door.

Estana arrived only a few minutes later. She looked completely calm and dignified, despite the haste it must have taken to arrive so quickly. "Good evening," she murmured, tilting her head towards Eric. "I trust there is no issue with your lady's purchase?"

Eric bowed to her slightly. "Of course not, Madam. Unfortunately, my lady apparently neglected to pack her cosmetics, and she has been unexpectedly invited to tea with His Grace, Duke Ahrlon. As she is unfamiliar with anyone in the city, and under some time constraints, I suggested we approach you..."

Estana smiled, her eyes flashing. "It is my pleasure," she replied. "Thanks to your note, I came prepared for such a contingency." She said, tapping an elegant-looking satchel that hung at her side. She looked over as Anika stepped out of the bedroom, and her face glowed with pleasure. "My dear! What a perfect choice for tea with Ahrlon. He simply adores that colour, and you wear it so well. Come, my dear, let me see you..."

Anika stepped forward glancing shyly at Eric. Eric

had to admit that the rich sapphire dress was absolutely stunning on her, accentuating her hips and bosom. Strapless, the neckline dipped in the front, displaying just the right amount of cleavage while showing her toned shoulders to advantage. "You look amazing..." he breathed, then hastily added, "...my lady."

"Now," Estana said, stepping up to study Anika's face. "You have such a clear complexion," she murmured, touching Anika's cheek tenderly. "And such lovely eyes. If you will allow me...?" she indicated her satchel.

Anika nodded. "Please," she said softly.

Estana hustled Anika over to the couches by the fireplace, making sure Anika's face was illuminated by the light shining in the windows. She withdrew several brushes and powders, and went to work.

When she was done, Eric could barely breathe. While he'd always known Anika was beautiful, Estana's cosmetics brought that beauty to shimmering life. He swallowed hard and looked away.

"That should do it," Estana commented, nodding to herself. "You have such wonderful skin tones, darling... and those eyelashes! The man you're marrying is fortunate indeed."

She rose to her feet and walked over to where Eric

stood. Eric fumbled at his belt for his purse, but Estana pursed her lips and shook her head. "Be very careful, child," she whispered to him, her lips barely moving. "Ahrlon is no fool, and if I can remember a face like yours after thirty-five years, you can rest assured that he can. Keep to the shadows, and let your lovely girl do the talking. She won't have to say much. She's captivating as she is."

Eric hesitated, and Estana laughed softly. Then she turned back to Anika. "It has been a rare pleasure to have an opportunity to work with such a lovely woman," she smiled. "Do have a safe trip to Almeri, my dear... and remember: a lady's greatest strength is often her own self-confidence. Demure women have a place, but honest confidence will often serve you better than misguided self-consciousness. You are a beautiful young woman. Let Ahrlon see that. And never fear his intentions. His new bride keeps him on a tight leash."

With a slight curtsy, Estana swept from the room, her soft laughter ringing in Eric's ears as she left.

"How do I look?" Anika whispered.

Eric looked up at her, his mouth suddenly dry. "You are... beautiful," he finally managed. He moved into the bedroom and came back with a silver hand-mirror. She stared at her reflection in the glass for a moment, her eyes wide.

When she looked up at him, he couldn't help but laugh. "You clean up really well," he told her softly. "Now, let's go visit the Duke."

Chapter 23

They hired a carriage to take them to the palace. It was a long trip, and Eric spent the time going over some of the finer points of etiquette. Anika spent the time staring out the window of the carriage at the pristine garden sprawling out before the palace.

She marvelled at the vast manicured lawns, lined with delicate flowerbeds and white marble fountains. Trees, neatly trimmed, rose gracefully in background, against the fading light. It was magnificent, and the beauty of the setting took her breath away.

The palace was no less stunning. While she had seen it from above, before they entered the city, seeing the shining dome and intricately carved marble, lit from below by carefully tended torches, made it seem something from a fairy tale.

The driver helped her down, and she thanked him softly. She paused there, before the grand entrance, as Eric strode up beside her, his chainmail gleaming red and gold in the torchlight. "Honest confidence," she murmured to herself as she straightened her shoulders and walked up the broad steps to the pillared doorway.

Eric handed the invitation to a painfully rigid-looking doorman. "Lady Anika to see His Grace," he said softly.

The doorman bowed stiffly. "His Grace is expecting you, Lady Anika. If you will please follow me?"

Anika nodded, and the doorman moved on silent feet into the cavernous palace entrance hall.

Anika did her best not to look around, fearing that she would lose her nerve at the sight of the opulence that surrounded her. Even so, she couldn't help but notice the artwork that hung, tastefully, along the walls. Suits of gleaming armour stood in alcoves at almost every corner, and one or two liveried guards stood at various points.

"His Grace takes tea in the courtyard in the summers," the doorman informed them as they passed what appeared to be a massive ballroom, gold gleaming on both the ceiling and along the floor. The doorman glanced at Eric's sword. "Your bodyguard will be required to relinquish his weapon with the guards," he added.

"Of course," Anika murmured airily, as though she had no concerns at all. "If His Grace can't protect me in his own home, no one can."

"Indeed," agreed the doorman, appearing mollified. He led them to an ornate door where two guards stood, watching them approach carefully. After Eric removed his sword and handed it to the guard on his right, the doorman bowed. "How shall I announce you, my lady?"

"Oh," she smiled. "Lady Anika will be sufficient, I think."

The doorman frowned slightly, but bowed again. "As you wish, my lady." He stepped through the door, which opened onto a beautiful garden, alive with night flowers and lightning bugs. "Your Grace," he announced. "Lady Anika has arrived."

A tall, broad-shouldered man with greying hair rose to his feet from behind a low table as Anika stepped through the doors. Beside him, a stunningly beautiful dusky-skinned woman, less than half his age, also stood, her dark eyes shimmering in the light of the torches along the garden wall. Eric felt his mouth grow suddenly dry at the sight of her. He recognized her immediately. He felt the last few hidden aspects of his memory click into place, and was about to whisper something to Anika when the tall man bowed slightly. "Lady Anika," Duke Ahrlon greeted her. "May I present my wife, Lady Rehann?"

Anika curtsied gracefully, her face raised. "It is my pleasure to meet you, your grace."

Eric bowed deeply, then retreated into the shadows beside the door, as befit a bodyguard of a noblewoman, but also because he knew that the woman standing beside the duke would recognize him instantly.

"I hear," Rehann commented softly, her voice faintly accented, "that you are going to visit someone in my grandfather's household."

"Your grandfather?" Anika inquired politely.

Rehann smiled gently, her eyes sharp despite her gentle tone. "Of course," she said. "Sultan Kysid ab Kyr'lasi."

Anika raised her eyebrows. "You are Sultan Kysid's granddaughter?" she asked, her voice mildly surprised. Eric shook his head, amazed by how well she maintained her composure. "It's a pleasure to meet you, indeed."

Rehann inclined her head slightly. "I am greatly curious to find out who, exactly, you are visiting."

Anika took a deep breath. "And I am surprised that I wasn't informed that one of Sultan Kysid's grandchildren had married the Duke of Floreni," she commented, her voice just loud enough for Eric to detect the note of displeasure in it. He smiled slightly, knowing the comment was directed at him. "Still," Anika continued. "I think your aunt would be displeased with me if I discussed who I was going to visit... and I've heard enough about her to not idly incur her wrath."

Rehann's eyes widened, then genuine sorrow filled them. "Then you haven't heard?" she whispered. "Word came a few days ago. I fear your trip will be in vain, Lady Anika. My cousin..." she bit her lower lip, which quivered slightly. "I'm sorry to be the one to have to tell you this... but my cousin, the only one you could possibly mean, was killed less than a month ago."

"Murdered," snarled Ahrlon, his face twisted in suppressed fury.

Anika blinked, glancing between Rehann and Ahrlon. "Murdered?" she repeated.

Ahrlon nodded vigorously, but Rehann touched his arm gently. "We can't prove anything, Ahrlon... and even if we could..."

"We both know who's responsible for his death, Rehann. Even if your uncle's man hadn't survived the attack and told us, who else but Ryas would dare..."

Anika coughed softly, and Rehann looked up at her, the grief in her face obvious. "Forgive us," she murmured. "This must come as a shock to you. We've had a few days to come to terms with it, but even so..."

Anika glanced over her shoulder at Eric, who sighed softly. Too many people were finding out about him, he thought. "It appears that the stories of my death have been... somewhat premature," he said softly as he stepped out of the shadows. "But it's nice to realize that I would be missed..."

Rehann stared at him as though she were seeing a ghost, and Ahrlon blinked in confusion until his wife, with a ragged cry, lurched around the table and threw herself at Eric, wrapping her arms around his neck and weeping into his chest. "He said you were dead!" she wept. "He said he saw you fall!"

"It's good to see you again, Rehann," Eric soothed, running his hand in small circles on her back. He glanced up at the duke, who was staring at him, his eyes wide and his mouth hanging open. "Your grace," he murmured. "Forgive the deception, but considering the circumstances, it seemed... prudent."

Rehann leaned back and stared up at him, her face streaked with tears. Then, very casually, she punched him in the stomach. "How dare you let me... let all of the family... believe you were dead! Sending that man with false information..."

"I didn't send anyone," Eric told her, coughing from the blow. "I assume it was Alhamid who came to you?"

Rehann nodded, her face dark.

"He was an assassin," Eric told her. "He set me up, left me for dead in the mountains. Anika is the only reason I'm still alive."

Rehann glanced back at Anika, who was standing calmly in front of the duke, her eyes sparkling. "You saved Eric?" she whispered. When Anika looked uncomfortable, she added, "Then we owe you a debt beyond words." She released Eric and walked gracefully over to embrace Anika, kissing her lightly on each cheek.

Ahrlon seemed to finally recover himself, and he shook his head. "You are the spitting image of your father," he murmured. Then, clearing his throat, he added, "If this assassin is still loose, we need to find him..."

"He's dead," Eric told them. "He found us here, in Heidal. Anika killed him."

There was a momentary pause, and then Rehann grinned at Anika. "You," she said softly, "are just full of surprises. I think this evening is going to be much more interesting than I had anticipated." She glanced at the table and frowned. "But we need another chair and some additional refreshments." She clapped her hands sharply, and the doorman poked his head into the courtyard. She conveyed her commands briefly, and then took Anika's hands and guided her to the table. "Come, Lady Anika... you must tell us everything."

*

Ahrlon leaned back in his chair, nodding. "You're right, of course," he commented to Eric. "This has all the sounds of a conspiracy to get Almeri to go to war with Prisia. To be totally honest, if your father landed on Prisian shores right now, there isn't a lord in the south that wouldn't welcome him with open arms... or in the west, for that matter. And with Masimor drawing Ryas' attention to the east... well, it would be an easy process to march on the capital."

Eric nodded slowly. "Unless my father came with ten thousand Almeri warriors at his back," he added.

Ahrlon coughed and took a deep breath. "Yes, well, that would be... less inviting," he agreed. "But considering the hash Ryas has made since the War of Succession... he didn't win himself any friends among the noble families, you know... well, even if your father came with Almeri...

support... I think all it would take would be some quiet discussions with a few of the older families."

"I think that was the bait that brought me here," Eric admitted. "Someone convinced my father that there was something to be gained by sending me to Prisia. Unfortunately, I don't know who it was that sent the message."

"Maybe it was a ruse from the beginning," Rehann mused. "If the Jiradin are involved, they could easily have sent a forged message to your father, requesting an audience. Gods know they seem to have their tentacles in everything."

Eric nodded. "That was kind of what I was thinking. But now... Rehann, how do you think Grandfather will react to news of my death?"

Rehann laughed, but it was without humor. "Oh, he'd get Uncle Kyvin to rouse the entire army..." she suddenly gasped very softly. "Oh, gods," she whispered. "Eric..."

"We're leaving tomorrow," he assured her. "No matter how quickly Uncle Kyvin can rouse the Almeri forces, they can't get provisioned for a voyage in less than a month, let alone get ready for an invasion. I'll be back in time to calm things down."

Rehann settled back in her seat, looking relieved.

Then she glanced at Anika. "So you really are going to visit a member of my grandfather's household," she murmured, thoughtfully. Then she smiled brightly. "You'll be my cousin!"

Anika blinked, and glanced at Eric. "Umm," she began.

"Oh, Eric," Rehann rolled her eyes at her cousin. "Please tell me you don't intend to let her slip away. I'll admit that she's too good for you, but even so..."

"I have every intention of asking her to marry me just as soon as we have a moment when we're not being chased by assassins or soldiers," he growled.

Rehann glanced around innocently. "I don't see any soldiers or assassins..." she observed.

Eric stared daggers at Rehann, and she clapped delightedly. At last he sighed and turned to Anika. "I've been waiting for the right moment ever since we got interrupted by Hilde at Gunther's, but..."

He slipped from the chair and knelt down in front of Anika, his face flushed. He reached out and clasped her hands gently in his. "Anika, will you..."

"My lord," the doorman called, appearing from the palace doorway. He glanced at Eric, kneeling before Anika, and cleared his throat. "Your pardon, my lord. There is a colonel from King Ryas' forces here to see you, Your Grace. He claims it is urgent."

Before Ahrlon could speak, a haughty-looking little man, wearing the white and green of King Ryas, pushed his way into the courtyard. His dark, oiled beard gleamed in the torchlight, a sharp contrast against his sallow skin. "Ahrlon," he began in a pompous, nasal voice. "I am Colonel Regis Penisston, of his majesty's sixteenth infantry, and I believe you have a traitor in your city." He glanced dismissively at Eric and Anika. "I need to speak with you immediately... privately."

Ahrlon rose to his feet, his face darkening dangerously. "Colonel," he said in a menacingly chill tone. "It appears you lack the social graces to recognize or employ the proper decorum when addressing a peer of the realm. I am engaged. I will deal with you when I deem it appropriate. Until then, you may speak with my chamberlain. He will escort you to the antechamber of my office..."

"I have no time for this," the arrogant little man sneered. "I am the son of Duke Henry, advisor to the king..."

"And I am the duke of Floreni!" Ahrlon snapped. "And you are in my home. Be thankful I don't have the guards stationed outside drag you to the cells and have you horsewhipped for your insolence!"

The little man flushed, his eyes narrowing. "I am here on behalf of King Ryas..." he blustered.

"Really?" Ahrlon murmured, his tone turning deceptively soft. "Well that changes things, of course. If such is the case, then surely you must have a dispatch from his majesty, which might excuse your temerity in barging into my home so rudely. I would be most interested to see that dispatch."

The little man squirmed slightly. "I have no dispatch, but the man we're seeking killed soldiers in your holdings... in Anidaron."

Ahrlon smiled coldly. "So you not only lack the etiquette to await my pleasure, you have the audacity to claim to be here on his majesty's direct orders, lacking the substance to prove your claim? You do know that some might consider that to be treason, do you not?"

The colonel, so full of himself a moment before, suddenly looked deflated, and glanced around nervously. "I only meant..." he began.

"Guards!" Ahrlon called. The two men outside the door stepped inside, their eyes alert. "Escort this man to the holding cells."

"Wait!" the colonel cried plaintively, his sallow skin pale and his eyes wide. He looked around wildly, and his gaze fell upon Eric and Anika, seeing them for the first time, and his eyes widened in shock. "Them!" he snapped. "They match the description! That man! He's the one from Anidaron!"

Ahrlon frowned and shook his head. "Guards. Take him. If he resists, subdue him. I will have the truth from him before this night is out."

The guards dragged the colonel from the room, screaming protests and accusations as they hauled him away.

Ahrlon turned and looked at Eric and Anika. "Do you have any idea what he was ranting about?"

Eric shrugged. "It sounds like he thinks we killed some soldiers in Anidaron," he replied.

The duke glared at him. "And did you?"

"Yes," Eric admitted without hesitation. "And if I could go back, I'd do it again... only this time I'd kill every last one of the murdering bastards."

Ahrlon blinked at the confession. "It would appear you left something out of your story," he murmured. "Perhaps you might explain why you've been killing the king's men in my territory? Not that it bothers me that you're killing Ryas' men... just that you did it in my territory."

Anika scowled. "They killed everyone in Anidaron... including my father."

Rehann rose from her seat, her face aghast. "What?" she demanded.

Ahrlon returned to his seat, motioning for Anika to continue. She and Eric alternated telling the story, and by the time they were done, Ahrlon's face was stormy, and Rehann was pale.

"It's the same bloody thing as before," Ahrlon muttered, almost to himself. "Ryas allows this kind of butchery... what manner of king allows his own soldiers to ravage the countryside?" He glanced up at Eric. "You had better go. I won't be able to hold him here for long. Ryas' elite," he spat the word, "have a certain amount of privilege. As the son of a duke, I have to release him. He's going to demand to know where you're staying..."

"Tell him we claimed to be staying at The Nightingale," Eric said. "Although how you're going to explain our presence here..."

"I often entertain unfamiliar merchants and nobility in the city," Ahrlon told him. "I try to keep tabs on the influential people that enter Heidal. I'll tell him you caught my attention, that you are a merchant dealing in spices from the Lerchan Confederacy. As it happens, I believe that there's a merchant staying at The Nightingale that is doing exactly that."

Eric smiled at the duke, rising to his feet. "You have our gratitude."

Rehann laughed wryly. "Oh, you don't have to thank him. He loves these little intrigues. It makes him feel young again."

"No, my dear," Ahrlon said, smiling at her. "*You* make me feel young again... these little intrigues make me feel like I still make a difference." He paused to study Eric for a moment. "You are a lot like your father, Eric," he said at last. "He and I knew each other quite well when we were younger. Let him know that I still harbour some strong sentiment."

Eric heard the emphasis Ahrlon employed on 'harbour'. Nodding slightly, he murmured. "I'm sure he'll be pleased to know he hasn't been forgotten by his old friends."

"He is remembered fondly by many in Prisia," Ahrlon agreed.

Anika rose from her seat gracefully and curtsied to Rehann and the duke. "It has been a pleasure to meet you both," she said softly. "Perhaps we will see each other again."

Eric bowed slightly to the duke and hugged his cousin tightly. "It was good to see you, Rehann," he murmured.

"Be safe, Eric..." she whispered back. Then she added, her tone echoing the nuances of her husband, "And I hope you come back to visit."

"Perhaps," he agreed cautiously.

Turning, he walked over and collected his sword from the guards, who had returned from dragging the colonel away. He glanced back at Anika, who was being kissed on both cheeks by Rehann. She blushed at something his cousin whispered in her ear, and smiled. Then, her head held high, she followed Eric from the courtyard.

Chapter 24

"As soon as that colonel is released, he'll have descriptions of us out to every soldier in Heidal," Eric muttered as they rolled down the cobbled drive from the palace. "We're running out of places to hide."

Anika smiled at him. "No," she said softly. "We're just refreshing our old hiding places. The colonel saw us in having tea with the duke... dressed like visiting nobility. Let's just go back to Gunther's."

Eric stared at her for a moment, and then he laughed softly. "That is... brilliant. A man like that would find it inconceivable for any guests of the duke to be staying in the shipping quarter... we'll have to arrange to have your trunks transported to the ship, but that should be easy. With a little gold, it shouldn't be hard to convince the concierge to deny we ever stayed at The Silver Chalice..." He shook his head. "Sometimes, you amaze me."

Anika smiled demurely. "I'm glad to hear it. Now, I believe you were about to ask me something when we were so rudely interrupted..."

"Oh, no," Eric said. "I'm not going to tempt fate again until we're safely out of Heidal."

"You already know the answer," she added softly. "I'm still here, after all."

He smiled his lopsided smile. "That doesn't take away from my need to ask it anyway." He stared across the carriage at her. "You were amazing back there, by the way. You acted as though you'd been born among the nobility."

She grimaced. "You could have warned me that your cousin was the duchess," she stated, her eyes accusing.

"Head injury," Eric replied, raising his hands innocently.

"Brain damaged, you mean," she muttered, and he laughed. "It came as a bit of a surprise, I have to tell you."

Eric took her hands in his. "You handled it better than I could have imagined," he told her. She smiled, and they rode like that in silence for a few moments.

"Eric," Anika commented at last. "Was it just me,

or did Ahrlon seem to be suggesting the same thing Captain Olaf suggested the other day?"

"Oh, he was doing more than suggesting," Eric replied quietly. "He was offering safe harbour to my father... and letting us know that the southern and western lords are ready to support his claim."

Anika shook her head. "Living in Anidaron, I never realized how much Ryas is hated," she whispered. "What could he have done that would have made everyone want to rise up against him?"

"Not everyone," Eric told her. "He has the support of the central lords, still. But I admit, it's hard to understand. I mean, Olaf explained it to some extent, but even so..."

The carriage lurched to a halt, and Eric stepped out, helping Anika down. He paid the driver and escorted Anika inside.

Willhem was waiting for them, his face pale. "Sir," he whispered. "There were soldiers here a little while ago. They were looking for some people. Gustav and I told them we hadn't seen anyone matching the description, but..."

Eric nodded. "Did they offer a reward?" he asked quietly.

Willhem nodded. "Twenty-five silver crowns," he

replied. "It's not enough to tempt me, but Gustav... he has a wife and three children. I think he might be considering..."

Eric frowned. "Is Gustav the concierge?"

"Yes," Willhem replied. "He's in the back right now..."

"Go get him," Eric said quietly. As Willhem darted into the back, Eric withdrew his purse and took out six gold hawks. When Gustav came out, he stared at Eric as though memorizing his face.

"You wished to see me, sir?" the concierge asked politely.

"I did," Eric replied. "I realized that I neglected to tip you for your gracious behavior when we arrived, and I wanted to correct that oversight." He placed a gold hawk on the counter. "In addition, I was hoping that you might arrange to have my lady's trunks taken to the docks tomorrow around midday. I'm not from around here, but I assume this," he placed a second hawk on the counter, "ought to cover the costs. You can, of course, keep the change." The concierge's eyes bulged slightly. "Now," Eric continued, leaning against the counter. "You strike me as a family man. Do you have children?"

Gustav nodded, his eyes wide.

Eric glanced at Anika. "My lady here recently lost

her father... it was an unfortunate affair. Some soldiers were killed. Now, however, I hear rumors that there might be soldiers poking around, looking for us in Heidal. And it is us," he added. "Needless to say, I am rather reluctant to be located. Her father was a good man, and he wanted nothing more than for his children to be protected. I'm sure you understand that sentiment. So," Eric placed a third gold hawk on the counter. "I would appeal to the father in you to help me protect my lady. It would be unfortunate if the soldiers looking for us happened to discover our location."

Gustav stared at the gold coins sitting on the counter, his face pale. "My lady," he whispered, scooping up the coins. "I am terribly sorry to hear of your loss. Of course, The Silver Chalice ensures absolute anonymity."

Eric smiled and patted him on the shoulder. "Good man," he murmured. "Now, Willhem, if you would come upstairs, I will show you the luggage that we need transported."

Willhem nodded and followed them up the stairs. When they reached the room, Eric turned to look at the youth. "I appreciate your warning," he told him, pressing the three remaining hawks into Willhem's palm. "You have done my lady and I, as well as Gustav, a good service."

"It's my pleasure, sir," Willhem answered, staring at

the coins. "But I don't need..."

"No," Eric agreed. "But need and deserve are different things. Every word I told Gustav downstairs was true. Those soldiers killed my lady's father, and I killed some of them... for that they've hunted us for weeks. You held your peace when you could have spoken to them about us, and you warned me of Gustav's uncertainty. You have earned my gratitude, and the best I can do in return is ensure that you are taken care of for a while. Take that gold and deposit it in one of the city's banks. Keep it for when you are married and a father, and use it to help protect your own family."

Anika watched from the background, a small smile on her lips. As Willhem walked away in a daze after being shown the trunks, she approached Eric. "That was a nice thing you did," she said softly. Then her expression hardened. "It almost made up for threatening that man's family, downstairs."

Eric blinked. "For... *what*?" he asked, genuinely confused.

She shook her head. "You... I thought... the way you talked about protecting children..."

Eric stared at her, stunned. "I would never, ever threaten children," he whispered. "Never."

She looked away. "I'm sorry," she said at last. "I think I'm just getting... jaded."

Eric closed his eyes for a moment. Finally he sighed sadly and walked without speaking to the tiny room where his pack was stored.

"Eric..." Anika said, her voice trembling. "Eric, I'm sorry. I should have known better. I do know better."

He emerged from the room with his pack. "You should change out of that," he said softly, indicating the stunning blue dress. "But bring it with you. You still need to appear like a lady when we get to the ship."

She saw the hurt in his eyes, but knew that there was nothing she could say to heal the pain her assumption had caused. Ashamed, she hurried into the other room, her eyes brimming with unshed tears.

*

It was a long, silent walk back through the city to Gunther's. The darkness around the buildings in the shipping quarter seemed to shift and writhe, occasionally disgorging a rough-looking figure who would follow them at a discreet distance for a while before deciding on easier looking prey.

Eric almost wished one of the footpads would try something.

The Sword and Satchel

Neither he nor Anika had spoken since leaving The Silver Chalice. The silence had grown into a living thing between them, malicious and gnawing at them both. Eric wanted nothing more than for something to lash out at, but the thugs in the shadows seemed to sense the threat of imminent violence roiling around him like a vast thundercloud.

He couldn't understand why her assumption had hurt him so badly. While his memory was still hazy, he was absolutely certain that he had never cared about how others thought about him... at least not enough for it to impact his behavior. What people thought of him was their problem, not his. He let his actions speak for themselves.

Anika was different. He cared about how she saw him, and the fact that she had been able to believe that he was capable of threatening innocents... it made him want to break something.

Worse, it made him question himself.

The Hearth was quieter than usual when he and Anika stepped through the doorway. The only patrons were a pair of dock workers he didn't recognize. Gwynn stood behind the bar, in Gunther's habitual place, and her eyes lit up when they walked in. Even so, she approached them as strangers. Eric assumed Gunther had told her about who he

The Sword and Satchel

was, and the presence of the dock workers made her cautious.

"Good evening," she murmured, bustling forward. The dock workers didn't even glance up as she hurried past them. "Are you here for a meal, drinks, or lodging?"

"Lodging," Eric replied gruffly. "How much?"

"A silver crown a night," she responded.

He grunted and handed her a silver coin.

"Right this way, if you please," she said, moving quickly towards the stairs.

They followed her up, and she led them directly to their old room. "I didn't expect to see you two back again so soon," she said softly as she opened the door. "Those soldiers came by this morning. Gunther told them you took off... but they demanded to search the inn anyhow."

Eric nodded. "I thought that might happen. They didn't hassle you, did they?"

"No," she replied. "We played the ignorant innkeepers. What would we know about the people who stay here?"

Anika smiled and took Gwynn's hands. "Thank you both so much. We don't want to put you at any risk..."

"Nonsense, girl!" she chuckled. "You saved my Gunther's life. You're as welcome here as the sunrise, you are. Will you be staying long?"

"Only the night," Eric replied shortly. "We'll be gone tomorrow."

Gwynn nodded. "Well, I can't say as I blame you. Assassins and soldiers... that's enough to keep anyone on the move. Now, if you need anything, just come down."

"We will," Anika smiled gently. "And thank you again."

After Gwynn left, Anika moved to sit down on the bed. "Do you think you're going to speak to me again anytime soon?" she asked softly.

Eric sighed. "Anika..." he hesitated, and then he swallowed his pride. "I'm sorry. I overreacted..."

"No," she told him quietly. "All the way here I thought about how I would feel if someone accused me of something horrible... especially someone who should know me." She looked up at him, tears on her cheeks. "I'm sorry, Eric. I... you are the best man I've ever known. You helped my brothers and me when you really didn't have to. You could have just walked away, let us find our own way to Lodi's, but you didn't. You kept us safe, you protected us... protected me..."

Eric crossed the room and wrapped his arms around her, and she leaned her face into his neck. "Anika," he whispered.

She sniffed softly. "I'm sorry I thought that of you," she said. "I think it says more about who I am than anything else I've ever done. Not only did I assume the worst about the man I love... *I* made that connection, about threatening his family. Doesn't that mean I considered it? Gods, you must think I'm a monster."

"No," he told her, leaning back to look her in the eyes. "I don't think you're a monster, and I don't buy the argument that because you read more into what I said than I meant, it means you considered it. That's garbage. If anything, I think that your reaction to what you perceived as a threat was courageous." She snorted derisively, but he shook his head. "No, really. You called me on it, even if I didn't mean it the way it sounded... It takes a lot of courage to do that, especially when it's someone you love."

She blinked and wiped her face with the back of her hand. "Eric," she said, smiling slightly. "I appreciate that you're trying to make me feel better..." she trailed off.

He laughed softly and kissed her gently on the head. "You're a better person than I am," he told her. "That's one thing about which I am absolutely certain. Now, let's just forget about this, and focus on what we've got ahead of us."

"Almeri," she agreed.

"We've still got to get there," he told her. "In the morning, we need to find out what ship we're on and let Willhem know, so your luggage gets there before we do."

Anika's eyes grew very wide. "It's really happening," she whispered. "I mean, I knew it was going to, but... I never actually imagined I would leave Prisia."

He touched her face gently. "You don't have to come, you know." He looked at her, his dark eyes sympathetic. "I would understand..."

She shoved him, and he fell awkwardly off the bed. "There is no way I would let you leave me behind at this point. I'm coming with you, Eric. It scares the blazes out of me, but I'm coming."

He grinned up at her. "Yes, my lady."

Chapter 25

"The ship is called *Al'Kysid Prisi*," Lars told Eric when they arrived at his office the following morning. Anika had slipped into a back room to change into her dress, and Eric was getting the last of the details they needed before the voyage. "It's a newer style of ship, I suppose. I don't know much about ships, to be honest, but it looks impressive. The captain's name is Saladan. He's expecting your arrival after the cargo is loaded, which should be finished in a few hours."

Eric nodded. "He bought the story?"

Lars glanced at Anika as she swept from the back room, looking like the noble lady she was pretending to be. He smiled at the sight of her, and shook his head. "He accepted the story. Whether he buys it or not will really depend on you. I told him that there were parties in Prisia who wished to prevent Lady Anika from solidifying an alliance with the Almeri, which explains the need for haste."

"So I need to appear important," Anika mused. She glanced at Eric. "I guess the dresses were necessary after all."

"Don't pretend to be disappointed," Eric snorted. "I know better."

"Eric," Lars said cautiously. "There are soldiers in town, looking for you. They haven't spoken to me directly, yet, but I've heard from a few of the other ship brokers that they've been poking around the docks."

Frowning, Eric ran a hand over his head. "I know. I'm hoping we can manage to avoid them."

"Do they know who you are?" Lars asked in a hushed tone.

Eric shook his head. "No, but if they manage to catch us, it won't take long for that to come out."

"That would make things... complicated," Lars said softly. "I suggest you keep a low profile until you board the *Al'Kysid Prisi*."

Eric gave the balding man a flat look. "I'll do my best," he murmured wryly. "I think getting captured would ruin my day."

Lars chuckled. "I imagine it would."

Eric handed Lars the letter of introduction he'd crafted the day before. "Here. I thought you'd want this back."

Nodding, Lars took the sheet and lifted his quill, writing 'cancelled' across the page neatly. "I will admit that I'm relieved. How much did you draw on it?"

Eric shrugged. "Not much of it," he replied simply. "Some dresses and the inn, plus fifty for..." he glanced at Anika, an eyebrow raised in question.

"For incidentals," she told him, smiling.

Lars raised his eyebrows. "Good. Well... good luck, and have a safe voyage."

They left the office and walked down the narrow street to the wider main road. "So," Anika said softly, running her hands down the front of her elegant blue dress. "What do we do for a couple of hours?"

Eric smiled. "I was thinking the open air market would be a good place to disappear. There are always a number of ladies dressed like that in the markets. It's the best chance we've got of hiding."

"We could go back to Gunther's," Anika suggested.

Shaking his head, he said, "Not dressed like that.

You'd draw the eyes of everyone in the district. Word would get back to someone." He shifted the sword on his hip. He'd left the long bow and pack to be sent to the ship with Anika's luggage, and now wore his bastard sword on his back and the shorter long sword on his sword belt. He looked the part of a bodyguard. "We just go to the market and blend in. We'll hire a carriage to take us to the docks sometime after noon."

Anika smiled. "Alright," she murmured. "I've been aching to see something other than the two dress shops you've taken me to, anyway."

They moved with the steady stream of people through the streets until they saw the wagons and awnings of the open air market. The rich smell of roasting meat and spices filled the air, along with the earthier scents of animals. The volume increased as they approached, and soon they were moving through a sea of people between the market stalls, dodging laughing children who raced after one another, and peering at the various items the vendors clamoured at them to buy.

It was just after mid-day when Eric realized they were being watched. Two green-and-white clad soldiers, both of whom looked vaguely familiar, were moving along the aisle parallel to them. Eric kept his eyes forward, using his periphery vision to keep track of them. Whenever Anika paused at a stall, the two soldiers would busy themselves looking at whatever the closest vendor happened to be selling.

"We've been spotted," he whispered to Anika as she held up a silver necklace. He noticed motion at the end of the market, where several more green-and-white uniforms had begun to weave their way into the crowd. "I think it's time to go."

Anika nodded, her face growing pale. She handed the necklace back to the vendor, smiling shakily. "It's very pretty," she told the man, "but I think I'll have to pass."

"Ten silver," the man argued. "It's a great price..."

Eric glanced at the vendor, his eyes cold. "I'd recommend you box up your expensive items," he advised softly. "It looks like the soldiers are planning a raid."

The vendor's eyes snapped up and scanned the crowd. He immediately spotted the uniforms moving cautiously into the crowd. "Those bastards!" he muttered. "We've all paid our rent here! They can't treat us like this!" He nodded his thanks to Eric, and waved at a vendor across the aisle. The second vendor glanced up, and moved through the throng of people.

"What's wrong, Jacques?" the second vendor asked

as Eric guided Anika away from the stalls. As they began working their way back towards the edge of the market, Eric heard one of the vendors cry out indignantly as a soldier bumped into her.

"What was that about?" Anika demanded as they moved.

Suddenly a shout went up from behind them, and Eric snapped. "Now, move!"

Chaos erupted around them as the market vendors, seeing the soldiers among them, suddenly began yelling curses and clutching at their merchandise. At the same time, the soldiers noticed Eric and Anika starting to pick up speed, and they stopped trying to be subtle, elbowing and shoving their way through the mass of people.

It created a panic.

Eric and Anika broke away from the market just as the other shoppers, finally noticing the shoving soldiers and frightened vendors, began to react. Screams and shouts chased them down the street as the market erupted, terrified people shoving one another in their haste to get out of the way of the soldiers. Like a broken dam, a wave of people burst out of the market, spilling into the street.

"Run!" Eric commanded, falling back slightly to delay any pursuit. "Go straight down the street, towards the docks!"

Anika stumbled forward, tripping over her long dress with almost every step. She glanced back over her shoulder to see the first of the soldiers break away from the crowd, his eyes scanning the street for them. Frustrated, she kicked off her delicate shoes and tried to increase her pace, but the flowing fabric kept getting tangled in her legs.

Eric was facing away from her, staring at the approaching soldier, his bastard sword in his hands. She growled under her breath and stopped trying to run. Eric backed into her. "Run!" he repeated as the soldier caught sight of them and started in their direction.

She grabbed the hilt of the sword at his belt and pulled it loose. He glared at her. "We can't fight them all," he snapped. "Our only chance it to get to the ship!"

"I know that!" she snapped back. Then she slashed the sword down across the fabric of her dress, between her thighs. The fine fabric parted easily beneath the sharp blade, and she turned to repeat the process on the back of the dress. Then she stepped on the edge of the dress and cut the hem off at her knees on each side.

Freed from the prison of her clothing, she turned and sprinted down the street. Eric, grinning like a madman, chased after her.

It was a mad scramble through the streets. Word of something happening at the market had obviously changed to rumour of an attack on the city, as people were fleeing in every direction. The sight of Eric, his sword in his hand, was enough to cause the people running towards him turn and run in another direction. Behind them, Eric could hear the sounds of pursuit. He glanced back to see four soldiers racing after them, their green and white cloaks flapping behind them.

"Keep going!" Eric called to Anika, preparing to turn and fight. "Get to the ship! I'll..."

City guards, wearing the grey and white sigil of Heidal, suddenly charged onto the street, colliding with the kings soldiers. Eric stared back in disbelief, but seized the sudden intervention and kept sprinting.

Several more soldiers appeared behind the four that had been following him, and the two groups – the kings' soldiers and the city guards – clashed into one another. The soldiers were screaming in frustration, and the city guard were yelling in rage.

There was no mistaking the ship. An aggressive-looking vessel with three masts, it stood alone at the end of the Long Dock. Sailors were standing on the deck and hanging in the rigging, staring at the chaos that had suddenly erupted in the city. A single figure stood on the dock beside the gangplank. Dark-haired and swarthy, he was peering at Anika and Eric, frowning, as they raced towards the vessel.

Three soldiers had managed to break free from the fighting, and charged after Eric and Anika as they drew closer to the wooden dock.

"Run, my lady!" Eric called out, fighting back a smile at the melodrama of his words. "I will deal with these ruffians!"

He spun around just before the edge of the dock, dropping into a defensive stance, his sword held in both hands. The three soldiers, panting, slowed as they approached him, their swords drawn.

"You..." the one in front gasped. "You're going to pay for what you did in Anidaron..."

Eric's eyes narrowed. "You were there, were you?"

The soldier sneered at him. "I was. I saw you."

"Was that before or after you started killing innocent women and children?" Eric demanded quietly. Before the man could answer, Eric lashed out, his sword slamming down on the soldier's weapon. The blow knocked the soldier back, and Eric followed up with a swift spin, catching the soldier beside the first man under the ribs. His third strike took off the leg of the man on the left, leaving only the soldier who had spoken.

The soldier's eyes widened, and he stumbled back a step. Eric pursued him, his eyes cold with fury. "If you were there," Eric growled, "then you know which one of us deserves what's coming."

"I was following orders!" the man screamed, but Eric's blade silenced him.

Wiping his blade off on the dead soldier's cloak, Eric glanced back up the street, where soldiers and guards were immersed in a vicious battle. Shaking his head, he turned and hurried up the dock towards the ship. "Captain Saladan?" Eric murmured as he drew near the man by the gangplank.

The Almeri captain nodded, his eyes watching the chaos behind Eric.

"Has Lady Anika boarded?" Eric asked unnecessarily.

"Yes," Saladan replied. "And I suppose we ought to cast off, before that mess clears up and people start wondering who started it."

Eric smiled slightly. "It would likely be prudent, captain."

The Almeri sailor shook his head slowly. "She must be important, to cause all of this," he mused softly.

*** The Sword and Satchel ***

"Oh, she is, Captain," he assured the other man before walking across the gangplank in search of Anika.

He found her standing at the stern of the ship, staring back into Heidal, her dress in tatters and her fiery red hair blowing in the crisp breeze. He walked quietly over to stand with her, leaning on the railing.

"You know I was joking, right?" he said after a moment. "I'm sure I told you I wasn't serious."

She glanced at him, her expression confused.

He gestured to her shredded blue dress. "I mean, you're halfway to wearing a dancing girl outfit, and just a few steps away from wearing chains. You didn't have to take me so seriously."

Chapter 26

"There's no way I'm going to remember all of this!" Anika protested, rising from the chair she was sitting in and stalking back and forth across the tiny cabin like a trapped cat. "Etiquette, language, history... you've had your entire life to learn this stuff, and you're trying to cramp it into my head in ten days!"

Eric sighed and sat back. "Five," he said softly.

She stopped and stared at him, tears threatening to spill down her cheeks.

"Anika, you're doing great!" he said, honestly. "Already you've got the basics of the language down. The etiquette is much the same as it is in Prisia, and knowledge of Almeri history is secondary..."

"Who cares which fork you use when you eat shrimp?" she snarled, grabbing her flaming red hair in frustration. "Or that you pass food with your right hand..."

"The people you'll be eating with care," he said quietly. "They won't say anything if you do it wrong, but they'll feel that you didn't care enough about them or their culture to learn how they do things."

She half-screamed and threw herself onto the narrow bed that was bolted to the wall of the cabin, covering her face with her arm. "Get out, Eric. I need a break."

Eric nodded and got up from the folding chair he'd been using. "Come find me when you're feeling better," he said. "I'll be on deck."

He stowed the chair in a small box beside the door to the cabin and left, walking up the narrow passageway to the ladder at the end. He climbed up onto the quarter deck and stretched, relishing the cooler air and the rich colours that spread across the sky as the sun crept toward the horizon. One of the sailors nearby glanced at him and grinned toothlessly. "*Istan*," he mumbled.

Eric nodded. "*Istan*," he greeted. It was strange, hearing Almeri spoken everywhere again. For the first time, it made him feel like he was actually going home. He closed his eyes and breathed in deeply.

"*Tul misra es Prisiani?*" the sailor asked.

Eric nodded.

"Of course his mistress is Prisian, you idiot!" the bosun growled, moving up from the main deck. "And the captain has already had to warn you about speaking Almeri on this voyage. While Lady Anika is aboard, you are expected to speak Prisian."

"Your pardon, Jubai. I forget. My Prisian... it is not so good, yes? Almeri is easier."

"I don't care if it means you don't speak all the way home, Yusef. No Almeri." The bosun turned to study Eric. "You are which, her bodyguard or her teacher?"

"I have the honor to hold both roles for Lady Anika," Eric lied smoothly, bowing slightly. "She is unversed in Almeri customs, and I was chosen for both my skill with weapons and my knowledge of court etiquette."

The bosun grunted. "You certainly have some skill with a blade," he acknowledged grudgingly. "That could be handy before too long."

Eric cocked his head to the side, quizzically. The bosun jerked his head to the left and spat over the railing in that direction. "Lookout spotted a sail, twenty degrees off the port stern, about an hour ago. Could be nothing, could be pirates... could be someone chasing your lady."

Eric raised an eyebrow. While he knew that the soldiers that had followed them to Heidal were persistent, the idea that they would pursue them over the Almerinthine Sea was ludicrous. Frowning, he glanced up at where Saladan was standing beside the pilot, by the ship's wheel, staring determinedly forward. "Is it permitted to speak with the captain?" he asked.

The bosun spat again. "Aye," he growled. "But he won't tell you anything more than that. Not until whoever it is that's following us gets close enough to see more than just the colour of their sails."

Eric nodded. "Still, I came up to speak with him about this decision to refrain from speaking Almeri. It inhibits the development of Lady Anika's grasp on our language. I was hoping he would consider rescinding it."

The bosun nodded and walked to the foot of the poop deck. "Captain," he called up. "The guard would like a word, if you've a moment."

Saladan glanced down at Eric and nodded, gesturing for him to join him. Eric climbed the ladder to stand beside the swarthy man. "Captain," he greeted softly.

"What do you need?" Saladan demanded gruffly.

"First," Eric replied, "I would like to ease any concerns you may have that the ship behind us, which your bosun mentioned, is pursuing Lady Anika. While we left Heidal one step ahead of her enemies, they are not likely to risk open war with Almeri."

The captain considered this for a moment, and Eric saw some of the tension leave his shoulders and neck. "Right enough," he agreed. "Then it's either chance or pirates, either of which I can handle."

Eric smiled at the captain's confidence. "Also, I would like to ask for you to allow your men to speak Almeri. I am attempting to instruct Lady Anika in the language, so she isn't quite as lost when she reaches Kisham. Hearing it used over the next few days would prove invaluable for her."

The captain considered this for a moment. "She won't take offense?" he demanded.

Eric shook his head. "I will explain the reasons," he said. "Though I hope your men will use language which is appropriate, while around her."

The captain glanced at the pilot, who stood staring ahead, his hands clutching the wheel. "Elan, you are relieved. I will hold the course for now. I will send for you later."

The pilot bowed and stepped away from the wheel. Saladan grasped the heavy oak wheel and watched the pilot descend to the quarter deck. Once he was certain only Eric was within reach of his voice, Saladan growled, "What aren't you telling me? You've got the crew fooled, with the way you talk and the way you act around Lady Anika, but I've seen men like you before... and you're no bodyguard."

Eric grimaced and shook his head. He'd guessed that the captain would suspect something was amiss. The man had proven quite astute in the limited interactions he'd had with Eric and Anika over the past few days. "I am working for Sultan Kysid," Eric said quietly, keeping his lie as close to the truth as he could without revealing his identity. "Lady Anika, while an important connection to lord Kysid, is part of the cover I needed while I was in Prisia. Sadly, that is all I can reveal to you, Captain. I trust that I don't need to comment on the need for continued secrecy?"

Saladan grunted. "I know how this game works," he muttered. "I saw enough of it while I was in the navy. If you're working for Kysid, it's good enough for me. You're sure that ship isn't after you?"

"I'm as certain as I can be, Captain. We may have caused a bit of a stir in Heidal, but not enough of one to warrant that kind of pursuit. Whoever they are, they aren't chasing us."

"You're good with a blade," Saladan commented.

"We may need you, if it comes to fighting. Tell Lady Anika to stay in her cabin, if we're boarded. Pirates are bad enough at the best of times, but sight of a woman on board would drive them insane. If you hear the bell sound, we'll need you on deck."

"Are they gaining on us?" Eric asked.

The captain nodded. "Not quickly, but they're gaining. If it's pirates, we'll know in a few hours. I've got more sail we can raise, which will draw the chase out a while longer, but the best case is around dawn tomorrow. Best get some rest tonight. Chances are good we'll need that sword of yours in the morning."

Eric turned and climbed back down the ladder to the quarter deck, and then descended into the passageway leading to the tiny cabins. He tapped lightly on Anika's door. Anika opened the door and grimaced. "I was hoping for a longer break," she admitted. "But I suppose I was just aggravated..." She moved aside and waved him into the cabin.

"The captain tells me that we're being pursued," Eric told her, smiling wryly as he entered. "Not that we aren't used to that by now, but this time it looks like whoever is following us isn't actually looking for you and me."

Her eyes widened slightly. "Who...?"

"It could be pirates," Eric replied, unconcerned. "Saladan requests that you stay in your cabin if we're attacked."

She frowned. "I can fight..." she began, but Eric shook his head.

"There's no need," he told her, taking the folding chair out of its storage compartment. "And apparently the captain thinks your presence might just... add fuel to a fire. Now, where were we...?"

Sighing, Anika sat down at the table.

"We were going over the long, exalted history of the Almeri Empire," she muttered.

Eric grinned. "I'm sorry," he said, innocently. "I can't say that I'm familiar with that particular place. Could you tell me about it?"

Glaring at him, she leaned forward in her chair. "You can't be serious," she growled.

He opened his eyes very wide and rested his chin on his hand, blinking quickly. Unable to help herself, Anika laughed.

"Alright," she murmured. "The Almeri Empire is one of the oldest kingdoms in recorded history, dating back over four thousand years," she stated in a flat monotone, reciting it from memory. "The only empire known to have predated it, which is still in existence, is the Yu'han Dynasty in the Far East."

"You make this so interesting," Eric observed sweetly.

"Oh, shut up," she snapped. "The current Grand Sultan, Kysid ab Kyr'lasi," she continued, "inherited the Empire at the age of sixteen after his father died in battle during the Almeri-Tunic War. He has held power for the last fifty-one years. During that time, he has expanded the territory of Almeri significantly, through a series of carefully controlled conflicts with the Tuni to the south and the Ithanic Empire to the east. Almeri has maintained an uneasy alliance with Prisia ever since the end of the Almerinthine War, nearly a hundred years ago.

"A significant amount of the Almeri Empire spans the vast Almerantic Desert. While much of the desert is considered hostile and inhospitable, it is home to numerous nomadic groups. Many of these nomadic groups are of Tunic descent, which is the principle cause of the tension between the Tuni and the Almeri. Likewise, the eastern mountain range, the Hiyan Mountains, has been a disputed region since Sultan Kymis, Kysid's grandfather..."

"Great-grandfather," Eric corrected softly.

Anika growled in frustration. "Kysid's *great*-grandfather, seized the territory... gods, your ancestors were greedy bastards."

"If you think the Almeri side of my family are bad, you should learn the history of Prisia," Eric laughed. "Yoland's great-grandfather makes Kysid's great-grandfather look like a cuddly kitten. Did you know he had the leaders of the minor kingdoms he conquered, now the various duchies in Prisia, burned alive?"

Anika shuddered. "That's horrible."

Eric nodded. "He was completely insane. I'd tell you more, but it would give you nightmares. It gave *me* nightmares as a child."

"Why do rulers get away with this kind of stuff?"

"Not all rulers are like that," Eric told her softly. "My grandfather..."

"Fought incessantly against the Tuni and the Ithani!" she protested.

"Not Kysid," Eric shook his head. "Yoland. He maintained the peace within Prisia for almost fifty years, despite repeated attacks by the Lerchan. He could have sent troops into the Lerchan territories, a lot of his nobles argued in favor of it, but he chose instead to focus on improving the welfare of the people in Prisia. He established the first education system in the history of Prisia, codified the laws, ensuring that all people – even the king himself – were subject to the laws of the nation..."

"That worked out well," Anika muttered, her words dripping sarcasm.

"It would have," Eric countered, "if Ryas hadn't seized power. My grandfather had a vision of what a ruler ought to be, how he ought to treat his subjects. He wanted to make Prisia into a nation everyone was proud of, from the nobles down to the simplest farmer. My father grew up listening to his plans..."

"So did Ryas," Anika pointed out.

"From what little my father has ever said about his brother," Eric muttered darkly, "I'm not sure 'listening' actually exists in Ryas' vocabulary.

"Anyhow," he shook his head. "All of that is off topic. You were talking about Almeri history."

Anika sighed. "Ever since the treaty between Prisia and Almeri, trade between the nations has flourished. The principle exports of Almeri include textiles, spices, fruit, and lamp oil..." she frowned at him. "Why do I need to know what Almeri exports? I don't plan on becoming a merchant."

"Conversation," Eric explained. "People like to talk

about what they, or the people they know, do. Knowing a little about the economy helps you to know what kinds of questions to ask to get people talking." He smiled at her. "You remembered almost everything I've been talking about," he said.

"Remembering this stuff isn't hard," she sighed. "The difficult part is finding a reason to learn it in the first place. I know," she held a hand up to forestall him. "I know that it will help me when I have to deal with your grandfather's court, but I can't help but feel like it's pointless. No matter how much you manage to cram into my head between now and when we arrive, I'll never be one of those Almeri princesses."

Eric smiled at her. "You know enough right now to get by. If you don't want to learn any more, it's not going to be an issue..."

She shook her head in frustration. "It's not like there's much else to do," she grumbled. "I can sit in the cabin and learn this, or I can sit in here and stare at the wall. Either way, I'm still just sitting in here. I might was well learn something along the way."

"Would you prefer to learn more about Prisia?" Eric asked. "I don't imagine that you learned a lot about history in Anidaron."

Anika shrugged. "Papa never really considered it important. While Mama was alive, she taught me about herbs and remedies, and how to read and write. After she died... well, the boys were young, and I had to help with them. I spent most of my free time helping old Patty with the village animals... when I wasn't acting as the healer. History... never really factored into things."

"I guess that's one of the biggest differences between village life and city life," Eric mused. "Practical knowledge versus theoretical knowledge, I suppose. It's hard to see the importance of a man who has been dead for two hundred years when you've got sick children in need of medicine, chickens that need feeding, and a cow that is in breach. In the cities, the focus is more on finance, history, and other less practical matters."

Pleased that Eric actually seemed to understand, Anika brushed a stray hair behind her ear, smiling. "But I guess I'm not a village healer anymore, am I? So... I guess I need to start learning new things. And since we're heading to Almeri, I guess it's more important to learn about how you do things there than it is to learn about the history of Prisia."

"Potentially," Eric agreed.

"Well, then," she braced herself. "What should I

know about the role of women in Almeri?"

Eric raised an eyebrow. "You mean, other than the dancing girls?" he asked, grinning.

Chapter 27

The ringing of a bell woke him, and he bolted upright, banging his head on the bulkhead above the cot. Groaning, he rolled out of the cot. He was wearing his leather armour, but had decided that wearing his steel chain armour while sailing across the ocean was unwise. He grabbed both swords, strapping his bastard sword on his back and the shorter combat sword around his waist, and stepped into the narrow passageway. Anika peeked out her door, and he grinning maniacally at her. "Stay here," he said. "I'll be back in a bit."

Without waiting for a response, he sprinted to the ladder and climbed to the quarter deck to the sound of shouted orders. Sailors were scurrying along the decks of the ship, but none of them appeared especially concerned. Eric glanced over the rail of the ship to see another vessel a few hundred yards off the port stern.

The second vessel was flying the ensign of the Almeri navy.

"What's going on?" Eric demanded of the sailor nearest him, a lean fellow with a ragged scar down the side of his face.

"I don't know," the sailor answered in Almeri. "The captain rang for all hands... that's all I need to know."

Eric glanced to the poop deck, where Saladan was staring through a spyglass at the other ship. Like all of his crew, he was wearing a short-bladed sword, but his stance seemed relaxed.

"It's not pirates?" Eric murmured softly, but the sailor beside him obviously heard him.

"So it would seem," he growled. "Lucky for us, I guess. They probably took us for pirates, too."

Eric shook his head, his tense muscles relaxing. He watched as the captain lowered the spyglass and waved to the bosun. "Drop sails," he commanded. "Prepare to be boarded."

The bosun started bellowing commands, and the sailors on deck began hauling lines and lashing them to the belaying pins. The ship slowed noticeably, and Eric moved to stand below the captain. "Is this normal, Captain?" he demanded.

Saladan shrugged. "It happens," he replied. "They will send someone over, check our manifest and examine our cargo." He smiled broadly. "It's better than pirates, I suppose. Fortunately, I'm not smuggling anything on this voyage."

Rubbing the bruise on his head, Eric climbed back down the ladder and knocked on Anika's door.

"It's nothing to be concerned about," he told her as she peered into the passageway. "The captain says..."

He was interrupted by the sound of something slamming repeatedly into the deck above, followed by screams and sudden shouts of surprise. Then the ship lurched to the side, and he was thrown against the wall of the passageway. Anika shrieked as she was thrown back into the cabin, falling over the edge of the secured table. Above them, the yelling and screaming took on a more frantic tone. Stumbling to his feet, Eric glanced into the cabin to make sure Anika was alright. When he saw her staggering to her feet, he pulled the door shut and bolted for the ladder to the quarter deck.

He was a few feet from the ladder when an

The Sword and Satchel

unfamiliar figure leaped down into the narrow passage, a dagger in one hand. The man was bare-chested, and several scars criss-crossed his dark skin. He grinned at Eric as he steadied himself, and then lunged towards him.

Eric jumped back and slammed his hand down on the sailor's arm, just above the wrist. The sailor grunted, and the knife clattered to the wooden planks. Not hesitating, Eric lashed out with his right foot, catching the man's left leg on the kneecap. The sailor screamed as the knee buckled, and Eric stepped forward, grabbing the man's still-extended arm and spinning abruptly, throwing the sailor to the floor.

The sailor landed hard, gasping, and Eric wrenched the arm he still held firmly around, jerking the shoulder from its socket with a sickening pop. Then he brought his foot down hard on the elbow and yanked up, snapping the arm like a twig.

The man squealed, and Eric released the mangled arm. Dropping down, he put the momentum of the fall into a strike to the sailor's exposed throat, crushing his windpipe. The man thrashed around for a moment, clutching at his neck with his good arm while the other flopped around uselessly. Eric didn't bother to watch the dying man; rising, he picked up the dagger the man had been carrying and strode to the ladder. Placing the dagger in his teeth, he climbed to the quarter deck.

The deck was a scene from a nightmare. Bodies, some still moving, lay in pools of blood, and all around him men were engaged in vicious struggles. Eric removed the dagger from his teeth with his left hand, drawing the short sword he wore on his belt with his right. Glancing around to assess the situation, he saw the captain standing on the poop deck, facing two sailors. An arrow protruded from the captain's right shoulder, and he held his sword awkwardly with his left hand.

Flipping the dagger so he held the tip between his fingers, Eric tested the weight. It wasn't designed as a throwing dagger, but it would do. He snapped his arm forward, hurling the knife at one of the two men facing the captain.

It wasn't his best throw, but it did the job, catching the sailor on the captain's right in the middle of his lower back. The sailor staggered forward, grunting, and the captain slashed down, hitting the injured man in the throat.

Eric seized the moment to dash for the ladder to the poop deck. The second sailor turned to intercept him, but the captain swung awkwardly at the pirate, forcing the man to jerk back and block the blow. It was enough time for Eric to scramble most of the way up to the poop deck. Before the sailor could react, Eric slashed out with his sword, severing the tendon in the back of the man's ankle.

The sailor lurched to the side, narrowly ducking away from the captain's sword, as Eric pulled himself the rest of the way onto the upper deck. Snarling, the sailor turned to face Eric, but his leg wouldn't hold him, and he collapsed to his knees. He managed to block Eric's first slash, but the effort left the man wide open. Eric kicked him in the face, and then drove his sword into the man's chest.

"I take it they aren't who they appeared to be," Eric commented drily to the captain, who glared at him.

"Save your smart-ass comments for later," Saladan snarled. "They're trying to take my ship."

Eric glanced down at the main deck, where a large ramp with steel hooks had been dropped onto the ship's rail. Dozens of sailors from the other ship had already boarded, and the fighting on the lower decks was intense.

"Hard to tell who is who in all of that," Eric muttered. He glanced at the captain. "Are you okay here?"

Saladan nodded, and Eric sheathed the shorter sword in favor of his bastard sword. "I don't suppose you have some kind of order to get your men to disengage and withdraw to regroup?"

Saladan shook his head, and Eric sighed. "Right. Well, hopefully I don't accidently kill the wrong people." He jumped down from the poop deck, moving towards the first cluster of sailors. He recognized one of the men and immediately cut down the sailor fighting him, cleaving the pirate almost in half from behind. Saladan's sailor nodded his gratitude and immediately launched himself at another pirate. Eric followed after, working in tandem with the man he had saved.

It wasn't pretty. More like slaughter than combat, Eric found himself playing the role of executioner. The sailor he recognized would engage a pirate who was attacking one of the other hands, and Eric would step in from behind to finish the pirate. Within minutes, the tide of the battle had turned, and the pirates began pulling back towards the ramp, calling for assistance from the other ship.

Once most of the pirates had been backed up to the ramp, Eric forced his way forward, clutching his sword in a two-handed grip. While many of the pirates obviously had some experience, none of them were ready to face a trained warrior. They fell away from him when he stepped into the front of the group of sailors, his blade moving like lightning. He scored hit after hit, though only a few managed to cut the pirates he faced deeply.

There was a cry from the other ship, and suddenly the pirates still on the deck of the *Al'Kysid Prisi* tried to scramble back to their own ship. Before more than four or five of the pirates had managed to clear the wooden ramp, however, the steel hooks slid free, and the ramp fell off the railing of the *Al'Kysid Prisi,* spilling nearly a dozen pirates into the water between the ships. There were a few screams, but they ended abruptly as the two ships ground against one another. Then the pirate ship raised one of its foresails and pulled away, leaving the crew of the *Al'Kysid Prisi* staring after the retreating pirates.

"Watch for archers!" Eric yelled as he saw some of the pirates moving into the rigging of the departing vessel, but the pirates seemed more interested in getting away than they were in retaliation for their lost crew. As the other ship added more sail, it picked up speed, rapidly widening the distance between them and their former prey.

"Jubai!" Saladan called down to the bosun in Almeri. "See to the wounded, and heave the bodies over the side." He leaned against the ship's wheel, his dark face tense. "I want every able-bodied sailor on deck in ten minutes," he added. "We may not be finished with them yet."

The crew immediately got to work, checking the

bodies. Most of the figures lying on the deck were unceremoniously thrown over the side of the ship. Only one or two were carried below, to be cared for by the ship's surgeon.

As Eric moved towards the ladder to the cabins, Saladan gestured to him to join him on the poop deck. Despite his concern for Anika, he climbed up, glancing at the captain's injured shoulder. "Are you alright, Captain?"

Saladan shrugged, and then winced at the motion. "I will live," he replied. "And I have you to thank for it." He paused for a moment before adding, "I dislike being indebted to anyone, but it would appear I am now in your debt."

Eric nodded very slightly. "You should have that arrow dealt with," he said, choosing not to acknowledge the debt openly. Some men, he knew, like the captain, would only be offended if he tried to diminish the importance of his actions. "If your surgeon is too busy, I'm certain Lady Anika would be willing to see to your injury. She is a talented healer."

Saladan smiled tightly. "Indeed? Perhaps she could join us here? My pilot... was among the first of our casualties. Sadly, that means I am... constrained to the helm."

"Don't you have a first mate?" Eric inquired, surprised.

The captain shook his head. "He got himself arrested in Heidal, before we left. If I'd had another few days, I could have bribed the guards to release him, but as it was..."

Eric frowned. "I'll go get Lady Anika," he said.

Anika was sitting in her cot when he opened the door. Her face was pale, and she threw herself at him as soon as he closed the door. "I was afraid... I heard the others being brought down to the surgeon, and when you didn't come..."

"I'm alright," he assured her. "But the captain took an arrow in the shoulder during the fighting. He can't leave the helm..."

Anika grabbed her satchel and nodded. "Let's go. It will be nice to be doing something useful."

He led her back to the captain, who was leaning against the ship's wheel, his swarthy skin looking pale. "The arrow may have struck the shoulder bone," she told him as she studied the wound.

He nodded and appeared to brace himself, but she shook her head. "As tough as you imagine yourself to be, Captain, expecting me to do this while you are standing, steering a ship is unrealistic. There's a good chance you will faint, either from pain or blood-loss."

Saladan frowned at her, but she glared at him, unwavering. Finally he sighed in frustration. Glancing at Eric, he growled, "Can you take the helm..." he paused. "You know, I don't even know your name."

"Eric," he murmured, cursing himself silently as soon as he said it.

Saladan's eyes narrowed for a moment, and then he blinked in surprise. "Eric..." he repeated softly. "I have heard that name in connection with Lord Kysid's house before..."

"Have you?" Eric asked. "Well, perhaps it was someone else."

Saladan smiled. "I presume there is a reason you wish to remain merely a bodyguard. Have you ever served on a ship before, Eric?"

Eric shrugged. "Once or twice," he admitted.

"And I think it was not as a common deck hand, was it? I presume you have some awareness of navigation?" At Eric's cautious nod, he continued. "If you do not mind, I would like to tell the crew that you are acting as my first mate for the duration of the voyage. After how you handled yourself with the pirates, I don't foresee any objections. But

I think, if you wish to remain... anonymous... I will introduce you as Sahri. It's a common name, and will not draw unwanted attention. Eric is much too Prisian, and while my crew are not educated, they are not stupid."

Eric nodded slowly. "That might be wise," he agreed.

The crew had begun to return to the quarter deck, and Saladan blinked at Anika. "If my injury can wait a moment or two more?"

She rolled her eyes and gestured for him to continue.

Saladan glanced at Eric and nodded towards the ship's wheel. Eric took it from him, and Saladan stepped to the railing of the poop deck to address the crew. He smiled when he saw how many of his crew were still able to perform their duties. "You fought well," he began in rapid Almeri. "But we have suffered a serious loss. Along with too many others, Elan, our pilot, was slain. Fortunately, Lady Anika's bodyguard, Sahri, has served as a navigator with Sultan Kysid's navy. I am naming him first mate until we arrive in Kisham. You will obey his orders as if they were my own."

The crew saluted with a chorus of "*A'sal, kalim,*" and Saladan nodded curtly. He turned to Eric. "You have the helm, first mate."

"*A'sal, kalim,*" he replied. Immediately he turned to Jubai. "Bosun," he called in Almeri. "Let's get this ship underway. Shake out the foresails and topsails, and ready the mainsails... and get someone to swab the deck."

"*A'sal, salasi!*" Jubai saluted, then turned and started barking orders at the other sailors.

Saladan turned to smile slightly at Anika. His knees buckled, then, and he almost fell, grabbing the railing with his good hand. "After you, Lady Anika," he murmured, gesturing to the ladder.

Chapter 28

The remainder of the voyage, while exhausting for Eric, went remarkably smoothly. The crew accepted him as one of their own almost immediately; initially, he knew, it was because of his role in staving off the pirate attack. The longer the captain remained incapacitated, however, the greater the sailor's respect for him grew.

He hadn't been lying when he'd admitted to having served on ships. His father hadn't seen the point, but his uncle Kyvin had insisted than any officer in the Almeri military needed to have a grasp on the roles of all branches of their forces, particularly if that officer was descended from Kysid. He'd been so adamant that Tindal had consented when Kyvin had arranged for Eric to serve for six months with one of the naval vessels. Eric, only seventeen at the time, had spent a month as a common deck-hand, two months as bosun on a different ship, and three months learning the officer's duties, including navigation, with one of Kyvin's most trusted captains. Eric had never thought he would actually need the skills he'd learned during those gruelling six months, but as it became apparent to the crew that he knew what he was doing, he was suddenly grateful that he'd been given the opportunity.

The captain's injury was more severe than it had initially appeared. Anika's guess that it had struck bone was correct, and the wound became infected. Anika spent the majority of her time in the captain's cabin, fighting to keep him alive. It took four days before she came on deck looking both exhausted and relieved.

"He's going to be fine," she told Eric.

He stared at her, blearily. "That's good," he muttered. "I'm guessing he won't be back up here before we reach Kisham, though."

She shook her head. "He needs to rest. From the look of it, so do you."

"I get a couple of hours here and there, when the winds are good and I can leave Jubai at the helm," he told her. "It's enough." He paused, suddenly, realizing that they were speaking in Almeri. "You seem to have picked up the language," he observed, smiling. "I take it the captain felt a need to do more than just lie in bed?"

She groaned. "I tried to say something in Almeri, when I first examined his wound, and he started ranting about how horrible my accent was. He decided to take it upon himself to 'continue my lessons'."

"He's done a remarkable job," he admitted.

She glared at him.

"I mean you've done a remarkable job," he corrected quickly, and she rolled her eyes at him. "You sound almost as though you've been studying Almeri for years."

"Yes, well, it hasn't been the most enjoyable four days I've ever spent," she grumbled. "At least you have a little patience for mistakes."

"Enjoyable or not, he's done you a great service. I don't think that I could have managed to get you this fluent in that amount of time." He smiled at her. "You speak the language better than ninety-five percent of all Prisians, you know."

"Only five percent of Prisians speak any Almeri," she countered.

"True, but of that five percent, I've never met a Prisian who could carry on a conversation this easily who hadn't lived in Almeri for at least a few years. You should be proud of yourself," he added. "That's quite an accomplishment."

She frowned at the last word and repeated it to herself.

Eric glanced down at the main deck and waved for Jubai to approach. The bosun walked swiftly to stand right below him. "*Istan, Lisini Anika*," he greeted Anika, bowing slightly.

"*Istan, Jubai*," she replied.

"Advise the crew that captain Saladan is going to recover," Eric told the blocky bosun.

Grinning, Jubai saluted. "Yes, *salasi*! The crew will be pleased." He turned and hurried down the deck. Once he was right beside the main mast, he bellowed out the news. There was a ragged cheer from the crew at the news, and Eric smiled.

"Did Saladan talk about what happened? I thought it was a navy ship."

Anika pursed her lips. "He said they sailed up as though to board, then dropped the ensign as they drew alongside. Archers in the rigging fired onto the ship as they pulled up some kind of ramp and fastened it to the side rail. He said it looked like they had done it fairly often."

Eric nodded. "I'll have to let my uncle know. A pirate ship pretending to be a naval vessel... he'll have them hunted down and hanged."

"How is it worse that they pretended to be a naval vessel? Shouldn't he hunt down pirates, anyway?" she asked.

He shook his head. "He tries, but piracy is hard to get rid of at the best of times. Mostly pirates know that unless they attack a naval vessel, there won't be much in the way of repercussions. The cost of tracking down ships that don't want to be found isn't worth the effort. But to pose as ships of the fleet... that's a new trick. When an Almeri captain sees a ship flying the ensign, he's obliged to heave-to. It's Almeri naval law. I'd never heard of the navy stopping merchant ships before, but from what Saladan said, it's not uncommon. Usually pirates don't fly a flag, which gives merchant vessels a bit of a fighting chance. If they see a ship without a flag, they have a good idea that it's potentially hostile. The ensign is supposed to be a symbol of safety. If pirates start using it to ambush merchants, well, it undermines confidence in the navy itself."

She nodded slowly, obviously struggling with some of the language. "That makes sense," she murmured.

He was about to add something, when the lookout

called, "Land!"

Eric glanced up, a small smile playing across his lips. He glanced at Anika. "It appears we made good time. I thought we might. We had the wind with us."

Anika peered ahead, straining to see, and Eric shook his head. "You won't be able to see it, yet. Not for a while. He's elevated and he's got a spyglass. Still, it means we're almost there."

"Kisham?"

He shrugged. "We'll see how close I was able to get us. I had to guess at where we were, and navigation isn't always as exact as sailors would like, but I'm hoping I got us to within a few leagues of Kisham. We'll know in a few hours."

The sun was well on its descent to the horizon by the time the land became visible to the rest of the crew. Eric used his spyglass to study the landmarks and smiled to himself. "Better than I'd hoped," he said softly, and Anika raised an eyebrow at him. "We should make Kisham before sunset," he told her, adjusting the rudder slightly. He handed her the spyglass and gestured for her to look.

The shoreline, barely visible to the naked eye, was much clearer through the glass. The coastline appeared to be pristine white sand, sloping gently up to dense, dark green trees, though she couldn't identify the type of tree. In the distant background, she thought she could see hints of jagged red stones, but it was hazy and hard to determine. To the east, barely visible, she saw what appeared to be a huge stone wall looming above the vibrant blue waters. "Is that Kisham?" she asked, pointing at the wall.

Eric nodded. "It's one of the oldest cities in the world," he whispered. "The wall you can see dates back almost two thousand years, to when the Ne'thuk, the tribes that once inhabited the eastern-most reaches of the Almerinthine Sea, used to raid the Almeri coast, in search of slaves to sell to the Far East."

She drew in a deep breath, her eyes wide. "How far away are we?"

"Still a long way, but we're closer than I could have hoped. Sometimes a plotted course will take you several hundred leagues east or west of your actual destination, depending on the winds."

Jubai hurried up to the foot of the poop deck. "What orders, *Salasi*?"

While Eric relayed a few quick instructions, Anika headed back below, to let the captain know their destination was only a few hours away.

"He brought us in close, did he?" Saladan asked

quietly, struggling to push himself up on his pillows.

"Kisham is within sight, with a spyglass," she replied, and the captain smiled slightly.

"He is a better pilot than I could have hoped, though we were fortunate not to have run into foul weather. Come, you must help me up. I cannot enter Kisham in bed."

"Saladan," Anika began, but the captain waved her objections away.

"I am the captain of the *Al'Kysid Prisi*," he said firmly. "And I will allow no other to stand at her helm when we enter the port." He grinned sheepishly. "I would never live it down," he admitted.

Shaking her head at the man's stubbornness, she moved to the side of his bed and helped him to his feet. "I think you're being an idiot," she told him bluntly. "But when it comes to men, I suppose that's a common trait."

Saladan laughed. "Perhaps," he agreed. "But our pride is what makes us who we are. It is what gives us strength when we have nothing left to give. I think your man, Eric, knows something of this."

Anika grimaced, but refrained from commenting.

"Now, Lady Anika," he glanced down at his bandaged chest and shoulder, blood staining the white cloth. "I need to make myself presentable." A smile flickered across his lips. "I suggest you do the same. That dress has more blood on it than my own clothing, and you will hardly make a good impression in Kisham dressed in yesterday's rags."

Anika flushed and glanced down at the outfit she was wearing. She had discarded the shredded blue dress as soon as they had boarded the ship, and had opted to leave her other fine dresses in her trunks, wearing instead the green dress she had purchased from Hilde. She hadn't changed out of it for the duration of the voyage, and her days of tending Saladan had made it impossible to take the time to even bathe properly. The dress, as Saladan had observed, was covered in dried blood, sweat, and salt.

"I... think perhaps that is a good idea," she agreed.

Saladan reached out with his good hand and took her hands in it. "You have my thanks, Lady Anika. I fear that the ship surgeon would not have shown the same degree of care. I would be short an arm going into Kisham, had I relied on his tender mercy."

Anika smiled broadly. "You are welcome, captain."

He frowned. "You still sound like a yipping puppy when you speak, however."

She glared at him for a moment, and then she laughed. "I have you to thank for being able to speak your language, captain. Perhaps if you didn't growl and bark so often, I would sound less like a yipping puppy."

Saladan stared at her for a moment, stunned, and then he laughed heartily. "Go!" he chuckled. "Let them see you for the lady you are."

Smiling, Anika left his cabin and hurried to her own to prepare.

Chapter 29

If Heidal had been eye-opening in its magnitude, Kisham was staggering. Not only was it a sprawling mass of buildings that seemed to stretch as far as the eye could see, the styles of the buildings and the vibrant colours the people wore were completely foreign to Anika's eyes.

Men in flowing saffron robes mingled with women wearing colours ranging from deep violet to crimsons as striking as Anika's own hair. They stood in stark contrast to the almost exclusively white buildings with blue tiled roofs.

Anika clutched Eric's arm as they stood on the edge of the gangplank, staring at the sheer number of people bustling about the busy harbour. Hundreds of ships were moored in the vast harbour, and dozens were lashed to the various docks. Saladan stood beside them, observing the organized chaos of the docks, his face impassive.

"Your assistance," the captain finally said, his voice subdued, "has been invaluable. I will not soon forget, *Sahri*. If you ever have need of me, I am at your service."

Eric dipped his head slightly. "I value the trust you placed in me," he replied quietly.

"Must you both be such stubborn, arrogant... men?" Anika demanded. "Thank you, you're welcome, nice to meet you, hope to see you again. There. Was that so terribly hard?"

The two men chuckled softly. "You have a way of circumventing the niceties of our culture, Lady Anika," Saladan commented wryly.

Anika sniffed and glanced away. "I'm sorry if I offended you..." she began after a moment.

"No offense," Saladan told her. "And I beg your pardon for implying such. I am simply not accustomed to Prisian ladies and their forthright nature. You have been most refreshing. Sahri, I do not know why you chose to travel unannounced, but I suspect there are reasons I do not need to know. If you need to leave in a similar way, I can use a man of your talents on my ship. And Lady Anika, if your visit to Almeri is not to your liking, I will gladly take

The Sword and Satchel

you anywhere you wish to go. Now, I must see to the unloading of my cargo. Jubai has seen your luggage down to a carriage."

Nodding one final time, Saladan turned and strode back onto the quarter deck, barking commands to the crew.

"Well," Eric murmured. "Are you ready to meet my family?"

Anika shuddered slightly. "Not really, but I suppose they deserve to know you aren't dead as soon as possible."

Eric grinned at her. "Let's go, then."

Together they walked down the dock to where Jubai stood beside a carriage. Anika's trunks were lashed to the back of the sleek, covered vehicle. He bowed to Eric, smiling. "It was good sailing with you, *Salasi*. I hope to see you again."

Eric nodded to the bosun. "You're a good man and a good sailor, Jubai. It was my pleasure."

Jubai grinned and bowed deeply to Anika. "*Lisini*," he said softly. "I wish you well in Almeri."

"Thank you, Jubai," she smiled.

Eric helped her into the carriage, checked that all of their luggage was accounted for, and moved to speak to the driver. "To Sultan Kysid's palace," he instructed.

The driver frowned. "They have closed the palace in

~ 364 ~

mourning," he advised. "They will turn you away."

"Perhaps," Eric said. "But go there anyhow. My orders are to deliver the lady to the palace, and I intend to obey."

"As you wish, *tali*," the driver assented, and Eric climbed into the carriage beside Anika.

"If they've closed the palace to visitors, how are we going to get in?" Anika asked softly as Eric sat down beside her.

"Passwords," Eric replied simply. "While interrupting my own mourning period is... unprecedented, I suppose, there are contingencies for almost any emergency."

The carriage lurched into motion, and Anika turned to stare out the window at the buildings as they passed. The light was fading, and torches and lamps were being lit along the streets, casting strange shadows along the walls. It was dizzying, and she finally sat back, resigned to miss seeing the sights of Kisham until later.

"Is it a long trip to the palace?" she asked after a moment.

"Fifteen minutes or so," Eric replied. He appeared nervous.

"What's wrong?" Anika asked softly, leaning in to him.

"It's just, in my haste to get here, I still haven't really had time to try and put all of the pieces together," he told her, his brow creased. "I know that someone tried to have me killed, and that it's likely someone in my grandfather's court, but I'm no closer to knowing who it is than when I couldn't even remember my own name."

"Does it matter? You're still alive, you're home..."

Eric sighed. "It matters," he whispered finally. "Someone I know wants me dead... or at least tried to have me killed to start a war. That kind of thing leaves a person... suspicious."

Anika smiled. "You'd be an idiot if you weren't. Still, you're not in Prisia anymore. Killing you here wouldn't accomplish the Jirad's goal."

Eric nodded, but his posture was still uneasy. "I know... it's just the idea that someone I know..." he shook he head angrily. "It's got me on edge, that's all."

Anika laughed softly. "Then we're both on edge. It's not every day a girl from Anidaron gets to meet the Grand Sultan of the Almeri... and the rightful king of Prisia..." she clutched her dress tightly in her hands, the smooth copper-coloured fabric gleaming slightly in the torchlight from outside the carriage. "And the mother of the man she loves, all in one night."

Eric wrapped his arm around her shoulders. "It's not that big a deal," he tried to reassure her. "They're just... family."

She shook her head. "To you. To me, they're all larger than life. I've heard stories about your grandfather since childhood. And from the stories I've heard about Tindal and Kyliandra... Eric, they're *legends* in Prisia."

Eric sighed. "You'll be fine," he promised her. "Honestly, I'm expecting that they'll be so surprised to see me that they won't even notice there's someone with me... for a while."

"That's not helping," she muttered, archly. "No one likes not being noticed."

"You'd rather be noticed by the Grand Sultan, the rightful king of Prisia, and the mother of the man you love?" he asked, feigning innocence.

"Oh, shut up," she grumbled. "It doesn't have to make sense, but I'd rather... be noticed, I suppose, even if it makes me uncomfortable."

Eric studied her for a moment, nodding slightly. "I think I understand."

The carriage slowed, and Eric glanced out the window. "We're here," he murmured as the carriage drew to a stop before a delicate-looking white wall. Two massive wrought-iron gates stood closed, and two guards in black robes stood on either side of the entrance.

"The palace is shut to visitors," one of the guards announced, stepping forward to stand at the window of the carriage. "If you wish, I will relay a message to the vizier."

"Stones fall silently," Eric murmured from the shadows of the carriage.

There was a moment of hesitation, and then the guard spun around. "Open the gate," he commanded to his partner.

The other guard paused. "But..."

"Now!" the first guard snapped. He looked up at the driver. "You will have to remain here. I will drive the carriage."

"Now look here..." the driver protested, but the guard reached for the heavy-looking sword at his waist.

"You will be reimbursed for your trouble," the guard said softly, death in his voice. "But if you do not get down immediately, I will be forced to kill you."

The driver stared down for a second, his face draining of blood. Then, muttering imprecations, he climbed down and the guard leapt nimbly to the seat.

The huge gates swung open silently, and the guard lashed the horses hard. The carriage lurched forward and careened up a tree-lined pathway so swiftly, Anika felt queasy.

Less than five minutes later, the carriage clattered to a halt, slamming Eric and Anika hard into the back of the seats. The guard leapt to the ground and raced to shout something unintelligible to the guards at the doors, who had begun moving towards them, their swords drawn. The two black-robed figures spun around immediately and sprinted into the palace.

"Get out of the carriage," the guard who had driven them up said coldly, drawing his sword. "And pray that your news is important enough to warrant this."

Eric climbed down and turned to assist Anika from the carriage. The two horses, lathered from the sudden run, stood in their traces, sides heaving.

As Anika stepped to the ground, a dozen armed men swarmed into the courtyard, their weapons drawn. In the midst of the group was a tall man with much paler skin than the others; his long dark hair, sprinkled with silver, was tousled as though he had been roused from bed. He strode forward, his sword drawn and his expression menacing. "What is the meaning of..."

Eric turned around, his dark eyes meeting the gaze of the older man. "Hello, Father," he said, very quietly.

There was a moment of stunned silence, and then Tindal Yolandson wailed, a broken cry of unimaginable joy and relief, and hurled himself at Eric, his sword falling forgotten to the stones of the courtyard.

Eric caught his father in a fierce embrace, as Anika stood uncomfortably to the side.

"They told us you were dead," Tindal whispered, pushing back to stare at his son, tears in his eyes. "Gods... I..."

"I almost was," Eric said softly, pulling away. "I would have been, if it hadn't been for Anika." He gestured for Anika to come forward, and then clutched her hand tightly. "She saved my life."

Tindal turned to face Anika, his face breaking into a broad smile. "Then you are more than welcome here." He glanced at the way Anika clutched Eric's hand, and his smile grew wider. "I look forward to introducing you to my wife."

"Father," Eric murmured. "The news of my death... is Mother alright? Grandfather?"

Tindal nodded. "Your mother is distraught, of course. She blamed herself almost as much as she blamed me. Your grandfather, well, he'll be pleased to see you... for several reasons."

Eric nodded, then moved close and draped his arm

over his father's shoulder. "It was a set up, Father," he whispered, leaning in. "It was intended to start a war. We need to talk, privately, after we see Mother."

Tindal's face grew stiff, and he nodded curtly. Then he forced himself to smile again. "Come! Your mother will be... beside herself."

Eric smiled at Anika, who continued to clutch his hand tightly, staring wide-eyed at his father. "The guards?" she inquired, her voice quavering.

"No one should know of my return, yet," Eric added in a whisper. "There has been more than one attempt on my life so far."

Tindal blinked, frowning. Then he nodded

"Return to your posts, and remain silent about this," Tindal called out to the guards in Almeri. "And send someone to Lord Kysid. Ask him to come see me in my suites."

One of the guards saluted crisply and barked an order to the others. In seconds, the courtyard was empty, except for the guard who had driven them in. He was climbing back onto the carriage.

"Ishtar," Tindal called. "You did well in bringing them in."

The guard smiled. "If I had known who it was..."

The Sword and Satchel

"Say nothing to anyone," Tindal reiterated. "Not until Lord Kysid announces my son's return. And bring their things inside," he added, gesturing at the trunks lashed to the back of the carriage.

Ishtar saluted and climbed back down from the seat. "As you command, my lord."

Turning, Tindal grasped Eric's arm tightly, as though to reassure himself that his son was actually there. "Welcome home," he whispered, switching back to Prisian.

They walked through the wide and airy corridors of the palace. Anika was in too much of a daze to really take in the beauty of the structure, but she couldn't help but feel the sheer enormity of the palace. While the ducal palace in Heidal had been lavish, this place was beyond her wildest dreams. She tried her best not to glance around too much, keeping her attention focused forward.

Noticing her distressed expression, Tindal smiled gently at her. "You are truly welcome here, Anika," he said softly in Prisian. "You would be, even if you hadn't saved Eric's life. It has been a long time since such a lovely visitor graced our hallways."

"It is gracious of you to say so, Lord Tindal," Anika murmured. "Forgive my distraction, but I've never dreamed of such a place. It is... beyond description."

Tindal nodded. "I understand what you mean. It struck me speechless the first time I came here, also. I would tell you about the history of the palace, but I'm afraid Almeri history is not my strong suit."

"Nor mine," she admitted. "Eric instructed me on some of the basics, before we arrived, but... it's all very new."

Tindal glanced at Eric. "I expect you have some additional news to share?"

Eric smiled slightly. "Perhaps. I thought my presence would be enough of a shock for one night, however."

"Where are you from, Anika?" Tindal inquired, changing the subject.

"A small village in the south of Prisia," she replied, glancing at her feet. "I... I was the village healer."

A hint of a smile danced across Tindal's lips, almost the exact expression she had seen so often on Eric's face. Before he could say anything, however, Eric cleared his throat. "Don't badger her, Father. She's had a lot to get accustomed to in the last month or so," he paused for a moment. "You knew her father," he added softly.

Tindal arched an eyebrow, glancing at Anika. "I did?"

Anika blushed slightly. "My father is... was Leif Svenson."

Eric's father tripped over his own feet, stumbling forward a pace before stopping and staring at Anika, his eyes wide with surprise. "You're Leif's daughter?" He threw his head back and laughed. "Gods! Let me look at you, child!" He peered at her, his face glowing with wonder. "I can see hints of him in you, sure enough. The hair, of course, but also in the eyes..." He shook his head, bemused. "I never expected to hear that name again, let alone meet his daughter..."

"We have a lot to talk about, Father," Eric murmured. "But it has to wait..."

"Of course," Tindal agreed, shaking his head again. "It's just... your father was a very dear friend of mine, Anika, a long time ago. It is an honor to meet his daughter." He glanced at Eric. "You have the gods' own luck to run into the daughter of Leif Svenson, son."

Eric chuckled softly. "Oh, believe me, Father... I don't know what I did to deserve their attention, but the gods have been watching over me more closely that I'm entirely comfortable with."

His father glanced at him quizzically, and then shook his head. "You'll tell me all about it... after you see your mother, of course."

Turning, he continued to guide them through the halls of the palace. Eric obviously knew where he was going, as his footsteps were sure and steady. Before long, however, he began to speed up slightly, and Anika realized they must be close.

An ornate door, carved from some rich dark wood Anika wasn't familiar with, came into view at the end of the hallway. A pair of guards, dressed in heavy black robes, stood to either side of the door. They bowed at the sight of Tindal, then glanced past him at Eric and Anika. At first, the sight of Eric didn't appear to register, and then their dark eyes grew wide. One of the guards hurriedly opened the door and stepped back, bowing low.

"Kyliandra!" Tindal called as he strode into the vast antechamber, his voice excited. "Kyliandra! Come quickly!"

There was silence for a heartbeat, and then a slender, stunningly beautiful woman stepped gracefully from a side entrance. Her skin was the colour of caramel, smooth despite the traces of silver in her lush black hair. She moved with the lithe grace of a hunting cat, exactly like Eric moved, Anika noted. Her luminous eyes were wide, and she stared at Tindal with concern, not even glancing at the two people who entered with him. "What? What's wrong?" she demanded, her voice strained.

Eric glided forward, his lopsided smile sheepish and meek. "Forgive me, Mother..." he began, his voice breaking.

Kyliandra staggered back a step, her hand flying to her mouth to stifle a stunned shriek. Then her knees failed her, and she fell to the ground, one hand outstretched towards her son. "Eric..." she whispered, tears brimming in her dark eyes.

Eric was beside her in an instant, kneeling to wrap her in his arms. "I'm sorry, Mother. I came as quickly as I could," he murmured into her hair.

"Eric," Kyliandra wept, her voice like broken crystal. "My son..." The dark princess turned her face to the ceiling, tears streaking her cheeks. "Thank you, gods!"

Gently, Eric rose to his feet, helping his mother up. She touched his face, her eyes fixed on his. "How?" she whispered.

Eric turned to look at Anika. "Mother," he said softly. "This is Anika. She found me, dying, and tended to my injuries. I wouldn't be here if it weren't for her."

Anika stared at the floor, feeling like an intruder on a solemn celebration. Kyliandra turned to look at her, and then moved gracefully over to stand in front of her. She reached out and placed both hands on Anika's cheeks, turning Anika's face to hers. A smile of genuine warmth, of heartfelt gratitude, lit the older woman's face. "Thank you," she whispered. "You are an angel. Thank you for giving me back my son."

"I... you are welcome," Anika murmured simply, glancing from her to Eric.

Kyliandra studied Anika for a moment, her face damp, and then she wrapped her arms around her and held her tightly. Then she released her and returned to Eric, pressing her face into her son's chest and weeping softly. "I thought we had lost you..." she whimpered.

Eric held his mother tightly, tears on his cheeks. "I'm sorry you had to go through that," he said quietly.

Kyliandra leaned back and wiped the tears away from her cheeks. She touched Eric's cheek with infinite tenderness, and then, quite deliberately, she pounded her fists on her son's chest. "How could you leave me to think you were dead?"

Eric danced back, laughing and rubbing his chest, though he was still wearing his leather armour. "It wasn't really my fault," he protested. "It's not like I sent the news."

Kyliandra glared at him, her eyes burning, and then she laughed. For the first time, Anika truly understood why

Lodi had said Kyliandra was 'fire and steel'.

"Lady Kyliandra," Anika said softly, "Eric was unconscious for several days, and unable to move for several more. Additionally, he received a significant blow to the head, which temporarily interrupted his capacity to recall memories. Had he been able to remember his own name, let alone yours, I'm certain he would have sent word to you as soon as possible."

Kyliandra turned to face Anika, one eyebrow raised. "Indeed," she breathed, her voice deceptively neutral. "Then I suppose I shouldn't be angry?"

"Not at him," Anika replied calmly, meeting Kyliandra's glare. "I thought, perhaps, you might reserve your anger for whoever plotted to have him killed... for whoever conspired to lure him into the mountains of Prisia and ambush him, leaving him to die."

Kyliandra hesitated, and then a small smile danced across her lips. She inclined her head marginally toward Anika. "Again, I thank you for saving my son's life. Now, perhaps we should see to finding you proper accommodations..."

Eric cleared his throat. "A moment, Mother, but there is something I promised I would do as soon as soldiers and assassins weren't following us." He grinned at Anika, and her eyes widened. Moving in front of her, he dropped to one knee. "Anika," he began.

"Eric!" Kyliandra hissed. "What are you doing?"

"Anika," Eric continued, ignoring his mother completely. "I've let too many things interfere with this already. Will you consent to marry me?"

Anika stared at him, a frantic giggle struggling to escape her lips. She swallowed hard, trying to ignore the venomous look Kyliandra was giving her. "Of course I will," she said softly. Then her gentle smile turned hard as granite. "But we need to discuss your sense of timing and choices of venue."

There was a suppressed laugh from Tindal, who covered his mouth and purposely turned away, his shoulders shaking. Kyliandra frowned at Eric, and then glanced at Anika. Her expression smoothened, and she smiled gently. "You must be exhausted after your voyage," she said. "And I would like a few moments alone with my son. Why don't I escort you to the courtyard, while I instruct a servant to prepare you a room." When Eric moved to object, glancing up from where he still knelt, Kyliandra stared coolly at him. "I will brook no argument, Eric. She is a guest in my father's home, and I will see her properly attended to."

Anika moved her hand in the gesture that indicated

all was well, a sign Eric had used countless times in the forests before Heidal. He relaxed slightly. "Of course, Lady Kyliandra," Anika curtsied slightly. "I appreciate your hospitality. It was a long journey."

"Tindal," Eric's mother said softly. "Please send word for Father to join us."

"I already have, Kyli," Tindal replied. He turned to Anika and bowed politely. "I look forward to seeing you again, soon."

Anika curtsied again, smiling at him sincerely. Then Kyliandra beckoned to her, and she followed the willowy woman out of the antechamber.

Chapter 30

Kyliandra guided Anika down an adjoining hallway, different from the one they had come down earlier. Anika followed the Almeri princess quietly, feeling slightly nervous.

"I frighten you, don't I?" Kyliandra asked in Almeri after a few moments of silence.

Anika smiled wryly. "I don't know that I would use the word 'frighten'. Intimidate, perhaps... but that's hardly surprising, given the circumstances."

"Indeed," Kyliandra agreed. "From your posture, you are not one of those Prisian hussies that call themselves 'ladies'. I assume that this is your first encounter with nobility."

"Not entirely," Anika replied. "We were invited to tea with Duke Ahrlon and Lady Rehann in Heidal."

Kyliandra smiled slightly. "Really? And what did you think of my niece?"

"She seemed pleasant," Anika said, "Though our visit was interrupted. She was genuinely pleased to discover that Eric was alive."

"Of course," Kyliandra nodded. "She and Eric grew up together. They are the closest in age of all the children." Her dark eyes studied Anika carefully. "And what of you, then?"

"Lady Kyliandra," Anika said calmly, "I am nothing more than a simple village healer. I realize that you likely think that makes me a poor match for your son, but..."

Kyliandra shook her head. "I do not judge people based on their birth, Anika. That is my brother's failing. I judge people based on their actions. Your actions, from saving my son to travelling across the Almerinthine Sea, speak louder than what your parents did or where you were born. And as for being a 'simple village healer'... well, simple village healers don't speak fluent Almeri."

"I'm hardly fluent, my lady," Anika protested. "I learned what I know from your son and the captain of the vessel that brought us here."

The Sword and Satchel

"And how, exactly, did you discover my son?" Kyliandra inquired.

"I didn't," Anika admitted. "My brothers found him. They discovered the battlefield and Henrik decided he wanted a sword. They literally stumbled over him. I was gathering herbs when Henrik dragged me back to help him."

"Did you recognize him?" Kyliandra asked.

Anika laughed. "No, Lady Kyliandra. He was an injured man, and I am a healer. I took him to my father's home and tended him there... until the soldiers came."

Kyliandra cocked her head. "Soldiers came looking for him?"

"Not for him, no. They came to raid our village for supplies. Their officer killed my father, and Eric helped my brothers and I escape."

The hallway opened into a stunningly beautiful little open-air courtyard, with ivy climbing every wall and a delicate fountain in the center. The scent of jasmine and the sound of water filled the air. Anika gazed around in open appreciation. "This is lovely," she murmured.

"Yes," Kyliandra agreed, glancing around. "I often come here when I need to relax. It seemed the most appropriate place to ask you to remain while your rooms are being prepared." She stared at Anika, her dark eyes piercing. "Anika..." she began, but stopped.

"I understand what you are trying to determine, Lady Kyliandra," Anika said, her gaze flinty, "and the answer is no. I did not know who your son was; I did not help him because he was the son of Tindal Yolandson and the grandson of Kysid ab Kyr'lasi. I am not some gold-digging trollop who sees your son as an opportunity to rise above her station. I love him. I was falling in love with him long before he even knew who he was. Now, if you are quite finished judging my character, I believe you wished to speak with your son alone?"

Kyliandra stared at her for a moment, and then she smiled slowly. "It has been a very, very long time since someone dared to speak to me like that," she said quietly. "Most of the women around here are meek little creatures that jump at the sight of me. You, however... I think I will enjoy your company, Anika of Prisia."

Turning, she gestured to a stone bench with a soft-looking cushion, beside the pond. "You can wait here while I speak with one of the servants. They will prepare your quarters. I look forward to speaking with you again."

Anika shook her head as Kyliandra walked away. "Fire and steel," she murmured.

The words caused Kyliandra to freeze halfway

across the courtyard. She turned, her gaze sharp. "What did you say?"

Anika smiled slightly. "It was how someone I know described you to Eric and me. He said you were 'fire and steel'. He was right."

Kyliandra stalked back towards her, her eyes blazing. "Only one man has ever referred to me in those terms," she said softly. "Who was this person you spoke to?"

"His name is Lodi," Anika replied. "He was a friend of my father's."

Kyliandra frowned. "This tale gets stranger and stranger," she mused softly. "Did Lodi recognize Eric?"

"He's the one who told Eric who he was," Anika said quietly. "We went there after my father was killed."

Shaking her head, Kyliandra turned away. "I look forward to hearing the rest of this story in the morning."

Anika watched her leave, and then she settled herself down on the cushion and stared around the courtyard.

The garden, for that's how Anika perceived it, was lush and verdant. Night-blooming jasmine, a stunning white and red lily she didn't recognize, and a small scattering of brilliant scarlet water lilies across the surface of the pool brought the garden to life in the moonlight and ruddy gleam

The Sword and Satchel

of nearby torches. She trailed her fingers in the water, suddenly feeling incredibly alone.

An old man, clutching a knobbed cane, walked softly into the garden, and Anika glanced up. His dark skin contrasted sharply with his neatly trimmed white beard and his mass of wild white hair. He smiled kindly and hobbled towards her. *"Istan,"* he greeted, his low voice rich and gentle. "I had not expected to encounter anyone here... especially a guest of such rare beauty."

Anika rose to her feet, her expression slightly sad. "I have only just arrived," she murmured. "Lady Kyliandra has sent for someone to arrange a room for me." She gestured to the cushioned seat. "Would you like to sit?"

The old man nodded and hobbled slowly around the pool. "My thanks," he said. "Age is a terrible thing. It robs the body of the things it once had, leaving only memories... which fade away as well."

Anika shook her head. "But it brings wisdom," she argued. "And the opportunity to see your children grow."

The old man chuckled. "True," he coughed, suddenly. "But wisdom is a poor substitute to health."

She knelt beside him, her head tilted. "If I had my things, I have some herbs that would help with that cough... and with your arthritis."

He smiled at her. "Truly? Are you a healer, then?"

She frowned. "Yes... at least, I was. Ginger, turmeric, or green tea..." she muttered. "Perhaps some thunder god vine or eucalyptus on the joints..."

The old man clasped her hands in his, smiling at her. "It is of little matter, child," he said softly. "I have grown accustomed to the pain."

She shook her head. "There's no need for it," she argued. "There are many herbs which help reduce swelling. Others reduce pain. I wish I had my satchel."

He leaned back and trailed his hand in the water as she had done only moments before. "What brings you to Kisham?" he asked quietly.

She sighed softly. "I came with a friend... I guess with my betrothed, now..."

"Truly? Have you seen the city, yet?"

She shook her head. "It was already getting dark when we arrived."

Smiling, the man took a deep breath. "I envy you," he said softly. "To see the city for the first time... it is a remarkable experience. It has grown much in the last few years, but it still is the beating heart of Almeri."

She smiled wistfully. "It appeared amazing from the sea," she agreed. Then she shook her head. "Forgive me, but I don't even know your name. I'm Anika. Do you work here?"

The old man grinned. "In a manner of speaking," he replied. "I am Kysid."

Anika staggered back a half-step, her eyes wide. Then she dropped into a deep curtsy, as Eric had taught her.

"Bah!" Kysid barked, coughing. "It's always such torment to see the effect my name has on people. It was so much nicer when I was just a charming old man in a garden."

"My lord..." she began, but before she could say anything more, Kyliandra swept into the garden leading a stately-looking servant in a dark red dress.

"Father!" she exclaimed. "There you are. I was about to have the servants roused to find you."

"And what requires my presence so badly that you would chase my servants from their beds?" Kysid demanded, his entire demeanour changing.

Kyliandra's face broke into a wide smile. "It was a lie. He's not dead! Eric isn't dead!"

Kysid stared at her as though she had gone mad. "Kyliandra..." he began, but then he glanced at Anika. "Ah," he murmured, relaxing slightly. "That would explain much. Is he in good health, then?"

Kyliandra nodded. "He is. I was just going to speak with him, to hear what exactly happened." She glanced at Anika. "Your room has been prepared, Anika. I'm certain you must be exhausted. Pentha will escort you..."

"I assume you arrived with Eric, then?" Kysid inquired, interrupting his daughter.

"Yes," Anika whispered.

"If you can forego your rest for a short time, child," Kysid said gently, "I would hear the story from both of you."

"Father..." Kyliandra began, but he gestured impatiently at her.

"It will be as I say, Kyliandra," he said, not unkindly. "I find that lengthy tales, particularly when about shared experiences, often are best told by all parties."

Kyliandra nodded. "As you wish, Father," she murmured.

Anika glanced at the servant beside Kyliandra. "Have my trunks been brought in?" she inquired politely. When the dour-faced servant nodded, Anika added, "Could you bring me the leather pack from inside the larger trunk? It has my medicines," she explained to Kysid.

Kysid chuckled softly. "You are determined that you can fix age, then, are you?"

"Not fix it," Anika countered. "But I can relieve

some of its less pleasant aspects."

Kysid jerked his chin at Pentha, who scurried off into one of the arched entrances to the gardens. Then he extended an arm to Anika, ignoring Kyliandra's startled glance. "Come then, Anika. Perhaps you can assist me more than this blasted stick."

Anika stepped forward and took the old man's arm. "It would be my pleasure," she said quietly.

Chapter 31

Eric was pacing in front of a wide window when Anika, Kyliandra, and Kysid entered Tindal's private office. His eyes searched for Anika first, brightening when he saw her. Then he stepped forward and dropped to one knee in front of his grandfather. "Grandfather," he greeted, his head lowered.

"It would appear that the tales of your untimely demise have been... exaggerated," Kysid murmured, placing one hand on Eric's head. When Eric stood up again, he added, "It is good. I had feared that grief might have broken your mother's mind when she said you were here."

Kyliandra snorted softly. Tindal, who was seated in a plush armchair behind his desk, laughed softly. He rose quietly and gestured for Kysid to take his place in the chair. Patting Anika's arm, Kysid released her and hobbled over to the offered seat. He sat down and surveyed the room. "You never were one for decorations, Tindal," he commented darkly, "But I doubt a few extra chairs would be amiss."

Tindal smiled at his father-in-law. "I have a servant bringing them as we speak, Kysid. I rarely have need of more than the one."

Kysid chuckled. "I assume the servants are bringing enough for all of us?" He gestured toward Anika significantly.

Tindal frowned, but Eric waved his hand. "I'll be fine standing, Father. There's no need to send for more."

Nodding, Tindal moved around the desk to join Kyliandra. "Eric has remained tight-lipped," he said softly. "Apparently he didn't wish to have to repeat himself."

Kyliandra smiled at her son. "I assume there is much to tell," she commented.

A knock on the door announced the arrival of chairs and a tray of refreshments. While the chairs were being placed, Pentha arrived with Anika's pack. Anika thanked her graciously, eliciting a smile from the stern-looking woman. Then, as the others sat, Anika moved to the desk and glanced at the tray. She opened the lid of a teapot and sniffed the contents.

"Mint tea," Tindal explained. "It's a common refreshment here."

Anika smiled at him. "I was hoping to brew some green tea with ginger..." she began.

Immediately one of the servants bowed and departed, and Anika stared after him, confused.

"He'll bring water," Eric told her softly, moving to stand beside her. "Did you have a good conversation with my mother?" he added in a whisper.

Anika glared at him. "She thinks I'm a gold-seeking hussy," she muttered low enough that only Eric could hear, digging through her satchel for the herbs she sought.

Eric bit back a laugh. "Well," he said, grinning. "It's good to see you're off to such a good start."

When the servant returned with a fresh pot of steaming water, Anika mixed some tea leaves and powdered ginger into the water. "Allow it to steep for a while," she advised Kysid. "It needs to be strong, and it will taste... different than what you're accustomed to."

Kysid nodded, smiling, and then gestured for her to sit. "Now, then," he said quietly. "Why don't the two of you tell us what happened in Prisia... particularly why word came to us of your death at the hands of King Ryas."

Eric frowned and began pacing. "That's a good question. Before we start, I need to know a few things. As Anika told you, Mother, I was hit in the head. Most of my memory has returned, but I can't recall who I was supposed to meet with in Prisia."

Tindal grimaced. "Estaves," he said coldly. "Julio Estaves is one of the most influential western nobles in Prisia. He sent a message to me, months ago, indicating that the western lords were... interested in establishing contact, in order to overthrow Ryas. You were supposed to meet with his men, who would take you to speak with him in his castle in Porth."

"Who brought you the message?" Eric demanded softly.

"It was delivered to Kyvin, who brought it to my attention," his father replied. "Estaves didn't know where I was, but it was a safe guess that if I was alive, I would be here."

Eric frowned, his mind spinning. "And what was your initial reaction?"

Tindal shook his head. "I don't trust the western lords, not after... the succession," he spat the word. "But Estaves had never done anything to me. He was a fairly young man during the War, and I'd met him a few times at my father's court." He shrugged. "But with this rebellion happening in the east, I thought it might be an opportunity."

Eric closed his eyes for a moment. "You thought it might be?" he pressed. "Or did someone suggest it might be?"

Tindal hesitated, blinking. "Well, I discussed it with Kyvin, of course. He agreed that it was something we couldn't dismiss."

Eric nodded slowly, but Anika could see a trace of tension in his shoulders that wasn't there before. "Father, I'm going to ask you something, and I don't want you to answer it yet. Not right away. Did you want to go yourself, and if so, who persuaded you to send me in your place?"

His father looked about to speak, but Eric held up his hand. "Just... wait. There's a reason I asked that, and you need to hear everything before that reason makes sense." He glanced at Anika. "Do you want to start, or should I?"

Anika shook her head, rising from where she sat to pour a cup of the green tea for Kysid. The sultan accepted it with a faint smile, but then grimaced at the taste. "Start from the beginning," she told Eric as she returned to her chair.

He nodded, then took a deep breath. "We made it to the meeting place without incident. We planted the banner, as directed, and then Alhamid told us he had orders to announce our presence to the men we were supposed to meet. About half an hour after Alhamid left, a party of soldiers in Ryas' colours charged out of the forest. They caught us by surprise, but we hadn't really started to set up camp yet. We'd been too nervous about what was going to happen next. When the soldiers attacked, we reacted exactly as we would if we'd been on patrol and nomads had attacked. Basic formation, with me centered. Hyrid died first, then Jordan, Sulmid and Revi. After that, things got too chaotic to know what was happening." He shook his head. Glancing over at Anika, he gestured for her to pick up the story.

It took a long time, and by the time they had finished, the first traces of light were creeping in the large window behind Eric. Kysid and Tindal were leaning forward in their seats, and Kyliandra was studying the pair of them with her dark eyes.

"So," Eric concluded, "here we are."

Tindal rose and walked over to the tray of tea and biscuits. The tea had grown cold twice, and each time servants had entered unobtrusively to replace the pot. Each time, Eric had halted the narrative until the servants were gone. He picked up a biscuit and nibbled on the edge. "That's a lot to take in," he muttered.

Eric nodded. "We skimmed over a few things that I need to discuss with you in greater detail. Right now, however, I want you to answer my question from earlier. Did you want to go to the meeting with Estaves yourself?"

"Of course I was going to go myself," Tindal growled. "And if I'd known the danger I was sending you into, I would never have allowed you to go."

"So who persuaded you to send me, instead?" Eric asked softly.

Tindal stared at his son for a moment, his jaw clenched. "I think you already know the answer to that," he said at last, turning and striding to the window, his hands clenched behind his back.

Kysid frowned and glanced at Kyliandra, who looked equally bewildered. "Tindal?" she demanded. When Tindal shook his head, she glanced at Eric.

"Uncle Kyvin," Eric said very quietly.

Tindal nodded, jerkily.

"Seven men came with me," Eric added quietly. "I knew six of them before I left, from working with them on patrol. I didn't know Alhamid. Why did he come along?"

Tindal turned around and swallowed hard. "He was the one who brought Kyvin the message from Estaves. He claimed he'd been chosen by Estaves because sending a

The Sword and Satchel

Prisian to meet with Kyvin would appear suspicious if Ryas learned of it."

Kyliandra still looked confused, but Kysid's face had grown pale, and he was leaning heavily on the arm of the chair. Anika found her eyes drawn to the old man, to the pain in his expression.

"Are you going to continue to be cryptic," Kyliandra asked, her eyes flickering between her husband and her son. "Or are you going to tell us why this is important?"

Eric turned to his mother, his face bleak. Before he could say anything, however, Anika rose from her seat, digging into her bag of herbs. Her sudden motion drew all eyes to her, but her attention was entirely on Kysid, who had suddenly stiffened, and was clutching at his chest.

"Get me more hot water!" Anika commanded, darting to the old man's side.

Kyliandra rose to her feet, her face draining of blood as she stared at her father. "What did you do to him?!" she shrieked.

"It's his heart," Anika explained, her voice tense. "I don't have time to bicker, Kyliandra. Get the water. Now!"

Kyliandra bolted from the room.

Kysid was gasping for breath, and Anika grabbed his wrist, checking for his pulse. She nodded after a moment,

The Sword and Satchel

---

then pulled a small packet of herbs out and held it under his nose. Kysid coughed and jerked his head away, but his rigid posture relaxed slightly almost immediately. "How long?" she demanded softly, staring at Kysid intently.

"A few months," he whispered. "They... have been more frequent in the last few days."

"Stress will do that," she said quietly. She glanced up as Kyliandra burst back into the room, a pot of steaming water in her hands. Gesturing for the princess to fill a cup, Anika drew another packet of herbs from the pouch and crushed them into the cup Kyliandra held out to her. "My father suffered from a similar problem," she told Kysid. "I've found that these helped."

"What is it?" Kyliandra demanded suspiciously.

"Hawthorn, valerian, and dried bilberry... with a touch of garlic and cayenne," Anika said, stirring the water. She glanced up at Kyliandra. "They help with circulation."

She handed the cup to Kysid. "I assume you have a personal physician..." When Kysid nodded, she asked, "What has he suggested?"

"Leeches," Kysid growled. "His advice is always leeches."

Anika nodded. "Typical," she said quietly. "And occasionally effective, depending on how he's using them.

I'll have to talk to him. These herbs can help. I will instruct one of your servants in how to combine them. I suggest you drink that tea twice daily. Most importantly, however, you need to rest."

Kysid leaned back in the chair, his expression sad. "Rest..." he chuckled softly.

Anika crossed her arms. "Yes," she said sternly.

Kysid sipped the tea. "It needs sugar," he commented, obviously wishing to change the subject.

Anika sighed and returned to her seat. Kyliandra stared after her for a moment. Finally she said, "I am sorry. I... thought you had..."

Anika glanced up at Eric's mother, a small, sad smile on her lips. "I am a healer," she said softly. "Not an assassin. But I accept the apology."

There was a long silence, during which Kyliandra moved back to her own chair, and Tindal returned to stare out the window at the sunrise. "Do you really believe he had a hand in it, Eric?" Tindal finally asked, breaking the silence.

Kyliandra looked up sharply, her eyes narrowing. Then she started to shake her head in denial. "You can't be saying..."

Kysid cleared his throat. "Kyliandra," he cautioned.

"I wish to hear what Eric is about to say... without interruption."

Eric's mother sat back, staring at her son.

"I don't want to," Eric said slowly. "But the more I hear, the more it seems to fit. Kyvin was the one to receive the message from Estaves, purportedly carried by Alhamid, a Jiradin. Kyvin encouraged you to accept the meeting, but to send me in your place..."

"But what does he stand to gain from it?" Tindal demanded, turning to stare at his son.

"An empire," he said softly. "He is Grandfather's heir. As the only other male directly descended from Grandfather, I am a threat to his position. Killing me would benefit him, if only by getting me out of the way. But it would do more. My death, at the hands of Ryas, would provide him with an opportunity to invade Prisia. It would, of course, be under Grandfather's orders, and you would be the figurehead, but he would be the one leading the invasion. And once Almeri forces were in Prisia..."

"But I wouldn't allow the Almeri to remain," Tindal argued. "After we overthrew Ryas, I would..."

"Do you really think he would actually let you take the throne?" Eric scoffed. "If I'm right, and he plotted to have his own nephew murdered, do you really think he would flinch at killing his sister's husband? You aren't even Almeri... and if he is who I think he is, that makes you less than dirt to him."

Tindal blinked, taken aback. "If he is..."

"The Jirad," Kysid whispered, nodding sadly.

Kyliandra was staring at Eric as though her son had morphed into a monster. "You can't honestly believe that Kyvin would... that my brother..."

"He stands to gain control of both Almeri and Prisia," Eric countered. "I'm guessing he's fully aware of your heart condition, isn't he, Grandfather?"

Kysid nodded again. "Of course," he replied softly. "He is my heir."

"And your attacks began shortly before Estaves' letter arrived," Eric added, speaking more to himself than to anyone else in the room. "That might have pushed his hand. As your grandson, my death would be a cause for retaliation. Once he becomes Sultan, though, my death becomes... less important. I'm only his nephew, though I'd also be his heir. But he wouldn't be seen as the instigating force, if the order came from you, Grandfather. His hands would be clean." He paused, and then he looked shrewdly at Kysid. "How did Kyvin react to news of my death?"

Kysid shifted, his shoulders slumping slightly. "He

said it was a direct attack on the Almeri Empire, that your murder by King Ryas was a declaration of war. He insisted that we respond in kind."

Eric nodded. "Righteous anger, indignation... but did he appear surprised?"

Kysid looked away, his eyes clouding. "No," he admitted. "I didn't notice it because I wasn't looking for it, but... it was as though he expected the news. He was already prepared to summon the legions."

Kyliandra rocked back, her face slack. "You can't really believe Kyvin would do this?" she demanded hoarsely.

Eric took a deep breath. "Do I believe it? Yes. Can I prove it? No. Fortunately, I don't have to. I'm not dead, so an invasion of Prisia isn't necessary. Whatever his plan was, it won't work."

Kysid shook his head. "But if he is the Jirad," he murmured, "then it is only a matter of time. Once I am gone, he will be able to take action on his own. Then he won't bother with the pretense of placing your father back on the throne. He will simply invade. The Jiradin are fanatics, and if he *is* the Jirad... which I begin to suspect may be true... he does not want anything less than total domination."

Kyliandra was shaking her head in denial, but there were tears in her eyes. "Why? Why would he..."

"For the same reason Ryas did it thirty-five years ago," Tindal growled. "Power."

Kysid closed his eyes. "That I could think this of my own son..." he moaned softly. "And yet, I do. Gods forgive me, I do." He looked up and his eyes were cold. "I will have him arrested..."

"Father, no!" Kyliandra cried. "There is no proof, only conjecture. You would not condemn any man without proof of the crime. I cannot... I will not believe that Kyvin plotted your death, Eric. There must be some other explanation, some other solution."

"There is one other way," Eric agreed, his voice barely audible. "I can challenge him to a duel. I can't prove his guilt, but I believe he is guilty. He won't be able to refuse... not and retain his honor. It becomes a civil dispute, resolved through combat."

"A duel?" Anika objected. "But how does that solve anything? If he's guilty, he might still defeat you. If he's not guilty, and you defeat him, you would be killing an innocent man... your own uncle."

Eric began to pace again. "The Jiradin believe that any who are not pure Almeri are not worthy of honorable combat," he began, thinking out loud again. "To the Jiradin, non-Almeri are no better than rodents. If he is a Jiradin... or the Jirad himself... he will detest the idea of having to duel a... mongrel. When I set the terms to first blood, he will insist on it being to the death. He will have to. I believe he plotted to have me killed, and based on what Alhamid said, the one who plotted to have me killed was a member of the Jiradin. If he's not a Jiradin, he will likely accept the terms of first-blood... and I will accept that it is possible it was not him who planned my death. If I lose, I will apologize and renounce any claim I have to the Almeri Empire. If I win, I will accept his apology and leave it up to Grandfather as to whether Kyvin remains his heir. Win or lose, the dispute ends."

"And if he's not Jiradin, but is so infuriated that you would believe him capable of murdering you that he demands a fight to the death?" Anika asked, angrily.

"He wouldn't," Kysid replied calmly. "Eric is family. He would respect that Eric could have set the terms to the death to begin with – and rightly so, given the complaint – and he would honor the family by accepting the terms." The old man glanced at Eric with appreciation. "It is a very Almeri solution."

"And if he is a Jiradin, and he demands a duel to the

death... and kills you?" Anika demanded. "Then you're dead."

Eric sighed. "I didn't say it was a perfect solution," he admitted, grimacing.

"You can't be serious about this!" Anika protested.

Eric smiled sadly. "Unfortunately," he said quietly, "It's the only way I can think of to stop an invasion that would cost the lives of thousands - tens of thousands – of people down the road. If you have a better solution, I'd love to hear it."

Anika glanced over at Kyliandra, who was staring at Eric with tears in her eyes. At the sight of the resignation in his mother's face, Anika bowed her head. "I don't," she admitted. Then she looked up at Eric, her eyes blazing. "You'd better not lose."

Chapter 32

Eric sat on the edge of his bed, resting his head in his hands. He stared at the floor, his mind racing. As hard as he tried, however, he couldn't come up with any plan which would be better than challenging his uncle to a duel.

A duel he wasn't certain he could win.

His uncle, he knew, was one of the finest warriors in all of Almeri. He was the commander of the entire Almeri forces, had fought in countless battles.

He closed his eyes, going over his conclusions again and again. He didn't want to believe his uncle would plot to murder him, but he knew with absolute certainty that it was true.

He felt the bitter taste of betrayal, like bile, in his

mouth.

There was a faint knock on his door, and he rose to his feet, moving slowly. He knew who it was going to be before he opened the door.

"You're insane," Anika growled, pushing past him.

"Look, Anika..." he began, but Anika spun and pounded her fists on his chest in a gesture remarkably similar to how his mother had acted earlier. This time he wasn't wearing his leather armour, and he staggered back a little.

"No!" she snapped. "You don't get to give me excuses. You lead me across the Almerinthine Sea to a completely foreign country, you propose to me, and then you tell me that you're going to have to fight your uncle to the death..." She whirled away, hissing like an angry cat, and stalked across the spacious room to sit down on the edge of his bed. Tears ran down her cheeks as she glared at him. "If you die... I don't know what I would do. You are all I have, now."

Eric moved across the intricately tiled floor and sat beside her. "He can't be allowed to get away with this," Eric said softly. "If I don't do this, sooner or later he's going to..."

"You don't know that!" she snapped. "You don't

know what he's going to do. You're guessing, just like you're guessing that he's the Jirad, that he's the one who tried to have you killed. You don't know. Not really."

"Can I afford to risk doing nothing?" Eric demanded, hotly. "If I'm right about him, about what he's planning, can I just... ignore it? I was born in Almeri, but I know that Prisia is just as much a part of me. If I'm right, and Kyvin becomes Sultan and invades Prisia, every person who dies in the invasion – *every single person* – will die because I didn't act now. That could include Harald and Henrik... and it would almost certainly include you, and my father, and possibly my mother. It would probably include everyone we knew in Heidal, everyone who helped us..." he shook his head.

"It's just so easy for..." she began, but Eric rose to his feet, cutting her off with a curt gesture.

"Easy?" Eric barked a laugh empty of mirth. "Kyvin is my uncle. I've known him my entire life. He was the one who insisted to Father that I do something valuable with my time, like train with the sword and join the Almeri army. He's the one who insisted I serve time on a ship, that I serve time in combat instead of hiding in the shelter of the city. I love and respect my father, but Kyvin is the one who demanded I become someone other than just the son of

Tindal Yolandson. When it comes down to it, Kyvin is the reason I am who I am... and he tried to kill me to start a war. For what?

"He betrayed the trust I have for him. And now I have to try to kill him... to kill the person who made me a better man. And to top it all off, I don't know if I can defeat him. He's the commander of the entire Almeri armed forces! He's spent his entire life with a sword in his hand. And if I don't beat him, if he kills me, I leave you here, in the middle of a foreign country as you so eloquently pointed out, with nothing... And you think it's *easy* for me?" he snarled.

Anika stared at him for a moment, her eyes wide.

"This is the hardest decision I've ever had to make, Anika," he said in a whisper, his head bowed. "And I hate the choice, but I don't see any other option. Believe me, if I did I would take it."

"Trick him into confessing," Anika suggested.

Eric smiled grimly. "How? Pretend to be a ghost and haunt him?"

Anika glared at him. "No," she snapped. "Have him come to a meeting with Kysid in... wherever it is that he meets with everyone important... and tell Kyvin that Alhamid told you everything before he died, that he named him the Jirad, and that he said your uncle was the one who plotted it all."

Eric considered this for a moment, but shook his head. "He would just deny it," he said finally.

"What if your grandfather invited as many suspected Jiradin, all influential lords, and you said that Alhamid told you that he, the Jirad, had been using the Jiradin... manipulating them to take the fall if things went wrong. Claim that Alhamid named all the major leaders of the Jiradin..."

Eric hesitated, his eyes growing distant, playing out the scenario in his mind. "He could still just deny it," he said quietly. "The Jiradin leaders would be nervous, but he could meet with them after to reassure them... it's not as though we could turn around and arrest them." He shook his head again. "He'd call our bluff."

"What if you added that Alhamid claimed that Kyvin was working with Ryas?" Anika persisted.

"To what end, Anika?" Eric sighed. "How would implying Kyvin was working with Ryas have any impact at all?"

Anika glanced around wildly. "There has to be some way to manipulate him into confessing!" she wailed. "If he confesses, Kysid can arrest him and you won't have to fight."

"I agree," he said simply. "But if there's a way to get him to confess, in front of witnesses, I don't know what it is."

Anika slumped forward, her shoulders shaking. "I don't want you to do this," she whispered through tears of frustration.

"I know," Eric said softly. "And I hope you can forgive me for doing it anyway."

She rose to her feet, wiping her tears away with the sleeve of her dress. "When?" she asked in a hushed voice.

"He's back in the palace tomorrow to report on the war effort. I'll challenge him then."

"Tomorrow," she whispered. "Then to blazes with propriety. I won't spend what could be our last night together weeping in a strange bed, alone." She strode across the room and grabbed the front of his shirt with both hands, pulling his head down and kissing him fiercely. Then she pulled him silently towards the huge bed.

Chapter 33

The palace was beyond anything Anika could have ever possibly imagined. Eric led her through rooms that could have easily held the entire village of Anidaron, buildings and all. The walls were made from spotless white stone she wasn't familiar with, and the open windows let the hot air blowing in from the desert flow through the halls, billowing out curtains of material so fine she could have cut it with a butter knife.

Priceless vases, atop fluted columns that stood shoulder high, stood in recessed alcoves. Carpets of exquisite workmanship and detail lay upon the delicate reddish-pink stone of the floors in rooms that seemed to drip chandeliers of crystal. Everything appeared to have been placed exactly, with meticulous attention to dramatic effect, and the effect *was* dramatic. Pieces of art from every culture Anika had ever heard of, as well as from some she hadn't, were displayed in various rooms. There seemed to be no specific pattern to the choices until Eric explained that each room was designed as a place to welcome dignitaries from the culture represented by the artwork.

The grand hall was vast, with a crystal-lined dome above, through which the sunlight was refracted in a rainbow of colours throughout the cavernous hall. The beauty of the refracted light stopped Anika in her tracks, her eyes wide. Sixteen intricately carved marble pillars were set in a perfect circle beneath the crystal dome; the ceiling outside the pillars was separated into panels by golden beams, each panel painted, in painstaking detail, with various events in the ancient history of Almeri.

The throne itself was on an elevated dais beneath the crystal dome, in a shaft of unfiltered sunlight. Eric explained that small mirrors in the very peak of the dome reflected the sunlight so that the throne was always perfectly lit. Carved from a rich, dark wood, and with red-velvet cushions, it actually looked both elegant and remarkably comfortable.

The grand hall was empty when they arrived there,

and the only sound was a faint tinkling of water from a small fountain against the far wall. "That fountain," Eric told her, shifting his sword belt slightly, "is the oldest thing in this city. This palace... this entire city, I suppose, was built around it. The facade around it has been reconstructed dozens of times, but the fountain itself is the original stonework."

She walked over to study the ancient stone. It was simple, really, after you looked past the beautiful stone carvings that surrounded it. It was a plain piece of what appeared to be simple slate with a small spout that the water poured from. On it, letters were etched, but Anika couldn't read what they said. She glanced at Eric, and he smiled.

"It says, 'From water, life'," he said softly. "When you live in a land as arid as Almeri, water becomes a very precious thing."

She nodded slowly. "How old is it?" she asked.

Eric shrugged. He looked incredibly different in traditional Almeri clothing, she realized. The saffron-coloured robes, combined with his short dark hair, made him look... regal, she decided. "No one really knows," he replied. "It's probably five... maybe six thousand years old."

She shivered, staring at it. The idea of a single thing lasting for so long was... "Beautiful," she whispered.

He nodded, his eyes on the simple stone.

There was a sudden commotion, and the two of them turned around to see Kysid, garbed in flowing purple robes, walking slowly into the hall, surrounded by guards. Several dozen other men and women entered slightly behind him, maintaining a respectful distance. As soon as Kysid mounted the dais, seating himself on the throne, the guards spread out to stand unobtrusively at each of the sixteen pillars.

Anika studied the faces of the others, who were engaged in conversation with one another. None of them looked anything like how Eric had described his uncle.

"He's not here yet?" she asked.

Eric shook his head, his hand unconsciously touching the hilt of his sword at the thought of his uncle. "He'll probably arrive shortly. It's tradition. Notice my parents aren't here yet, either. The sultan arrives first, usually followed by his ministers, then the royal family, and finally followed by the regional representatives."

Anika shook her head. "I don't really understand how the Almeri government works," she admitted. When Eric turned to speak to her, she raised a hand to forestall him. "I know you told me on the ship, and I'm sure it's important to you, but I really don't actually care."

He laughed softly.

There was a slight stir, and Anika saw Kyliandra and Tindal, as well as another woman, slightly younger-looking than Kyliandra, enter. Tindal was dressed in Prisian clothing, unlike everyone else in the group. He was also wearing a sword. Kyliandra and the woman with her were both dressed in the royal purple robes that denoted Kysid's family.

"That's my aunt, 'Rissa," Eric said, nodding at the woman with Kyliandra. "Rehann's mother."

"Rissa?" Anika asked. "That's an unusual name."

"Kyrissa," Eric explained. When Anika raised her eyebrow, Eric continued. "The royal designation in Almeri is 'ky'. It's like 'prince' or 'princess'."

"But not you?" she blinked.

Eric smiled. "Not in Prisia, but my legal name in Almeri is actually Kyric ab Kyr'lasi ni Yolandson. The northern Prisian tradition of the son inheriting the father's given name as his surname doesn't exist here. Here, names are passed down generation to generation."

"I prefer Eric," she muttered.

Eric smiled. "So do I."

A few moments passed, and more people entered the grand hall. Eric frowned. "I expected him to arrive before the regional representatives," he commented quietly.

Apparently, so did Kysid. The old man looked around the room at the gathered men and women, glowering. "And where," he demanded, "is my son?"

There was a long silence. Many of the regional representatives shuffled their feet and glanced around, confused. After a few moments, however, the sound of many booted footsteps could be heard on the stones in the hallway.

A tall, hawk-nosed man with dark hair laced with silver strode into the room, surrounded by several guards. Unlike everyone else, Kyvin was fully armoured. His chainmail gleamed in the reflected light from the dome above, and his sword hung easily at his hip. He waved to the men with him as he entered, and they fanned out around the grand hall like Kysid's guards had done, though standing further back than the others. One of them stopped a few feet in front of where Eric and Anika stood, not even glancing at them.

"Ah, Kyvin," Kysid greeted his son.

"Father," Eric's uncle replied in a deep, raspy voice, bowing his head slightly. "I was delayed."

Kyvin wasn't as broad across the shoulders as Eric was, but he looked lean and lithe, despite being well into his middle years. A neatly trimmed beard and deep-set dark eyes gave him a vulpine look. He moved with the same kind of feline grace that Anika had begun to associate with all of Eric's family. Watching him, she suddenly felt very afraid.

"I was arranging the last details of the boarding process with Admiral Hyth. Troop ships..." Kyvin continued, but his father raised a hand.

"There will be no attack on Prisia," he announced calmly.

There was a moment of absolute silence, and then everyone in the room began speaking quietly amongst one another. Kyvin's face had grown pale for a moment, and then his forehead creased and blood flushed his cheeks. "But Father!" he objected. "Those *pradtha* killed... no *murdered* your own grandson! How can you sit there, the Grand Sultan of Almeri, and not take action against such a direct declaration of war?"

Eric had begun to move into the crowd. He'd chosen to wear the saffron-coloured robes for exactly this reason. His presence, likely because his appearance was so vastly different from how it once had been, went completely unnoticed by those gathered.

"Tindal! Kyliandra!" Kyvin called out, glancing over at Eric's parents. "Surely you agree that Ryas deserves nothing less than to be hunted down and killed for murdering your only son!"

"There will be no invasion!" Kysid repeated, loudly. "Ryas is not responsible for the death of Eric."

"But Father, we have first-hand accounts..." Kyvin began, not noticing as Eric moved to stand only a few feet behind him.

"Perhaps you should have arranged for a more reliable witness," Eric said softly, and Kyvin spun around, his eyes fastening on Eric in stunned disbelief. "Or a more reliable assassin, Uncle," Eric added.

"You... it can't be," Kyvin murmured, off-balance. Eric smiled coldly.

"Are you surprised that your effort to have me killed, to start this little war, failed, Uncle? Your assassin confessed everything before he died."

Kyvin's face paled slightly, and any doubt in Eric's mind about whether his uncle had plotted his demise disappeared in that instant.

"I... don't know what you're talking about," Kyvin stammered, still stunned.

"Really? I find that hard to believe," Eric said calmly, moving slowly towards his uncle. "Your assassin seemed quite certain about who sent him. He was absolutely convinced that he was acting for the greater good of Almeri... that he acted on your orders."

Kyvin retreated a step, and then he straightened, forcing himself to his full height. "The idea that I would attempt to have you killed is insanity," he proclaimed.

"He also told me all about your little scheme... with the Jiradin. I never suspected that you might be the Jirad."

Kyvin's eyes widened slightly, and Eric knew he'd hit the mark. His uncle shook his head fiercely. "You've been misled. Alhamid lied to you."

Eric paused, a slight smile playing across his lips. He glanced up at his grandfather, who had fallen back into his seat at the last comment, his expression dark. "Have I?" Eric asked softly. "It's possible, I suppose... except I never told you the assassin's name, Uncle."

Kyvin blinked, and then suddenly he went for his sword, screaming, "Guards!"

The room exploded into motion.

The sixteen guards that Kysid had brought into the chamber with him immediately drew their weapons, spinning to face the men Kyvin had brought. Kyvin's men were outnumbered, but Eric had absolutely no doubt that every single one of the eight warriors was a dedicated Jiradin who would fight to the death for their leader.

Eric had drawn his own sword as soon as Kyvin had moved, and he stood facing his uncle amidst the screaming mob as the regional representatives scattered in an effort to escape.

"I was going to challenge you, Uncle," Eric told the older man, circling him carefully until he had placed himself between Kyvin and his grandfather.

Kyvin noticed, and a cold smile crossed his lips. "Just because I'm willing to order the death of a mongrel like you, do you really think I would kill my own father?"

"Yes," Eric replied, his eyes never leaving the older man. "I think you would kill him without hesitation or remorse because you realize that there is no way, now, that you will ever be sultan."

Kyvin's face tightened. Then he feigned a slash at Eric, who barely shifted. "You believe that my father would disown me? I am his heir!"

Eric chose that instant to strike, his blade breaking through a hasty defense and catching Kyvin across the side. The chainmail his uncle wore deflected the blade, but the older man grimaced and backed away. "You are a traitor who tried to force this nation into a war which would end up killing thousands," Eric retorted, his dark eyes burning into his uncle's.

"The destiny of the Almeri is worth the loss of life," Kyvin hissed, lunging at Eric, who danced back, slapping the sword away with a deft motion.

"You've lost, Uncle," Eric told him. "You can't win. Your men are outnumbered..."

Kyvin risked a swift glance around the grand hall. His men were being badly pressed. Two of them were badly injured, though they were still trying to defend themselves. The others were still fighting to get to Kyvin's side, but the royal guards were well trained, and Kyvin was too close to Kysid. Tindal had placed himself at Kysid's side, his sword drawn in case anyone managed to reach the dais.

Snarling, Kyvin whirled around and dashed toward the entrance to the hall. Eric pursued him. He was faster than Kyvin, and they both knew it.

Just before the archway leading to the halls of the palace, Kyvin twisted and grabbed someone cowering to the side of the entrance by the hair. It was Eric's aunt, Rissa. Kyvin placed his sword blade at Rissa's throat, and Eric skidded to a halt.

"Kyvin..." Rissa whimpered. "What are you doing?"

"Be silent," he snapped at her. "If you pursue me, I swear I will slit her throat," he snarled at Eric.

The Sword and Satchel

"She's your sister, Kyvin!" Kyliandra screamed from where she stood behind Kysid and Tindal. "Let her go!"

"Be silent, you whore!" Kyvin shouted, spittle spraying from his lips. "Be glad it is your sister and not you. If it was you standing here, I would kill you just to wash away the stain of your disgrace! You shamed the house of Kyr'lasi when you lay with that *pradtha* you hold so dear, the king of nothing." He inched his way backwards, and Eric kept his eyes locked on his uncle.

"Uncle," Eric whispered. "You know I can't allow you to..."

"Her blood will be on your hands if you take a single step, mongrel," Kyvin spat. Rissa closed her eyes, a tear tracing its way down her cheek. "I will not hesitate..."

A sudden motion from behind Kyvin caught Eric's eye. Before he could register what it was, Kyvin shrieked and the sword fell from his hands. He released Rissa and spun around, backhanding his assailant, knocking her to the floor. Then Kyvin bolted from the room.

Anika knelt on the floor, blood dripping from her mouth... and from the blade of a long, thin stiletto still clutched in her hand. Eric glanced after the fleeing prince, but dropped to his knees beside Anika.

"Anika..." he murmured.

"Go after him!" she snapped, wiping the blood from her lip.

Eric nodded and lurched to his feet. Before he could race after his fleeing uncle, however, one of his uncle's guards slammed into him from behind, his shoulder driving into Eric's kidney and knocking him into the corner of the archway.

Eric spun desperately, his sword slashing at his attacker, but the guard blocked the blow. "For the Jirad!" the man bellowed and struck.

The blade of the guard's sword caught Eric in almost precisely the same place Eric's strike had hit his uncle. The guard grinned as Eric staggered back, but then he saw the glint of steel under the saffron robes Eric wore.

Eric stepped forward, his blade moving with almost inhuman speed. The first strike caught his opponent across the stomach, tearing through flesh in a spray of blood. His second took the man's sword arm off at the elbow, the blade and forearm clattering to the ground. His third strike nearly beheaded the guard, who spun away from the impact and crumpled to the ground in a pool of spreading blood.

A second of Kyvin's guards was charging towards them, but he was running at Anika instead of Eric, his sword raised. Eric didn't hesitate. He threw himself between the attacker and Anika, catching the sword strike on his own blade and deflecting it. His momentum carried him past the guard, and he had to spin around, his blade a silver blur.

The second guard didn't have time to recover his balance from the intended strike, and Eric's blade caught him at the collarbone, cutting deep into his chest. He staggered back, screaming, and fell to his knees, blood spurting like a fountain from his severed artery.

When Eric glanced around, all of Kyvin's other guards were down. He glanced down at Anika; she was still kneeling on the floor, but she was holding his aunt gently in her arms as Rissa sobbed quietly, her eyes fastened on the second guard, who was still writhing on the floor. "Are you both alright?" Eric asked.

Anika looked up at him, shaking her head. "She's pretty distraught," she said softly, "But we aren't hurt."

Eric glanced through the archway, but he knew there was no chance of catching up to his uncle. Instead, he knelt down beside his aunt. "Auntie Rissa," he murmured. "It's over. You're safe, now."

Rissa shifted her gaze from the dying man to Eric's face. "Eric..." she whispered. "They said you were dead. Did... did Kyvin really...?"

Eric nodded. "He did, but it isn't important anymore." He extended his hand to her. "Come," he said. "Grandfather will want to see you're alright."

Rissa took his offered hand, and then glanced at Anika. "I don't know who you are," she said quietly, "but thank you."

Anika rose to her feet, smiling. "You're welcome."

"You," Kyliandra's voice echoed through the great hall, "have a habit of saving the lives of the people in my family, Anika."

Anika looked towards the dais, where Eric's parents stood, shoulder to shoulder behind Kysid. Tindal still held his sword, and there was a long dagger in Kyliandra's hand. Kysid remained in his throne, his expression unruffled. "I happen to be in the right places," she explained.

"Why didn't you kill him?" Tindal demanded. "You could have slipped that knife between his ribs..."

"It would have required a very precise strike," Anika told him as the three of them approached the dais. "And while I'm familiar with where the internal organs are, I couldn't be certain I would be able to kill him before he could kill Eric's aunt... so I aimed for a nerve cluster in the neck area. It causes people to drop whatever they are holding."

The Sword and Satchel

The guards around the dais shifted uncomfortably as Eric approached, glancing at the sword he still carried in his hand. Eric smiled wryly and sheathed his weapon.

"Good thing you were wearing armour under that ridiculous robe," Tindal grumbled at his son. "You left yourself wide open."

Eric rolled his eyes. "He hit me from behind, Father. I was off-balance."

Tindal shook his head, trying to hide a smile. "Excuses..."

"Tindal," Kysid interrupted. "Now is not the time for levity... though I know it is simply your method of coping with stress."

"My apologies, Kysid," Tindal murmured.

Kysid looked at Rissa. "You were not hurt?" When Eric's aunt shook her head, he glanced at Eric, his eyes sad. "It was as you thought," he said finally. "I did not want to believe it, but there is no escaping from it."

Eric sighed. "I'm sorry, Grandfather. I had hoped..." he shook his head. "I was hoping I was wrong."

Kysid nodded. He looked around the grand hall, at the bodies of Kyvin's guards lying on the floor. All of the regional representatives, as well as all of Kysid's ministers, had fled the room. "Guards," he said finally. "Remove the bodies and have servants come to clean the floors." He glanced around again. "And have my vizier and my seneschal come immediately to my private chambers. I need to have word of Kyvin's betrayal sent to all of my nobles."

He rose slowly to his feet, looking suddenly older than Eric had ever seen him. Kyliandra was at his shoulder immediately, helping him descend from the elevated throne. As he neared Eric, Kysid paused, and then reached out and patted him gently on the shoulder. "Come see me later," he said quietly. "There are matters we must attend to."

Eric nodded, and Kysid looked past him at Anika. "I wish to thank you," he said simply. "As Kyliandra said, you seem to be a blessing to all of those within this house." He looked from her to Eric, meaningfully. "And I sincerely hope that your presence here becomes... permanent... as soon as possible."

Anika curtsied deeply, and Kysid shook his head. "I still liked it better when you thought I was just a kind old man in a garden, Anika. Don't change just because everyone around you tells you how they think something ought to be."

Kysid reached out towards Rissa. "Kyrissa," he murmured. "Come. I would have you and Kyliandra with me right now."

Rissa took her father's arm, and the three of them walked slowly from the grand hall.

Epilogue

Eric stood in silence, leaning against a waist-high wall that overlooked the palace gardens. He stared down at the neat rows of flowers and shrubs, feeling the hot, arid breeze blow across his skin.

Footsteps behind him caused him to turn. He expected Anika, but it was his father, instead. "Hello, Eric."

"Father," Eric greeted.

"It's official," Tindal said quietly. "Kysid has disowned Kyvin and made you his heir."

Eric shook his head, turning around to lean against the wall again. "I never wanted that," he whispered.

"I know," Tindal agreed, moving to lean on the wall beside him. "It isn't what I wanted for you, either. I wanted..." he sighed. "Well, I guess what I wanted isn't important."

Eric closed his eyes, feeling the wind on his face. "I never told you," he said suddenly. "The captain we met in Heidal..."

"Olaf," Tindal supplied, smiling wistfully.

Eric nodded, opening his eyes. "He asked me to tell you something."

"Really?" Tindal said, raising his eyebrows.

Eric stared out across the gardens to the vast, grey-brown landscape that stretched out before them. Almeri was huge, he knew. There were a thousand miles of desert, with only the occasional oasis to be found. Only the coastal areas were truly hospitable. It was a brutal land, but it had forged him in its fires. It was his home.

But so was Prisia.

"He asked me to tell you that 'the bitch was right', that you all 'should have listened to her from the beginning'," he repeated from memory. He turned to look at his father. His father was smiling, his eyes distant.

"They never liked your mother," he confided. "They thought she made me weak. They didn't know that she is the strongest one of us all."

Eric nodded. "Anika's like that. Fire and steel."

Tindal laughed. "That was what Lodi always said about your mother, though he wasn't being complimentary."

Eric took a deep breath. "Ahrlon asked me to tell you something, too. He wanted you to know that your friends haven't forgotten you... that they would be overjoyed if you decided to come home."

Tindal snorted. "Some, maybe," he muttered.

"Father," Eric said quietly. "Every person who figured out who I was, from a common dress-maker to the duke of Floreni, spoke of you with reverence. Every last one."

"What are you saying, Eric?" Tindal demanded softly.

"I'm saying that this..." he waved a hand to indicate Kysid's decision to name him his heir. "This changes nothing. You sent me over to find out if the western lords would support you if you chose to return. I didn't speak to Estaves... but I did speak to Ahrlon. I don't know if the western lords would rise up under the Black Hawk, but I know the southern lords would... and so would every single soldier who served under you in the War. Ryas is engaged in Masimor's rebellion... which from everything I've heard is the direct result of Ryas' mismanagement of Prisia.

"I want to go back, to talk to Estaves... or one of the

other western lords..."

"Eric," Tindal objected. "The last time I agreed to you going to Prisia, you nearly died."

"This is the second time an uncle of mine has tried to betray his family," Eric growled. "Ryas is running the kingdom, the kingdom your father worked so hard to stabilize, into the ground. His soldiers terrorize and murder civilians under the guise of military action, and Ryas not only does nothing, he *condones* it! Father, were you willing to go to war because you believed Ryas had me killed?"

Tindal straightened. "Of course! You are my son."

"And the people of Prisia are your people!" Eric argued, turning to stare angrily at his father. "How is it that my life is so valuable that you would lead an army across the ocean to kill your brother, but the lives of hundreds... thousands... of men and women just like me and Anika don't deserve the same? Your brother stole your birthright. If that was all he did, if he had proven to be even a moderately good king, I wouldn't say anything about your decision to hide here for the rest of your life. But he isn't, Father. He's a tyrant, a despot, and he shouldn't be allowed to continue ruining the lives of the very people you swore to your father to protect when he named you his heir."

Tindal seemed to stagger under his son's words, and

he turned away to stare out across the desert, as his son had been doing when he arrived. He took a deep breath. "You think I am a coward?"

Eric laughed. "No, Father. I think you felt that going back would hurt more people than it would help... and maybe that was true, once. But it isn't true anymore. You've been avoiding listening to reports from Prisia. Look at them. Look at what Ryas is doing..."

"I have," Tindal confessed. "When I received that letter from Estaves, if it was actually him who sent it, I started having reports delivered to me. It was what made me willing to take the risk of sending you there. What Ryas has done..."

"Can be undone," Eric said softly. "Let me go back. Grandfather will object, but I'm not of any actual use here, except to parade around as the next sultan. It's not like I can replace Kyvin as the commander of the military. But in Prisia... over there Anika and I can find out exactly how much support you would have for your return. We can speak to the western lords... maybe even with Masimor and the eastern lords involved in his rebellion. The people of Prisia deserve it."

"And if Ryas catches you?"

Eric chuckled. "He may be a tyrant, but he isn't

stupid. Even he would hesitate at killing Kyric ab Kyr'lasi ni Yolandson, heir apparent to the sultanate of Almeri. He'd lose that war."

"How is this different from what Kyvin wanted?" Tindal demanded.

"The difference is that with Kyvin, you'd be coming back to Prisia with an army of Almeri warriors, and he'd kill you as soon as he could. If I'm right – and Father, I know I'm right – you won't need Kysid or the Almeri. The lords of Prisia will support you with everything they have."

Tindal stared out over the desert, drumming his fingers on the wall. "Let me think on this," he said softly.

Eric smiled. "Of course." He paused, then glanced at his father again. "Lodi asked me to tell you something, too. He said to tell you he's still angry at you, and that you still pull your shots on release."

"I do not!" Tindal grumbled, glancing away and smiling at memories from days long past.

*

The wedding took place in the grand hall. The throne had been removed, and Eric knelt beside Anika in the brilliant sunlight. His dark eyes gazed deeply into her vibrant green ones. He was only vaguely aware of the hundreds of people who had crammed into the hall to witness the ceremony.

"Do you, Kyric ab Kyr'lasi ni Yolandson, Eric Tindalson, take Anika Leifsdottir to wed, forsaking all others?" the priest asked in his nasal voice.

"I do," Eric whispered.

"Anika Leifsdottir," the priest continued, stumbling over Anika's name the way most Almeri did. "Do you take Kyric ab Kyr'lasi ni Yolandson, Eric Tindalson to wed, forsaking all others?"

"I do," Anika murmured, her eyes gleaming brightly.

The priest droned on about the sanctity of marriage for several long minutes, but Eric didn't really listen. He was too caught up in the sight of his bride, the sunlight shining on hair that looked like the essence of fire itself, the eyes that were greener than the finest emeralds. Finally, the priest took each of their hands, placed them together, and wrapped a gold ribbon around them.

"May the gods bless this union," he concluded.

Eric and Anika rose and turned to face the crowd.

"It's a good thing crowds don't make me nervous," Eric whispered from the side of his mouth, barely moving his lips.

Anika bit back a smile and waved politely to the gathered people, the lacy sleeve of the brilliant saffron dress she wore sliding up to bare her arm. "I have a surprise for you," she whispered back.

"Really? What?"

"If I told you, it wouldn't be a surprise," she replied, smirking slightly.

"Please?" he murmured as they began walking down the dais.

She grinned wickedly. "Underneath this hideous gown your mother insisted I wear is a dancing girl costume... and there are gold chains in the bedroom."

Made in the USA
Charleston, SC
13 April 2015